FORBIDDEN

Also by Lee Sato

The Jara Quinn Series

Hornet's Nest

FORBIDDEN

BOOK TWO IN THE JARA QUINN SERIES

BY

LEE SATO

A Launch Point Press Trade Paperback Original

For permission requests, write to the publisher at publisher@launchpointpress.com or "Attention: Permissions Coordinator" at

Launch Point Press
4804 NW Bethany Blvd, Suite I-2, #148
Portland, OR 97229

www.launchpointpress.com

ISBN: 978-1-63304-084-7
E-Book: 978-1-63304-085-4

Editing: Raven's Eye Editing
Formatting: Anne Battis
Cover Design: KLRCOVERS.COM

Printed in the United States of America
First Edition June 2026

Acknowledgments

To my partner Mary, thank you for your unwavering support, love, and encouragement. You've put up with my late-night writing sessions, writer's block, and occasional bouts of "plot panic." I wouldn't have made it without you... and honestly, I'm still not sure how you survived some of those drafts.

To my friends and family, thank you for buying my first book, telling others about it, and even helping me pester bookstores on my behalf. Your cheerleading, and gentle reminders that "yes, you should finish the second book" made all the difference.

A huge shout-out to my publisher, Jodi Zeramby at Launch Point Press, and to Cindy King from Raven's Eye Editing. Thank you for challenging me and for cleaning up the parts I swear made sense at the time I wrote them. I also want to thank Roderick Brydon at klrcovers.com for another brilliant cover design. You always listen to what I want and make it happen.

And to you, dear reader, thanks for sticking around for part two of this journey. I hope you enjoy it as much as I enjoyed writing it.

Dedication

This book, as well as the series, is dedicated to my partner, Mary. Her belief in me turned words into worlds and dreams into pages. Her love was the quiet force that steadied my hand and inspired my heart. Thank you for being my love and my muse.

Epigraph

There is a charm about the forbidden that makes it unspeakably desirable.

-Mark Twain

Prologue

I watched the light drain from his eyes. His longing for an unforgettable night was no longer a dream, but a haunting memory imprinted on the shadows of the evening. I caught my reflection in the mirror. I hadn't realized I was smiling. I looked back at him, sitting there, and took a mental inventory of everything. I had found the perfect dress, the perfect shoes and bag, the perfect makeup. Now, for the finishing touch, the scent that was so comforting, yet so dangerous. Everything had to be perfect. No matter how many times I did this, it had never gotten old. I'd created something beautiful and unforgettable. I took one last look at my masterpiece.

Everything was perfect.

I met him the other night in the parking lot as he left work and knew immediately he was the one. Men were so easy. Flash a smile, toss your hair, pretend to be helpless, and they're hooked every time. He was no different. We'd had our evening together, and it was time to part. I leaned down and gave him a sweet kiss, then tucked the handkerchief into the bag and reluctantly left him.

I walked through the cool evening air as it started to rain. I was as giddy as a child, not minding the few raindrops splashing against my skin. Each one highlighted how alive I felt in this moment. The world was my playground. He gave me his all. I couldn't have asked for more. A night between us that would never be forgotten.

Chapter One

Having settled into a rare night off, Detective Tess Goodwin was savoring the quiet solitude of her home. The soft glow of the television illuminated the living room, where a glass of beer sat on the table beside a plate of reheated leftovers. Tess had seen this movie before, so she turned the volume down low, threw a blanket over her body, and cozied in for a night of relaxation. She relished this brief respite from the demanding nature of her profession.

Tess was a detective with the Connecticut State Police (CSP), the kind who never clocked out mentally. Even with the case technically wrapped, her mind was still running through inconsistencies, replaying witness statements, second-guessing every decision. However, her body craved a reprieve, and she dozed off on the couch before ever touching her beer.

The tranquility of the evening was shattered by the insistent ring of her phone. Glancing at the screen, Tess sighed. She recognized the department's line, and she knew all too well what that meant. Reluctantly, she removed her blanket and reached for the phone. A terse voice delivered the news she anticipated. Another incident had occurred, and duty called once more. The caller provided an address, the digits echoing in Tess's mind like an unwelcome refrain.

Closing her eyes for a moment, Tess prepared herself for the task ahead. The movie's dialogue lingered in the background, a stark contrast to the gravity of the situation. With a sigh, she rose from the couch, the glass of beer now a forgotten companion on the coffee table. Tess ran her fingers through her short blonde hair, trying to comb out the tousled strands from her restless nap. She made her way into the bathroom, brushed her teeth, and splashed cold water on her face attempting to wake up. She looked in the mirror. Having seen too much in her career, her once bright and sharp blue eyes were now dulled by exhaustion. She threw her clothes back on and adjusted the sleeves of her button-down shirt. She rolled them up, revealing toned forearms. The faded scar near her wrist was a souvenir from a case long closed but never forgotten. Her toned body was slumped, still feeling the fatigue in her muscles and bones. She finished dressing, grabbed a thermos of coffee, and made her way to her vehicle. She climbed into the worn seat of her car and paused, readying herself for what she was about to see. Thunder rolled, mimicking the thoughts in her head...then the raindrops fell.

Flashing lights from police cars, fire trucks, and ambulances pierced the rainy curtain, casting an eerie dance of light and shadows on the surrounding trees. Yellow crime-scene tape crisscrossed the area, creating a boundary between the mundane world and the grim reality within. The tape fluttered in the gusts of wind, its color vivid against the gray backdrop of the rainy woods.

Tess reluctantly trudged through the mud. Her badge hung heavily on her belt, not just in weight but in responsibility. She knew this scene all too well. Other than the weather, the scene was pristine. The air was thick with the scent of rain-soaked earth and death. Police officers moved with purpose through the sodden underbrush. They meticulously marked evidence and took photographs, their expressions hidden beneath hoods and soaked hats as they gathered information. The incessant rain complicated their work, turning footprints into indistinct impressions, washing away potential clues, and casting a gloom over the already foreboding setting.

Amidst the chaos, the detective homed in on the well-dressed body, seemingly untouched by the elements. The figure, adorned in a dinner dress and clutching a brown purse, was perched against the dumpster as if casually taking a moment's rest. Every article of clothing was immaculate. Tess repressed a shudder at the eerie contrast between the pristine appearance and the sinister reality of the scene.

No cause of death was obvious at first glance, even to the detective's keen eye, but she knew it was just a matter of time before a small incision would be found on the inner thigh, a deliberate slicing of the femoral artery. It would have taken only a few minutes for this person to bleed out and die. The lack of blood at the scene indicated a methodical execution that occurred elsewhere. There were no obvious signs of struggle, except a slight disfigurement to the face. Tess knew one more thing without examining the body. If you looked closely enough, you'd realize the body was that of a male, not a female.

Recognizing the potential link to a past criminal case, Tess briskly made her way through the rainy night toward her car, leaving the crime-scene techs to do their jobs. The urgency in her steps mirrored the seriousness of the situation. The previous case had been a peculiar one. The suspect pled guilty, despite a lack of substantial evidence connecting him to the crimes, and was sentenced to a hospital for the criminally insane instead of prison. This was the fourth murder since his incarceration. Tess was well aware of the intricacies surrounding this case and the possible involvement of other family members. Revisiting the psychiatric hospital's records was a crucial step to ensure Andrew Branson was still securely confined. The possibility of his involvement in the current crime scene couldn't be ignored, given the similarities in *modus operandi.*

Pulling out her phone, she apprehensively dialed the number.

"Connecticut Valley, may I help you?" The female voice on the other end exuded professionalism, crisp and composed. Yet an undertone of reluctance lingered, as if the speaker were handling the call with a subtle weariness or disinterest.

"Hello, this is Detective Tess Goodwin of the Connecticut State Police. I'm calling to confirm the status of Mr. Andrew Branson."

"Code word please."

Tess gave the code word and held her breath. She awaited confirmation, hoping to either eliminate Mr. Branson as a potential suspect or uncover a chilling connection between the past and present crimes involving the wealthy Branson siblings. The night held secrets, and she was determined to unveil the truth hidden beneath the layers of mystery and rain-soaked intrigue.

"Yes, Detective, Mr. Branson is still here and is in solitary confinement."

Surprised, but relieved, Tess continued her inquiry. "May I ask when he entered solitary confinement and why?"

"Mr. Branson tried to attack his lawyer and brother on their last visit. It's been about two or three weeks now."

"Thank you for the information. Please let me know if Mr. Branson's status changes in any way."

Tess breathed out a sigh of relief. She racked her pounding brain. Since Mr. Branson had an alibi, she wondered who could have possibly committed this murder. She walked over to the coroner, who had just arrived. Dr. Edgar Bryant, a short, pudgy man, had been a coroner for the state of Connecticut for the past twenty years. He too had seen this scene before. Dr. Bryant made his way over to the body and shook his head.

Setting down his bag and putting on gloves, Dr. Bryant turned to Tess. "Hello, Detective, another one I see."

"I'm afraid so, Doc, at least by first glance it is."

"And that maniac is still locked up?" The doctor's eyes searched Tess's for an answer.

"Yes sir, I just called and confirmed. He's in solitary confinement again too."

A soft "damn" escaped the doctor's lips, as he looked over the body and shook his head again. "If it wasn't so macabre, it would almost be art. Tess, I'll call you when I get ready to do the exam."

Tess nodded her head, then turned and walked to her car. She climbed into her Ford Police Interceptor and sat for a bit, listening to the rhythmic percussion of raindrops on the roof. She stared at the yellow tape surrounding the area and all the technicians gathering evidence. She knew they wouldn't find much, if anything. All the crime scenes had been this way. This was the fourth body that had been found since Tess arrested Andrew Branson five years ago. He had been sentenced to Connecticut Valley Mental Health Facility for the Criminally Insane and was under constant medical care and supervision. The confirmation from the hospital about Mr. Branson's current status in solitary confinement provided a momentary sense of relief, but it also deepened the mystery surrounding the crime scene before her. Tess couldn't shake the feeling that a dark force was at play, connecting the past atrocities committed by Andrew Branson to the ones now. There was no way Andrew could be doing this, but the similarities of these last crimes to the ones that he was arrested for were remarkable. Could this be a copycat? If so, they had intimate knowledge of the prior crimes. Tess's head was starting to pound harder. She thought this nightmare was over when she arrested Andrew Branson, but the resurgence of these gruesome crimes shattered that illusion.

She had checked and double checked her work, then even triple checked. Andrew Branson had murdered at least five men, drained them of their blood, disfigured their faces, dressed them in women's clothing, and posed them. Frustration and confusion mounted as Tess questioned herself. Had she missed something in the investigation? Was there a detail she'd overlooked? The relentless pounding in her head demanded answers.

Tess slammed her fists against the steering wheel. The echoes of her scream left her to grapple with the unsettling truth that the nightmare was far from over.

Chapter Two

Upon reaching Katerina's family estate in Greenwich, I let the sense of familiarity and comfort envelop me. I felt a mix of nostalgia and relief as we stepped through the front door, returning home after a relaxing and eventful time in France. I knew I needed to call my supervisor and tell him I was back, but I needed to digest our trip a little more. Honestly, I wasn't in a hurry to get back to the FBI. After being injured during my last case, thoughts of quitting were in the forefront of my mind. The trip to France did little to ease my reluctance to return to work. The journey was a whirlwind of researching Granny May's journals, deeds, and contracts, a task that proved both exhausting and rewarding. The family matriarch's legacy extended beyond her life, and the discoveries made during our trip added layers to the intricate family history.

The shadow of Granny May's tragic demise lingered in the background, a result of Katerina's father, Senator Charles Lansing, seeking retribution over financial matters. Charles, with a political career stained by embezzlement and identity fraud, had escalated to the heinous acts of kidnapping and murder. His incarceration in a federal penitentiary marked a severed tie with the family and left behind a complex web of emotions.

We quietly entered the home and carried our luggage to our room. Jetlagged, we gave each other a knowing smile, acknowledging it was good to be home again, then collapsed onto the bed.

Katerina rolled onto her side and faced me. "Jara, do you really have to go back? Surely the FBI doesn't need you right away. I want more time with you."

I looked into her pleading pools of green and brushed back a strand of her red mane. "Nothing would make me happier than to hide away with you forever, but I promised to go back. I feel it's something I have to do, even though I may not want to."

Katerina huffed and turned her back to me. "Of course you do. Agent Jara Quinn reporting for duty to save the world."

I wasn't going to argue with her. Our time in France was as close to perfection as anything could have been, but we both knew it was time to return to reality.

The enticing aromas of garlic and rosemary wafted through the air, drawing us downstairs to the kitchen where Katerina's mother was tending to the roasting chicken. Always radiant, Victoria turned with a beaming smile. Steaming pots and pans abandoned, she dropped her utensils and ran to us.

"I thought I heard you two sneak in. I am so glad you are finally home. I have missed you so much." Victoria went back and forth to each of us, embracing us harder each time. We helped her set out plates and silverware on the island, a favorite spot of mine. We laughed and caught up, telling of our adventures that hadn't fit on the postcards and texts we'd sent. After a fabulous meal and great conversation, we all crashed for the night.

Routine and purpose blended in the days that followed, as we settled back into the rhythm of everyday life, Foundation business and laundry equally important. Katerina went with her mother to the Foundation to learn of the progress made with recovering the funds embezzled by Mr. Lansing.

I called to check in with Travis O'Ryan, my friend and former liaison from DHS. After the case with Mr. Lansing, Travis returned to the FBI. Although we were partners, he acted as if he was still my boss. Since he helped save Victoria, I gave him that one.

"Oh, you're finally back from gallivanting around the world, huh?" Travis joked. "How good of you to return to the real world and us little people."

"Come on, Travis, are you saying you missed me? We weren't gone that long. Besides, the FBI wouldn't let me work until I healed up more."

I went off the road when I was shot, wrecking my Defender and shattering my scapula. I had one hell of a concussion. Victoria had it worse. She was placed in an induced coma after the kidnapping. She was still recovering. My shoulder still bothered me, but I did my PT exercises religiously while in France.

"I go in tomorrow for my clearance exam. I'm a little nervous," I confided to Travis, "but I don't think it will be a problem. I feel good."

"Well, we need you, so don't think you're coming back to sit on your ass and read emails. We have work to do. Meet me after your exam. We have a lot to go over." Travis said.

I hadn't heard Travis that serious since I was in the hospital. My mind started racing.

"Okay, Travis, spill it. What's going on? What has you so worked up?"

"Damn, I wasn't supposed to talk to you about this until you're cleared, but I need your help, as in yesterday. We were asked by CSP to help with an investigation of a series of murders. It's come to us because one of the bodies was found in Manhattan."

"I get the cross-state issue, but what's really got you worked up? Why is this so different? You've worked with serial killers before."

"Yes, but not when the killer is already sentenced and locked up."

Now I got it. The FBI juices started flowing and all reluctance evaporated. I was ready to work.

Chapter Three

I was eager to look up what I could about the Branson case, and I delved into the details. Andrew Branson had been convicted of five murders spanning the years 2014 to 2020. The extent of his atrocities left a chilling uncertainty regarding the number of actual victims shrouded in the darkness of unsolved mysteries.

Andrew hailed from a prominent and affluent family in northern Connecticut. His father's death in 2014 triggered a series of events that plunged the Branson family into turmoil. The family fortune was secured in trust funds for Andrew and his two siblings. The peculiar nature of their triplet status played a role in Andrew's conviction. Alan and Andrew were identical twins, sharing the same DNA markers. Alibis and other factors had to be thoroughly looked into. Antoinette, Toni, being female and a fraternal triplet, her DNA was not tested. Alan's alibis were allegedly ironclad, clearing him of any involvement in the murders.

Toni Branson lived mostly in Europe. She made occasional trips back to the United States, notably for her father's funeral and the subsequent trial for her brother. According to my findings, the Branson family tragedy continued when Mrs. Branson died of COVID-19 in 2020, just prior to Andrew's trial.

The more I uncovered, the more intricate the web of the Branson family's saga became. Loss and murder cast a pall over their once-gilded existence. I felt a lingering sense of unease, wondering about the untold stories and hidden truths that might further unravel the dark tapestry of the Branson family's history.

Although CSP Detective Tess Goodwin was credited for the arrest, it seemed the investigation ended prematurely when Andrew Branson confessed after a trace amount of DNA was found on the last body in 2020. Testing confirmed the DNA came from a Branson male, and with Andrew's confession, the prosecution ended further investigative work and filed murder charges against him.

Andrew made a plea deal with the state, but due to a backlog of cases during the COVID-19 pandemic, he was not seen in court for sentencing until 2022. He had been held in a county facility until his hearing. He made an Alford plea, which was odd. Usually, those were made with defendants when the prosecution has more than enough evidence to convict, whether innocent or guilty, and the defendant did not admit to the crime. The Branson case was the opposite. The defendant admitted to the crime, and all the prosecution had was a small amount of DNA and a barebones confession. The judge sentenced him to prison for life with no parole, but for whatever reason, Mr. Branson's sentence was modified so he would serve his time in a mental health facility for the criminally insane. The reason for this was redacted in the file.

I continued reading about the murders themselves. As stated in his arrest record, Andrew was caught after leaving a trace amount of DNA at the very last crime scene. Before that, all the crime scenes were pristine and exactly alike, except for a small disfigurement of the victim's face. There was no DNA, fingerprints, hair, or anything to tie anyone to these crimes. All five victims had signs of being confined and were absent of blood. Other oddities of this case were that all the victims were male but disguised as females, wearing expensive dresses and holding purses. None of the victims were gay, crossdressers, drag queens, or transgenders.

As I was going over all of this, the name Tess Goodwin kept nagging at my brain. *I know that name.* I went back to my emails. There were three unopened emails from Detective Goodwin. I opened and skimmed them all. She explained the cases she'd closed regarding Andrew Branson and the murders that were occurring now. She was asking for the FBI's help. I wondered how she got my name and email, but my name had been in the news a lot over the past year. The emails were dated two months ago, while I was still in France. I started to write back, but after all this time, it would take a whole email explaining why I hadn't responded earlier. I found her cell number in one of the emails and decided to call.

A distracted and impatient voice answered. "Hello, this is Tess."

"Hello, Detective Goodwin, this is Special Agent Jara Quinn. Sorry, I haven't gotten back to you sooner regarding your emails, but I was out of the country and technically not cleared for duty."

Her voice seemed to relax after hearing my name. "Please, call me Tess. No problem. I totally understand. I'm sorry for having bothered you. I'm at my wits end on this case, and I didn't know where to turn. I hope you don't mind me emailing you directly."

"No, not at all. And please, call me Jara. I understand, though, you already were able to get FBI involvement. Is there anything else I can help with? I'm not officially back yet. I return tomorrow for my physical and debriefing."

I could hear papers rustling and phones ringing in the background. Tess must be at the station. I heard a door close, and the background noise faded.

"Agent Quinn, I mean Jara, once you get some time, I would love to get your opinion on this case." Her voice was almost pleading. "I feel I may be too involved to see clues that are right in front of me. Another body was discovered just yesterday, and I'm afraid there will be more. Can I send you some of what I have?"

"Sure, I'd be happy to help. To be honest, I think I'm already on the task force that is assigned to your case. I'd be happy to see what our involvement is going to be. I'll call you when I know. Is this the best number to reach you?"

"Yes, thank you. I need all the insight I can get. Talk soon."

I read through the emails again and printed out all the reports Tess sent me. I must have been deep in thought because I didn't hear Katerina come in until she came up behind me and put her arms around my shoulders. She was kissing my neck before I realized she was even there.

"Wow, that must be some interesting reading if I have to go to this length to get attention." She pretended to pout.

"Maybe I waited purposely for you to greet me that way." I pulled her down on my lap and kissed her.

She laughed. "Well, you know, I don't like to be ignored."

"Me, ignore you? Never!"

Victoria walked in, and it was obvious she had been crying.

"Mom, what is it? What's the matter?" Katerina got up and hugged her mother, then led her to the couch. Victoria dabbed her eyes and started to explain.

"A good friend of mine, Jerry Hatfield, was found murdered yesterday. His wife, Susan, is beside herself, and the police won't tell her anything. They keep asking about her husband's lifestyle. They've asked if he was gay or a crossdresser or something."

"Was he?" I ask. "A crossdresser I mean."

Victoria looked up, wide-eyed. "Why are you asking that? The man was murdered! What would that have to do with anything?"

"Victoria, I'm sorry if I sounded callous. I meant no disrespect. Some other murders have occurred lately that have the same cross-dressing element to them." I looked at Katerina. "That was what I was reading about when you walked in. I may be working on this case."

Both Victoria and Katerina stared at me.

"And? Is that all you're going to tell us?" Katerina demanded.

"Kat, I'm not even back to work yet, so yes, that is all I'm going to say."

Victoria started crying again. "So there have been others?"

"I'm afraid so, yes. I received some emails from a detective in the Connecticut State Police while we were in France. She had asked for FBI help, and we are now involved. I spoke with Travis earlier. He told me the FBI is putting together a task force. If I'm cleared, it sounds as if Travis and I will be on it."

"Please Jara, if there is anything you can do," Victoria cried, "I'd be forever grateful. This family is very dear to me."

Katerina hugged her mother tightly as they cried together on the couch. I put my head in my hands, and my shoulders slumped as a feeling of helplessness washed over me.

Chapter Four

I woke early the next morning feeling unrested and nervous. I wondered if the stiffness in my left shoulder would prevent me from being cleared. I let the warmth from feeling Katerina's body curled around me ease my nerves. She was still sleeping soundly. She has been my rock, my cheerleader, and my love. She never allowed me to get discouraged with my physical therapy, and our relationship grew even stronger in France. We had a lot of heart-to-heart discussions about my returning to the FBI and her leaving her job in Boston to work at the Foundation. We both need to keep busy.

I kissed her on the forehead and disentangled myself from the bedding. Stepping into the shower, I felt my muscles relax as the hot water soaked over my body. I closed my eyes and tried to clear my mind, welcoming positive energy to my soul. I guess it worked because I felt a familiar pair of hands gently rubbing my back and shoulders.

"I thought maybe you needed a bit of help relaxing," Katerina said. She continued to rub my stiff muscles while kissing my neck. "You know you have nothing to worry about regarding this clearance. All your medical and physical therapy reports have shown continuing improvement, over 90 percent mobility in your shoulder, plus you have kept up with your counseling appointments. Do you have her report?"

"No, I believe she sent it directly to the FBI. Something about needing it to be in a sealed, confidential envelope. I don't think she'll say anything surprising. I mean as in nothing she hasn't already said to me and that we have worked on. I don't know what I'll do if they don't clear me."

"I can think of a few things." Katerina seductively moved her hand to my breast and pulled me to her.

"Although that would be an amazing way to spend my time, I'm afraid you would get bored after a while." I laughed and brought her hand to my lips.

"I am never bored with you, nor do I think I could be. Life with you could never be dull. And if the unthinkable happens, we'll figure it out. The FBI is not the only place you can work, you know. Many places could benefit from your expertise, me included." Katerina smiled and kissed me passionately. We made love in the shower until the alarm went off, saying I needed to leave for my appointment. Katerina began laughing as I ducked out of the shower and grabbed my clothes.

"Well, I almost was able to keep you here, but I guess once a G-man, always a G-man. Anyway, you look great in a G-man uniform."

I looked down at what I was wearing. Yeah, black pants, white shirt, black shoes, and a black jacket. Nodding my head, I laughed too. "Have to keep it simple for US government folks."

I threw my hair back in a ponytail and kissed a naked, gorgeous Katerina, then reluctantly walked out of the bathroom.

"Wait a minute. G-man, you're going to need this." Katerina handed me a modified, black shoulder holster with a black and silver Glock 19. I looked down at the glistening silver barrel and custom-made grip in awe.

"How—"

"I talked to Travis. He said the FBI was going back to Glocks now, and I knew your gun was gone, still stuck in evidence."

Next to the Glock was a smaller box.

"Go ahead and open it," Katerina urged.

The Smith and Wesson J-frame Ladysmith had a wooden handle and a silver barrel. I still had my Ruger for my ankle, but this Ladysmith was amazing.

"I know you like to be prepared for anything. I hope you like them." Katerina was beaming.

"I love them. Thank you so much. I can't believe you thought of this!" I was stunned. I picked one up, then the other. They were beautiful. Yes, guns could be beautiful.

"I know how important today is for you. I just wanted you to know how much I support you."

I sat the boxes down and took Katerina's hand. Two things hit me at once. One, Katerina was still naked and two, I was going to be late.

Chapter Five

I made it to the New Haven FBI field office and gave my halfhearted apologies for being late.

"I guess you aren't used to all this traffic so early in the morning." Travis winked at me.

"Yeah, traffic, traffic was bad. That was it," I answered, sheepish and red-faced.

Ignoring the exchange between Travis and me, Supervising Special Agent Jack Stewart motioned me down the hall to his office. "So, Miss Quinn, are you ready for the last leg of your return-to-duty process?"

"Yes, sir. Looking forward to it."

SSA Stewart had a large but comfortable office. Sports pictures, commendations, and a small medal hung on his walls. His desk was an organized mess. Stacks of folders and books covered it, but he seemed to know where everything was. I saw no pictures of his family or friends. There was one photo of a military unit, but I couldn't tell which branch. SSA Stewart was a tall, muscular man, with dark, short, cropped hair, approximately in his fifties. He was a very sharp dresser, even in his FBI black. He pulled out a stack of folders and a couple of manila envelopes. I noticed a couple were from my doctor and one was from my therapist. I pulled out a chair across from his desk and set my briefcase down.

"No, no, no," he said, smiling. "I don't want to be that formal. Let's sit over here." He motioned to an area with a couch and two chairs. "Anything to drink,? Coffee, water, or soda?"

"I think I've had my fill of coffee." I didn't want to seem like I was fidgeting due to caffeine. "Water is fine. Thank you."

He pulled out a couple of bottles of water from a small fridge in the corner, grabbed the stack of folders, and sat down in one of the chairs. I sat on the couch and placed my case beside me.

"I hear from Travis you got some new weapons. I'm very excited to see how those perform."

I laughed. "Don't you mean how I perform?"

He gave me a warm smile that caught me a bit off guard. "I'm not really worried about your performance, Jara. I've been reading that you took some pretty good shots under pressure. I don't think a still target will be much of an issue for you."

I relaxed a bit on the couch. "Well sir, I have been in a few pressure situations, but definitely not by my choosing."

As I crossed my legs, I looked down and saw I was not wearing the socks I had originally picked out. In my rush and distracted state, I grabbed the socks on the bed. They were black...with red letters saying, *Takes no shit! Loves a redhead.*

Noticing my socks, SSA Stewart smiled. "Adding a little flair to the standard black, huh?"

My face went beet red, as I hurriedly uncrossed my legs. "I am so sorry. I, uh, I must have grabbed the wrong pair."

Chuckling, SSA Stewart leaned over and pulled his pant leg up, exposing a bright-orange pair of socks. "We all need to show some individuality. It makes the team perform more efficiently. Success for the team is achievable when individuals strive to be their best selves and bring those qualities to the group. Although we are all unique, we share common team goals."

Nodding my head in agreement, I said, "Still, other socks may be a better fit."

"You have to admit, though, someone loves you and has your back. Now let's get down to the matters at hand."

SSA Stewart pulled out a couple of the folders, nodding his head up and down. "Uh-huh, yes, uh-huh. Okay, yes, that sounds about right."

I drank my water as I watched him go through folder after folder. I glanced around the room again, taking in the photos and letters of commendation I had missed before. There was a Navy Cross, a Navy Distinguished Service Medal, a Purple Heart, and a Silver Star. He must have noticed me looking at the awards.

"Ignore those," he said, nodding his head to the wall. "I hung those up because it looks good as a boss. Every one of those medals was earned by being in a unit, not that I did anything extraordinary or by myself." He looked over at the Purple Heart. "Except I guess that one. Being shot is something personal, don't you agree?"

I felt a twinge in my shoulder. I had never felt more alone than when I was shot and lying on the cold ground. I had thought of the people I loved and wondered if I would ever see them again. I must have teared up because I felt a tissue being handed to me.

"I'm sorry sir, but you are correct. I took being shot very personally. Had I stayed conscious longer, I might have gotten a little angry."

"Angry enough for revenge?"

I let out a sigh. "No, not revenge. More like justice. Justice for all the people who were harmed by the person who shot me and the person who was behind it. Granted, I was angry later and, honestly, embarrassed. I had never been hurt on the job before. I felt I had let people down."

"Uh-huh." SSA Stewart looked through more papers. "So are you over that now?"

"Over it?" I shrugged my shoulders. "Well, the case is closed."

"Yes, the case is closed, but are you over it? You know, the pissed-off feeling of being shot and almost dying. The feeling that you let everybody down and allowed Mrs. Lansing to be kidnapped. Are you over that yet?"

SSA Stewart had taken on a different tone, one that wanted to get under my skin. I felt my face get hot and my jaw tighten. Then I looked down at my socks. *Takes no shit*. Exactly. I'd take no shit.

"Sir, respectfully, yes, I am still angry, but not at what you're saying. I had no control over being shot, or I would have chosen not to be. I didn't let anyone down. I did everything I could to the best of my ability. My job was to protect the people under my care and to catch the son of a bitch that caused it all. Sir, I did that. What I'm angry about is that it took me this long to know what is important. I only have control over myself and my actions. And it is 100 percent okay to rely on persons that you trust."

"Is that all?" he asked, one eyebrow raised just slightly.

"No sir, if I may, I need to use your bathroom. The coffee and water have kicked in."

A loud, guttural laugh came from this once-stern face. "Good, good, asking for what you need when you need it. Turn right and go down the hall. It's on the left."

I headed to the bathroom, still hearing that laugh. I returned to his office a few minutes later to find no one there. I sat for a moment, wondering if I had blown it, when Travis walked in.

"Talk about making an impression. You got the old man to laugh. What did you say?" Travis seemed baffled.

I smiled and shrugged my shoulders.

"Well, whatever it was, you are now wanted at the firing range." He motioned me down the hall to an elevator that took us to the basement.

The FBI had multiple ranges, but we were going to the one in the basement. I took off my jacket, checked my pockets, and asked Travis to check the back of my shirt.

"The back of your shirt? What the hell for?" I showed him my socks and he smiled. "Katerina."

"I'm just making sure there are no other surprises."

I did find a note in my jacket pocket. *My love, whatever you set your mind to do, do it with conviction, courage, and caring. I love you, K.*

As I approached the entrance of the indoor firing range, the heavy door swung open with a weary creak, revealing a world of controlled chaos. Stepping inside, I was greeted by the sharp scent of gunpowder and the rhythmic report of gunfire, punctuated by the metallic clang of casings hitting the floor.

The firing range was well-lit, bathed in the sterile glow of bright, fluorescent lights that illuminated a row of pristine shooting lanes. The stark contrast between the harsh lighting and the dimly lit hallway created an immediate sense of focus.

The recurring thud of gunfire grew louder as I approached the firing lanes. Overhead, the ventilation system hummed, its low-frequency vibrations melding with the symphony of controlled disorder in the range.

I took in the details. The shooting stall was separated from the adjacent lanes by sturdy partitions, creating a sense of individualized space. Directly ahead, a series of standard B27 targets had been set up, plus, those that popped up labeled *friend* or *foe*. The electrically controlled target retrieval system hung at the end of the lane, its cables ready to transport the panels to various distances at the touch of a button. The floor beneath my feet was paved with rubberized mats, muffling the footsteps of shooters and lending an air of professionalism to the environment. Empty shell casings littered the floor, glinting under the bright lights like discarded confetti.

As if on cue, the ambient noise of shots fired and the mechanical whirr of the target retrieval system stopped. SSA Stewart's booming voice echoed in the room. "What are we waiting for? Let's get to the fun part."

I put on my goggles and ear protection, sat my gun and ammo on the stand, and readied myself to start.

"Anytime, Agent Quinn."

I loaded my gun, took aim at the target, and squeezed the trigger, emptying the clip of fifteen. Not bad, mostly center mass and a couple of headshots.

"Not bad for the first day back," boomed SSA Stewart. "Do it again."

I did a few more targets. *Boom. Boom.* To my right, SSA Stewart was shooting over my target. I continued, and he kept shooting. I reloaded and shot again. Shots came from my left. Another agent. I reloaded and kept firing. Out of the corner of my eye, I saw a friend target pop up, then another. I yelled, "Hold your fire. Hold your fire. Friendlies in the area."

The firing stopped. A foe target popped up. I tapped two in the chest and one in the head.

"Well, well, Quinn, it looks like you haven't been away a day. 96 percent on standard shooting and quick reflexes on friend or foe. You didn't even miss a beat with the distractions. I'm quite impressed. Meet me upstairs in my office," SSA Stewart ordered, as he turned and left.

Travis looked at me in shock.

"What?" I slipped into my jacket.

"What the hell just happened? A 96 percent on your first day back, and you not only got the old man to laugh, but he said he was quite impressed. Not impressed, but quite impressed. What the hell, Quinn? Are you trying to make us all look bad?"

I put my gun and holster back in the briefcase and laughed. "Must be the socks."

Chapter Six

We made our way upstairs and locked up our guns. We were heading toward Stewart's office, when we heard a voice behind. "Agents, he's waiting for you in the conference room." As we turned, a young gentleman motioned the way. Travis opened the door to the boardroom. Sitting around a long table were SSA Stewart, plus a male and a female not dressed in the usual black FBI attire.

SSA Stewart stood up and introduced us. "Special Agent Jara Quinn, Special Agent Travis O'Ryan, please meet Detective Tess Goodwin and her partner, Detective Jacob Donovan, from the Connecticut State Police."

I thought it wise not to mention the conversation or emails Detective Goodwin and I had exchanged. We all greeted each other and took our seats. Detective Goodwin mouthed *thank you* to me. My gut instinct to keep my mouth shut was right. SSA Stewart pulled a large board over to the table. On the left half were five sections, each with names and crime-scene photos. On the other half, were three sections, also with names and crime-scene photos.

"Agent Quinn, I apologize for throwing you into the ring right away, but this case needs all hands on deck ASAP," said SSA Stewart, not apologetically.

"I understand, sir. Since we are going to be working closely together, please call me Jara. I'm still getting used to the agent title."

Detective Goodwin stood up and made her way to the large whiteboard at the end of the room. "Thank you, SSA Stewart. I might as well jump right in. Please call me Tess, by the way. As you can see, the board is split in half." Tess aimed a small laser pointer to a picture of Andrew Branson. "On the left are the five murders Andrew Branson confessed to and was convicted of. On the right half are three murders that have occurred since Mr. Branson's arrest. We had one more two nights ago. I'll get you all that information soon as I can. From what we have determined so far, Mr. Branson has been locked up under 24/7 supervision and has had no means to commit these crimes. Also, all of Mr. Branson's mail has been seized. He has only received two visitors, his lawyer, William Payne, and his brother, Alan Branson. His sister, Antoinette, goes by Toni. She hasn't been seen since Andrew's sentencing." Tess put down the laser and turned to face us. "There's a theory that we're looking at a copycat, but the details of the case are too unique. Only someone with intimate knowledge could be committing the current murders. Each of you has a stack of folders in front of you. Each folder holds copies of the murder book on one of these cases, and all the crime-scene photos."

I was impressed by the way each of these cases were handed out. The murder books, which had the autopsy, forensic reports, sketches of the scene, crime-scene photos, and interviews, were actually quite thin. They included lists of names in different colors. Tess must have seen me looking at the color-coded names.

"As Jara has already found, there are lists of names for each case. They are color-coded to show if more than one pops up on any other case, whether as a witness or a suspect. So far only a couple of names have been found on multiple lists, other than Andrew Branson. When you look through the three later cases, and the most recent one, no names crossover. The only details that are similar or even the same, are the cause of death, disfigurement of the face, and the cross-dressing and posing of the victims."

Tess's voice strained with frustration as she continued. "One case stands out. The very first crime scene was found in 2014. It was the only one with blood at the scene, and there was a lot of it. All of the cases were male victims, and as I said, were cross-dressed. The face is disfigured enough that, at first glance, you couldn't tell the sex other than by the clothes. A misdirect. Also, all the victims have a small incision on their inner thigh at the femoral artery. The cutting of the femoral artery and the exsanguination were all the same. Since there is no blood found at the other scenes, there has to be another area in which the murders were committed. We haven't figured out, even with the first five, how Andrew and the new killer subdued their victims and moved them to another area. We also haven't found the area where the blood draining and clothes changing occurred. Andrew would not discuss any of this in his confession, nor would he say how he chose his victims."

"So Tess, if Andrew didn't say how and where he killed these victims, what made you and the court sure Mr. Branson committed them?" The contents of the folders certainly didn't make me certain.

Tess pulled out five sheets of paper and a marker. She took one sheet of paper and taped it to the board with the first crime scene, then followed suit with the other four pieces of paper. "With each murder," she's circled DNA numbers, "four of them only had the victim's DNA, but on the fifth"— she pointed to a piece of clothing—"there was a large sample and an exact DNA match to a male in the Branson family. After bringing in both Andrew and Alan Branson and confronting them about the DNA, Andrew confessed to all five murders. He included the victims' names and locations of the bodies. He explained his fascination with making people into something they aren't. Although he took the Alford plea and didn't say any of this in court, his polygraph showed he was telling the truth about being responsible for each murder."

"But now you have four more, exactly the same, correct? What does Andrew say about these?"

"He refuses to discuss them with me. I have tried a few times to reinterview him, but he is either in solitary confinement, or his lawyer isn't able to be present."

"Tess, would it be all right if I tried to talk with him?" I asked. "Maybe a new face will interest him and get him talking a little."

"I can try and arrange it, but don't hold your breath." She let out a large exhale. "When I called after the last murder, Andrew had been put into solitary again, this time for attacking his brother and lawyer."

"Seriously? Has he displayed aggressive anger before? Other than the faces, these murders appear calm and controlled."

Tess shook her head dejectedly. Her partner reached over with a comforting touch, but Tess glared at him. He withdrew his hand as if she'd bit him.

"I am so over this case! I thought for sure we had the right guy and it was done. Instead, Andrew has been locked up, and

Alan has alibis for each of the new murders. Just to be sure, I checked in on Toni. She is still living abroad, although we haven't laid eyes on her."

SSA Stewart stood. "Well, you have all the material in front of you. Jara and Travis, I want you to work directly with Tess and Jacob. Help them with whatever they need."

We all looked at each other around the table and nodded in agreement. Everyone shuffled out of the room except for Tess and me.

Tess walked over to me and quietly said, "Thanks for not saying anything about our conversation and my emails. I think I went a little outside the chain of command on that. I appreciate you not ratting me out."

I organized the folders according to what I wanted to look at further and put them in my briefcase. "No problem. I figured when SSA Stewart introduced us, he wasn't aware of our talk. Let's meet up tomorrow and see where we want to start on this. I have some ideas, but I want to read over what you gave us first." I walked over to the whiteboard and took pictures of it all. I grabbed my stuff and started to walk out the door.

Tess called after me. "Jara, I am very glad we will be working together on this. I hope you can see something I haven't."

I stopped and turned to her. "Tess, is your partner going to be a problem?"

A look came over her face, both surprised and questioning. "My partner? No, I don't think so. Why?"

"I saw how you glared at him, and how fast he pulled his hand away."

"Oh, that. Well, to be honest, we have had a bit of trouble lately. We've worked together since before the first murder. You could say we became quite close." Tess started to fidget, rocking from one foot to another. "Everything was great until Andrew Branson's sentencing. Then the next murder happened. I guess I became a bit self-absorbed. Anyway, we still work well together but just not as close as we used to be."

"Hmm, I guess the details of all that are for another time." I smiled. "See you tomorrow at your building. nine a.m."

"Sounds great. Again, thanks, Jara."

Chapter Seven

It felt so good to be heading home to Katerina, driving my new car. I never really owned a new car before. I decided to splurge when my specially rebuilt Defender 110 was totaled, but with something a bit more practical. When I said that to Katerina, it took her twenty minutes and a bunch of tissues to stop laughing and crying.

"Practical? You are never practical," she said between fits of laughter. "No matter what you buy, you're going to modify it into a beast of some sort."

I laughed too, thinking of all the modifications I'd made to my old Defender. It kept me alive, though, when I was shot off a bridge. I stayed with the Land Rover make but decided to get a Range Rover Sport. On top of the spectacular detailing, I added bullet-resistant glass and side panels, a new biometric safe, a large gun safe compartment, and a kickass, secure computer system. I pulled into the drive thinking I could almost live in this car.

No one was home. *That's unusual.* I made my way into the den to throw my briefcase and jacket on the couch, then to the kitchen to grab a beer. I saw the note right away. *If home before us, please place in oven at 350 degrees. Love K*

I did as I was asked without even opening the lid to the roaster, then grabbed a beer and headed back to the den. Shoes off and shirt neck unbuttoned, I pulled out my folders from the meeting. The day must have worn me out more than I thought because I woke to Katerina's voice.

"Oh my god," she said, her voice more of a shriek.

She was standing over me, holding a crime-scene photo with one hand and the other over her mouth.

"I am so sorry." I grabbed the photo out of her hand. "You weren't meant to see those."

I shoved the photos into piles and placed them back into their folders.

"Is this...well, is it a photo of Mom's friend?"

"Yes, this is the case, but no, Victoria's friend is not one of them. Anyway, I don't want knowing a victim is a friend of the family to cloud my judgment."

"Cloud your judgment? Wouldn't it make you want to work harder? It's Mom's friend. You must solve this." Katerina was pacing like a tiger readying itself for an attack.

"Victoria's friend or not, all of these victims are equally important. I need to help solve all of these, not just the one."

Victoria walked in with a confused look. "What are you girls arguing about? I could hear you in the driveway."

"We're not arguing, Victoria..." I stammered.

"Yes, we are! You don't want to solve Mom's friend's case," Katerina shouted as she walked away from the desk.

I slammed the rest of the papers into my briefcase. "When did I say that? I said all of them are important, all of them need my attention."

"Show her the pictures."

"Show her what? The crime-scene photos? No, not even you were supposed to see those. There is no way I would want Victoria to see her friend or anyone else in that way."

"Girls, stop it. I don't want to see those photos, and I want all of them solved. Now quit arguing and get ready for dinner. Jara, thank you for putting in the roast. It's almost ready. Now get yourselves together. Do what you have to do to get over this and come into the kitchen. It's been a long day." Victoria was visibly tired, her eyes puffy and red. "And Jara, I take it then that you were cleared to work again? I'd like to hear more about that, even if my daughter doesn't." Victoria shot a look toward Katerina.

"Mom..." Katerina said sheepishly.

"Thank you, Victoria." I smiled. "Let me get this all put away."

Victoria left for the kitchen, as I took the rest of my folders and locked them in my briefcase. Katerina reached over and touched my shoulder. "I'm sorry. I wasn't thinking. Seeing that picture shocked me a bit. I know what you do, but I guess I never realized what you see. I am so sorry."

I stood up straight, my back to Katerina. I was still angry. She'd lashed out, but I was also angry at myself for being so careless. I let out a long sigh and turned around to face her. "I never wanted you to see that side of my job, of who I am."

"I know you. That is not all of who you are. If anyone can do this, it's you. I saw how you handled my father. I would expect nothing less of you on this. I'm sorry. I overreacted."

My body relaxed a bit, and I took Katerina's hand. Head down, I let out another sigh. Katerina kissed me on the forehead.

"So did you kick ass today or what?" She giggled a little and I joined her.

"Well, thanks to you, I took no shit."

We walked arm and arm, still laughing, into the kitchen. Victoria looked up. "First yelling, now laughing. Oh, to be young again. So Jara, other than this case, how was your first day?"

I pulled up my pant leg, showing her my socks. "I took no shit, Victoria."

Chapter Eight

I decided to get an early start on my second day back. I was already playing catch-up on this new case. I stopped by the FBI office before heading over to the CSP building. Only a few of the lingering night staff were there, so I headed straight to my desk. It was nice to have a place to land. I was organizing my desk, putting up a few personal items, and making sure the lock worked on my desk drawers, when what I thought was a cleaning lady startled me.

"Hello, Miss Quinn. So glad to see you are doing all right. I was worried about you," the lady said softly.

"Hello. I'm sorry, are we acquainted?"

"Oh yes, I didn't mean to startle you. I saw you were here and wanted to say hi. I used to work for Victoria Lansing's mother, Granny May. Mostly at the Foundation, but sometimes at the house. I miss her so much." She reached out her hand. "I'm Anita Burris."

I remembered her face from Granny May's memorial. She looked a bit different though. Anita was possibly in her late sixties or early seventies, but you wouldn't know it at first glance. Her posture was poised and graceful, as she looked around the room with quiet confidence. She seemed to be taking inventory of her surroundings. There was a timeless elegance to her, silver hair styled with intention, not vanity, and skin that showed the soft, weathered traces of experience rather than surrender. She wore her clothes the way some people wore armor, tailored and effortless, with a pair of classy boots that had clearly walked more than one continent. I sensed she had seen enough to no longer be surprised. She and Granny May must have had many experiences together.

"Oh yes, you were at the memorial. Good to see you again," I said, as I shook her hand.

"I won't keep you. I just wanted to say hi. If there is anything you need, feel free to let me know. I'm the cleaning and maintenance manager here." She laughed as if she'd told an inside joke. "At least, that's what they call it."

I wasn't sure what she meant by that, but I decided not to ask.

"Well, good to know, Mrs. Burris. If I have any issues, I'll make sure to let you know."

Mrs. Burris smiled and nodded her head. "I'm here early most mornings. Again, good to see you."

"Oh, Mrs. Burris, I do have one question. Is there an out-of-the-way, unassigned room I could possibly use?"

"My yes." Her face lit up. "In the basement, on the other side of the shooting range. They made it into a conference room, but they never use it. I think the proximity to the range made it less than ideal. It's mostly quiet though. Do you want me to get it cleaned up for you?"

"That would be fantastic. I owe you a huge favor. Thank you."

I figured I'd go check it out after I returned from CSP. Sounded promising. I had finished my organizing when I heard a familiar booming voice greet Mrs. Burris as she left.

"Travis, I thought you were going straight to CSP?"

"I was, but drove by and saw your car. Thought we'd ride together. I've been dying to get into that car of yours."

I threw the materials I thought I'd need in my bag, and we headed out. Travis walked straight to my Range Rover's driver's side.

"Oh no you don't."

"Oh come on, let me drive at least once. Remember, you owe me for saving your life."

Laughing, I walked to the passenger door. "For the love of God, fine, if it will keep you from whining."

We made it to CSP in record time, thanks to Travis's lead foot and the lack of traffic on the roads.

We pulled up to a large cement building with a rounded middle and two rectangular sections at each end. The station was quite impressive, to say the least. We found our entrance and made our way in to meet Tess, who was waiting inside the door. She seemed distracted but was pleasant for this early in the morning.

"You, okay?" I asked.

"Yeah, a bit tired is all. I've been here all night getting things ready." She ushered us inside. Photos of officers, newspaper clippings, and state police patches lined the walls of the hallway. We turned into a large conference room filled with file boxes and whiteboards. At first glance, it appeared to be a disorganized mess, but then I saw how each pile was organized as its own case.

"Sorry for the mess," as if Tess read my mind. "I tried to organize it all but ended up going through it again."

"So where do we start?"

Jacob walked in looking as tired as Tess.

"You here all night too?" Travis inquired.

"Yep. When she stays, I stay."

Tess rolled her eyes. "Whatever. So let's figure out how to do this."

I walked around the room, looking at each case pile.

"I have an idea. Since you two have worked so much on the older cases, let Travis and I go over those, while you two focus on the new ones. We're still interested in anything new you might find, but it might help you to see things differently. If you aren't focused on the old cases, you can treat the recent cases as unrelated to the Branson murders."

We all agreed and split off to separate sides of the room. It had been a minute since I worked on cases with this much evidence.

"Let's dig in." Travis sat down by the last case pile and took inventory. I started on case one.

Steven McCleary, age thirty-one, a Caucasian male, found September 2014. Mr. McCleary was found in a parking garage, sublevel three, sitting against one of the concrete columns. It was hard to make out the clothing he was wearing due to all the blood. The notes indicated he was wearing a dress and had a tan handbag. The handbag, which was used and worn, had absolutely no blood on it, whatsoever. An embroidered handkerchief was found inside the bag, also with no evidence of blood. His face had multiple superficial cuts, but there was no evidence of Mr. McCleary being bound or gagged. There were no obvious signs on how Mr. McCleary was subdued. The coroner recorded a deep cut on the right groin area had severed the femoral artery and stated that Mr. McCleary would have bled out in a few minutes. Nothing explained how or when Mr. McCleary was put in a dress, where his other clothes were, or how there was blood on everything but the purse. There were no shoe prints in the blood, nor handprints on the clothing. No DNA was found, other than Mr. McCleary's. It was also noted that none of the cameras in the parking garage were working at the time of the incident. The garage was attached to a large, professional building that housed multiple offices. It was learned Mr. McCleary had worked at one of these offices.

Case number two. Thomas Mason, age twenty-nine, a Caucasian male, was found March of 2015. Mr. Mason was found in a parking lot leaning against a parking attendant stand. He was dressed in a yellow print dress, yellow heels, and a tan handbag. There was nothing in the handbag except a yellow, embroidered handkerchief. Mr. Mason's face had been a bit disfigured, but no other significant injuries were found. A small, half-inch laceration was found on the inside of Mr. Mason's right groin. It appeared to have punctured the femoral artery. No blood, semen, or any other secretion was found at the scene. The clothing appeared expensive, but all the tags had been removed. The handbag was not worn but seemed less expensive. The only article that stuck out for me was the handkerchief. According to the notes, Mr. Mason had no ties to the parking lot or the surrounding area.

Travis had been looking through case five, when I asked him, "Travis, can you look through these two other cases and see if there was mention of a handkerchief found at the scene?"

Travis shuffled through cases three and four. All cases had the male victim wearing an expensive, colorful dress, heels, and a generic, tan handbag. Cases one through four each had a handkerchief either in the purse or in the victim's hand. In case number five, the victim had the handkerchief in his mouth. The small amount of Branson DNA was found on that handkerchief.

"Now that's a difference," I said. "Maybe minor, but definitely off script."

"Hey Tess," Travis called out, "do your cases have a handkerchief or anything like it?"

"Yep, all of them, and all embroidered. All were found in the purse with the victim."

I looked through the boxes and found pictures of the handkerchiefs, but not the actual handkerchiefs themselves.

"Tess, do you still have those handkerchiefs in evidence?" I was feeling hopeful but knew this was only day one.

"I believe so. They're all locked in the evidence room. The one found in the mouth of victim number five had a bit of damage, but the others were in perfect condition."

"I would like to see those if I could, and the actual purses. Am I allowed to take them with me to my office?"

"I'm sure you could, but I'll go make sure." Tess walked out, leaving her partner awkwardly staring at us.

"Jacob, are you okay?" I asked.

"Yes, I'm sorry. I can't believe I didn't have those up here for you." He started shuffling papers around.

"No problem. But if you don't mind, may I have a new copy of the evidence list in each case, old and new?"

"Uh, well, yeah sure. Did you lose yours?" Jacob asked a bit snidely.

"Oh no, nothing like that. I like to see the original list from each case I work on, plus the copies. Just being thorough, I guess." I smiled, trying to keep things civil.

"Sure. Then I'll get those together." Jacob moved to gather the lists.

"Travis, could you give Jacob a hand with that?"

Travis gave me a strange look, shrugged his shoulders, and went with Jacob.

Tess returned with eight boxes and an evidence card. "Here's the evidence boxes for the earlier five and the latter three. The fourth and most recent one, I'm not able to release. It's still being processed."

I signed the evidence transfer form and took the first five boxes to my side of the room. I put on a pair of surgical gloves and opened the first box. In it was a plain tan purse and a handkerchief. I took the purse out, looking it over. It didn't appear to be an expensive purse, but well-used. The handle, clasp, and bottom were all worn, as if it was a woman's daily purse. I pulled it out of the evidence bag and opened it. My mind floated with memories of my own mother's purse. That distinct smell of gum and cigarettes, stale money, and my mother's perfume. I didn't recognize this perfume scent. I put the purse back in its bag and pulled out the handkerchief. A flower pattern was intricately embroidered on the edges, and it also had a perfumy smell. After putting everything from the first box away, I went to the second. This purse was the same type, but there were no wear marks or smells. Same with the other three. All the handkerchiefs were embroidered the same as the first and had the same perfume smell, with only a slight bit of difference.

I held one of the handkerchiefs up. “Hey Tess, has anyone ever figured out what perfume is on these?”

“No. I know one of the forensic guys was going to try and do a breakdown of it, but since Mr. Branson confessed, they aborted. They felt it would be a waste of money.”

I lifted the handkerchief to my nose again. I could smell flowers, with a hint of an earthy, woodsy scent. I’m sure there was a lot more to it than that, but I think I got the main ingredients.

“Did you ever ask Mr. Branson what perfume this was?”

Tess furrowed her brow. “I asked him, but he wouldn’t give me a straight answer. He never gave me a name. He kept saying ‘It’s forbidden,’ then he’d laugh. I think the women in his family wore it, but I’m not sure.”

There were photos of what I assumed was the Branson family in the main file. The victims didn’t necessarily look like his mother, or his father for that matter.

“Tess, by the way, have you been able to set up a time for me to talk with Mr. Branson?”

“Actually, yes, I have. I was going to tell you that but got sidetracked.” Tess rolled her eyes toward Jacob as he returned. “We have an appointment next Wednesday, at the hospital, at one p.m. I hope that works for you.”

“Perfect. I’ll have time to set up my questions. Thanks, Tess.”

Travis and Jacob carried in multiple stacks of paper.

“Here they all are. Not sure why you want these. You already have copies.” Jacob scoffed, as he dropped them in front of me.

Travis rolled his eyes. “I have the originals for the last three murders. I have a feeling you’re wanting me to copy all these for you too?”

I grinned. “Travis, you know me so well. That’s why we’re so great together.”

Travis huffed as he grabbed an empty file box and put in all the evidence lists. "I'll be right back, Boss, if you think of anything else I can do for you."

"Well, I wouldn't mind a Dr. Pepper if you're going by a machine."

"I'll get right on that, Boss." Travis gave me a mocking salute as he left.

Tess and Jacob had been watching our banter. "Are you really Travis's boss?" Tess asked.

"Not hardly, but sometimes I do get a bit demanding."

"Sometimes?" Travis said over his shoulder.

"Go get my copies, Travis," I said laughing. "Actually Tess, Travis was my Homeland liaison and head of the task force. He is a great leader and an even better partner and friend. I trust him with my life."

Tess nodded her head. "It's good to have people you trust, especially if it's your partner." She looked over at Jacob and glared.

"Whatever, Tess," Jacob said. "You know you can trust me. Have I ever let you down?"

"Honestly, are we really going to get into this now, Jacob?" Tess responded back.

"If you feel you can't trust me or depend on me, what am I even doing here?" Jacob shoved a box out of his way.

"Oh my god. Seriously, Jacob, grow up. I don't have time to coddle you and stroke your ego. Show some maturity, will you?" Tess turned to me. "I'm sorry about this. As you can obviously tell, we have some things to work out. Don't worry. It won't affect our working together."

Travis returned with two file boxes as I stood up.

"Well Tess, I think you need to get your house in order here, or it will affect the investigation. We can't have any drama distractions while we're trying to solve these cases. It's hard enough as it is. Is there anything else we need to know?"

Travis looked at me then to Tess. "What did I miss? Is there something I need to know about?"

"It's all good, I promise. It will not affect our working together, right Jacob?" Tess walked over to him.

"Oh no, no. It's not going to affect anything. Tess is right, always right," Jacob said sarcastically. "We'll get it worked out."

"Fine." I grabbed the evidence boxes of the first two murders and the evidence lists Travis copied. "I'm leaving for the day. I need to return to my office for a bit, then home. Travis, are you ready?"

"Sure, I need to grab a few things and I'll be down."

Tess grabbed one of the boxes for me. "I'll walk down with you, if that's all right."

"Great, I could use the help."

We walked silently until we reached my Rover.

"Nice ride. Not FBI standard issue, I assume." Tess said, admiring my car.

I gave a chuckle. "Not hardly. My last car basically died to save my life. I wanted to make sure this car could do the same."

We put all the evidence in my locked compartment and the boxes in the back.

Tess gave a low whistle. "Nice setup back here."

"Yeah, I put in a few extras for just this purpose. So what do you want to say to me? I'm sure you didn't walk down here just to see my car."

"You're right." Tess shifted from one foot to the other. "I wanted to reassure you that Jacob and my issues aren't going to be a problem."

"So far, I'm not reassured, but that is your business. You handle it as you see fit. As long as it's not hindering our case."

Tess gave a deep sigh. "Jacob and I used to be lovers, as well as partners. Nothing steady, just basically something to do. Hell, we were together all the time, and no one else really understands our jobs and what we see every day. It just seemed natural that we would sleep together."

My mind flashed back to Katerina when she saw the crime-scene photo. "I get that. I do. I hide a lot from my partner. At least I thought I did."

Tess nodded. "I broke it off entirely before the trial. I was so angry and bitter that they took Branson's confession as gold and dropped everything else."

"Did you want to keep working on this?"

"Yes. I don't think Branson committed these murders, at least not all of them. But I couldn't prove it. Then they shut down all forensic work and said we have our man, patted me on the back, and closed it all. Then, after the conviction, the new bodies started to drop. I know they all are the same killer, and I want the chance to prove it. I guess I took out all my anger and frustration on Jacob, so even our friendship and work relationship suffered. I'm not sure what he wants from me, but right now I can't give any part of me to anyone."

I listened as Tess went on about her frustrations with the case. I knew what that frustration felt like. Travis came down with the other boxes and some folders. He locked them in the back and turned to me. "Ready to head out?"

"Sure." I looked over to Tess. "Thank you for explaining this to me. It makes more sense now. We're going to work out of our building the next couple days. We'll keep in touch. I'm looking forward to meeting Mr. Branson."

Tess backed away from the car. "Thanks for listening. Talk soon."

Travis and I rode back to the office in silence. When we reached the parking lot, Travis turned to me. "So what the hell is going on? You're having me do double work, and the other half are arguing like a lover's quarrel? Spill it. What do you know?"

I told Travis what Tess had said. "Now about the copies. I was skimming through some of the evidence and there were discrepancies. Things on the list they don't have and things we do have but are not on the list. I'm trying to see if it was a mistake at the beginning or if someone is not giving us all that we need. And if I find out someone is trying to sabotage our work, there will be hell to pay."

"Damn. Second day and you're already stirring up trouble. Okay, okay. We'll go through it all again. Are we taking this all in tonight?"

"Yes, most of it. I have a place for us to settle in. Down in the basement there's a room that should be perfect. Mrs. Burris set it up for me."

Grabbing the boxes, Travis shook his head. "Seriously, you're already getting favors. How do you do that?"

"Guess it's just my sweet personality."

As we carried things in, I heard him mumble, "Sweet personality, my ass."

We made our way to the basement and found the conference room. Mrs. Burris was right. It was perfect. She'd added many much-needed things. One huge coffee maker, multiple cups, five large whiteboards, five long tables, comfortable chairs, a pull-out couch and coffee table, and a large basket full of blankets. There was a note on the first table.

Jara,

It was so nice to see you. I took the liberty to add some things to this room. Hope you like it. I had it scrubbed from corner to corner. Markers and more cabinets will be here tomorrow. Also, I put in a work order for two new locks on the door, one keyed and the other coded. Please let me know if there's anything else you need. Please tell Mrs. Lansing and Katerina hi for me.

Anita.

Travis chuckled. "So Granny May pulled out another one for you, huh?"

"You don't have to join me down here, Travis, if it isn't to your liking."

"Oh no, no, I never said that." He flopped himself down on the couch. "I was figuring it couldn't just be your sweet personality."

"Oh, bite me," I said, smiling.

Despite our laughter, I could tell by how he looked that Travis had started to feel as tired as I felt.

"Let's head home, begin fresh tomorrow." I locked up the evidence in the cabinets. I found one lock on the room door and secured it, then Travis and I went our separate ways. I couldn't get the perfume smell from the handkerchiefs out of my head.

Chapter Nine

I made it home just as Victoria and Katerina pulled into the drive. Perfect timing. What a lovely sight to come home to. I smiled as I walked over to greet them.

Katerina pulled her briefcase out of the car and turned to me. "Can we go back to France? This work thing is for the birds."

Victoria snickered. "Day two and my newest employee is already disgruntled."

"It's only because my boss is a total dictator." Katerina flashed Victoria a grin. "But honestly, it's nice working with Mom again."

"We brought home carryout," Victoria said. "I hope that's okay."

"Perfect. I'm starving," I took two large bags from Victoria. "Too busy to have lunch. Oh, and by the way, do you know an Anita Burris?"

"Of course I do." A knowing smile creeped over Victoria's face. "She was good friends with Matka. She ran the day-to-day of the Foundation like clockwork, plus did some other things for Matka that she wouldn't talk about. Why do you ask?"

"Well, I ran into her this morning at the FBI building. She said she works there as head of maintenance and cleaning. Not sure what else she does, but she seems like she has a bit of pull." I told them about the room that Mrs. Burris arranged for me and how quickly it was done.

"Yes, sounds like the magic she would do at the Foundation. You think she might want to come back?" Victoria asked.

"If today was a slice of what she can do, I'm keeping her."

We finished dinner and cleaned up. Katerina grabbed a bottle of wine and a beer for me, and we headed to the patio. When we reached the lounge chairs, she was holding my beer but wouldn't hand it to me.

"What's up? Holding my beer hostage?"

"Why yes, I am. What woman have you been around today?"

"Are you jealous, my love?"

Katerina leaned over and sniffed my neck. “You’re wearing perfume. You rarely wear perfume, so you’ve had to have been close enough to get it from someone.”

“Yes, sweetheart, I have been with this hot other woman. I’m just ignoring the serial killer.”

She backed up, her smile escaping her face, quickly replaced by concern. “So you believe they’re all connected?”

“Actually, I’m not sure yet. Just getting started. Can I have my beer, please?”

Katerina handed me the bottle. “Fine, but back to this other woman...”

I smirked. “I kind of like this sexy, jealous look on you.”

“Oh, you don’t want to see me really jealous, missy. They don’t call a red-haired, green-eyed woman a devil for nothing.”

“I promise, my love, you have nothing to worry about. The case has some evidence that is a bit, well, odorous. It’s perfume, but I can’t place it.”

“Evidence, huh? So that’s your story. By the smell, I was thinking it had to be an older woman. You into older women, Jara?” Katerina teased.

“You are a year older, my dear, so yes, I guess I am. Why do you ask that?”

Katerina took me in her arms and took a deep breath. “If I had to say, the perfume you have on is a good twenty years old, if not older. The scent is stronger than it should be.” She smiled again. “Yes, definitely a rose scent, violets, jasmine, and...” she sniffed again, “I think some sandalwood. Yep, sandalwood. What a unique mixture.”

I sniffed my clothes and hands. “How in the hell can you tell all that?”

“Sweetheart, perfume is a lot like wine. It can smell amazing together, but you can also distinguish each individual fragrance. If it is a high-end perfume and stored correctly, it should hold its scent, perhaps grow stronger. Cheaper perfume can sometimes smell like vinegar or bug spray over time. This is definitely a high-end perfume.”

“Good to know. So, high-end huh, that helps.”

Katerina sniffed again. “I haven’t smelled this before. It’s very nice.”

I took my beer and sat on the big lounge chair. Katerina sat down beside me. It was nice being home and sitting on the back deck watching the boats in the harbor, smelling the flowers from the garden, and being beside Katerina.

After a long silence, she asked, "Are you in any danger?"

"No. Well, I don't think so. Right now, I'm stuck in an office going over boxes and boxes of evidence. I might get a paper cut though."

She smacked me on the arm. "I'm serious. Since these murders are still happening, do you think you will be focused on? I can't go through almost losing you again."

I took another drink of my beer. "Honey, you know I can't promise anything, especially regarding the FBI, but I will do my best to stay safe and come home to you every night."

"You'd better," she exclaimed, as she laid her head on my shoulder.

I couldn't stop thinking about what she'd said about the perfume. Who could I go see about identifying this scent?

"Hey Kat, do you know anyone that could help me figure out what the name of this perfume is? You seem to know so much about all of this."

"I know a couple places in New York that specialize in fragrance consulting. I could call a couple of them. Would that help? We could take a trip into New York City and see Chase."

"That would be awesome. We haven't seen your brother and Abby since we got back. I'll get permission to take the stuff I need." I started to get up to call Tess.

"Wait a minute, Jara. Not tonight. You'll call tomorrow, and you'll wait for permission tomorrow. Got it? The nights are mine."

I sat back down. "Okay, okay," I smiled. "Yes, the nights are yours. But can I at least refill our drinks?"

"Of course, but hurry it along." Katerina smiled.

I took her glass back in and headed to the fridge. After I refilled her wine and grabbed another beer, I sent off a text to Tess about taking evidence across state lines. I brought our drinks back out to the deck.

"So did you get your question answered?" Katerina asked with a sly grin.

"What? What do you mean?"

"I know you probably texted Travis, or whoever you are working with, about the evidence. Once you get an idea in your head, you can't let it go."

"You know me so well. Yes, I texted the detective in charge at CSP. This may be the break I'm looking for."

"I'll let it go this time because other than my father's, I have never seen you work on a case. I need to get used to this, I guess." Katerina sighed.

I turned and looked her in the eyes. "Kat, I'm sorry. I do get laser-focused when I'm on a case. I will try to balance my time and energy. It will be good for me to learn that."

"So how about your first lesson tonight." Katerina turned, and in one smooth move was on my lap facing me.

"How can I say no to a such a gorgeous teacher."

We kissed deeply, our bodies intertwined with each other on the lounge chair. We were pretty sure Victoria had gone to bed, so we continued our passion. We ended up making love multiple times. Not bad for my first lesson.

Chapter Ten

I left early the next morning to get to the office. I'd received multiple texts and a few missed calls from Tess, so I called her on my way to work.

"It's about time you called me back. Sending me a cryptic message like that, then not answering my calls or texts. Drove me crazy. What is going on? What are you thinking?"

"Sorry, sorry, sorry. Uh, something came up after I texted you. I wasn't in a position to get back to you. Again, I'm sorry. But about my question, can I take your evidence across state lines? Since the FBI is part of this case now, I think I can, but I wasn't sure about any evidence from the last case."

"I'm pretty sure you can, as long as it stays in your possession. You are FBI, ya know, so you can cross state lines."

There was a hint of either bitterness or anger in her tone. I was going to let it pass but rethought and knew I had to address the tension.

"Tess, are you pissed about something? Our involvement maybe? Remember you requested us to be here."

Tess let out a deep breath. "No, I mean yes, God, no not really. It grates on me that a task force had to be formed. I know I asked for your help, but I am pissed I couldn't solve this myself. Since one of the bodies was found in New York, I know the FBI had to come in. But I have worked so hard on this...It angers me I haven't figured this out yet, and now I'm being second-guessed."

"Who said I'm second-guessing you? I'm looking everything over to get all the information I can to familiarize myself with the cases. I'm not second-guessing you! I hold no judgments on who did what right or wrong. My only concern is to catch this son of a bitch that is doing this. If your ego can't handle this, I'm sorry. You got the wrong agent to think I am going to placate your feelings. I ask questions to learn and make informed decisions, not judge. We need to work as a team. This isn't just your case anymore." There was silence on the phone. I hadn't realized how angry and defensive I had gotten. "Tess, I'm sorry for my outburst. I get it. I get defensive about my cases, and I would expect nothing less from you. I'm just trying to get to the truth. That's all."

Tess sighed again. "I'm sorry. I am very protective about my work too. This has been over a decade of my life, and I thought it was over. So yes, take the evidence. May I ask what you are taking and where you are taking it?"

"Of course." I figured it would be best to keep Katerina's name out of this for now. "There are people in New York City that, for no other way to put it, hire out their noses. They either make perfume or figure out what is in existing perfumes. I thought I'd give it a shot."

"Wow, that's a good idea. Never knew there were people that could do that. My forensic guy can only tell me what's in it, not the name. When are you going? Want me to come along?"

"Thanks for the offer, but I think it is best to keep the crimes separate. I'm only taking one item, the handkerchief, from three different cases for comparison. Is that okay?"

Another long pause and a deep breath, then Tess said, "I guess you're right. I'll get it ready for you. What do you need?"

I could hear the disappointment in her voice.

"Thanks Tess. I have the evidence from the older crimes, so I need the handkerchief and purse of the first victim of the new murders. I'll come grab it later today, if that's okay?"

"Sure, see you then." And the phone clicked.

Chapter Eleven

I made it to the office, checked in at my desk, and went downstairs. The workers were already there installing the special locks on the door. I smiled and moved past them. The room was even better than I remembered from yesterday. Coffee was already brewed, and a small fridge had been brought in. The TV and CD player on a table were new, also a projector and screen sitting in the corner. I saw a note.

> *Jara,*
>
> *I hope I am making this room to your liking. Let me know what the fridge should be stocked with. I brought down a few more cabinets for equipment. Also bringing down evidence gloves and boxes. Let me know if there is anything else you need.*
>
> *Anita*

I wanted to be a smartass and write that I needed a hot tub and a massage therapist, but I was afraid I would get them. How would I explain that? I was laughing when Travis came in.

"What's so funny?" he asked, then started looking around the room. "I see your fairy godmother paid us another visit. This is going to be nice. Have to keep it a secret or everyone will be down here."

"Agreed."

I started pulling out the evidence, setting each case on its own table.

"Travis let's go through the evidence list and see what we have and don't have. We might get a better idea of what we are looking at."

Travis pulled out the copy of the list we were given and the copies he'd made of the original.

"Both of these lists match perfectly. The originals all bear Tess's initials. Looks like she went over these many times."

We matched the list with everything we had.

"Not a single thing wrong or missing, but then again, I would expect nothing less from Tess. I'm afraid, though, if I say anything, it will come out like a backhanded compliment. I'll keep my observations to myself."

My phone rang. Not looking at the screen and thinking it was Tess I answered, "Okay, you do great work."

"You bet your ass I do," Katerina replied, "but in what context are you referring?"

I know I turned many shades of red. "Uh, in every context, my dear."

"Uh-huh."

"Okay, I thought you were my CSP colleague. I was trying to give her a compliment."

"Her?"

I heard the inquisitive tone in her voice. "Uh oh, is the green-eyed demon coming out? Yes, the lead detective from CSP is female, but you have nothing to fret over, my love. Actually, she may be the one in trouble. She already has a complicated history with her male partner, and Travis has his way with women."

"Okay, well as long as it's them doing the fraternizing and not you."

"I promise, my dear." No way was I going to tell her how attractive Tess was. Katerina would find out if and when they ever met. I heard an indistinguishable mumble under Katerina's breath but thought better of asking her what she said.

Katerina let out another sharp breath. "Well, I called to tell you we could run into the city on Friday if you want. I contacted a place I know in New York, and they are excited about this perfume. They own a business which makes designer fragrances for people. They can sniff out anything."

"Sounds exciting, wish I had that talent. I'll make the arrangements. Thanks, love."

As soon as we hung up, I called Tess with the news.

"I'll stop by on my way home to pick up the evidence. Have we learned if the handkerchief was hand or machine stitched?"

"It was hand-stitched. Also, if you noticed, each of them has the same pattern. I also learned the purse was not an expensive one, but it was popular in France. It was made by Dofan up until the 1970s. I think you can still buy some vintage ones online. I even think they had a company in New York," Tess said proudly." If you're going, you might want to confirm that."

"Thanks, Tess, I will. This is great, not sure where this is heading, but it's at least a lead."

We hung up and I told Travis what Tess had said. "Maybe we are finding out new things on this old case."

Chapter Twelve

After a full day of going over all the evidence, I left the office and headed to CSP. Tess had a purse and a handkerchief all ready to go and the paperwork ready to sign. *Can't say she's not efficient. I wonder about her partner though. Can't say how I feel about him yet.* He hadn't done enough one way or the other to get an opinion.

I locked the evidence in the back of my Rover and headed home. Victoria and Katerina were coming home late. I had fixed dinner and headed to the den when I heard them arrive, talking a mile a minute. I called out to them. "Dinner is in the kitchen, wine is in the fridge, and I'm in the den."

Katerina came straight into the den with a large smile on her face. She was almost giddy as she hugged and kissed me. "We found one of the accounts where Dad stashed the money."

Katerina's father embezzled over $270 million of the Foundation's money. The authorities, with the help of Victoria and Katerina, had been looking for it ever since.

"That's wonderful," I said. "How much?"

"Over $50 million, plus the interest it has accrued. It's in an offshore account, of course, but the authorities feel this bank will work with us. We may have to go there when the time comes to prove it as ours." She flopped on the leather couch.

"We?"

"Well yes, we, silly girl. I'd love if you could come with me, but I know you are deep in this case. Mom will probably go." A devilish grin slowly spread over her face. "Probably for the best anyway. That way I won't get distracted."

"So where did you find this money?" I asked, curiosity creeping in as I thought of ways I could distract her. "And when are you going?"

"In the Caribbean, of course," she said, her sly grin not leaving her face. "Not sure when, maybe within the month. Honestly, I have a feeling it will take many trips."

I fell for the tease. "Maybe I can make one of those trips," I said. "I love seeing you on the beach."

Katerina came over and kissed me. "Yeah, maybe," she said, as she turned to walk back to the kitchen. "That is, if you can leave your detective."

"You mean the task force, right?" I yelled after her. I heard her faint giggle and pouted for a bit. Her job was taking her to the islands, and I was only going as far as New York City.

We all went to bed early that night. I tossed and turned, but Katerina slept like a log. I think the excitement of going to New York City and the islands had worn her out.

The next morning, I went to my Rover and checked on my evidence. I pulled out the boxes they were in.

"Oh, a Dofan. Where did you get that old thing?" Victoria had come up behind me.

"Well, damn. I should bring all my evidence home so you and Katerina can identify it. How did you know what it was?"

"Oh, Matka and I both had one. A French purse at a reasonable price. You know how she liked to be classy but frugal." She laughed. "That one seems new, like you bought it from a vintage store. Even then, I would think it would have some wear on it."

I stood there shaking my head. Might as well take a chance. I pulled out the handkerchief and opened its bag. "Does this look or smell familiar?"

Victoria leaned over. "From what I can see, the cloth is a high-end silk. I love the hand-stitched embroidery. It's very pretty."

"How can you tell it's hand-stitched?"

"I can't be positive. Silk is a bit hard to embroider, but embroidery was all the rage then." She pointed to the design. "See, you can tell by the stitches and the different thicknesses of the embroidery thread. If it was a machine, it would all be the same."

"How do you know all this?" I asked, as I put the items back in the lockboxes.

"Being fancy was a thing back in my day. A one-of-a-kind handkerchief, handbag, and scarf made you stand out." A nostalgic smile spread across Victoria's face. "By the way, the perfume on the handkerchief is also French, but I'll be damned if I can place it."

"Well, aren't you a wealth of information?" I smiled. "I'm taking these to a nose hound, or something like that, in New York. I'm hoping they can tell me the brand."

"I'm sure they can. Who knew French fashion and perfume would enter into your case?" Victoria gave a genteel laugh and walked to her car. She got something out, then went back inside, still softly chuckling.

So I have two votes on a Dofan purse, hand stitched embroidery, and French perfume. Won't be calling Victoria or Katerina to the stand though. It's time to confirm everything.

I got to the office and went straight to the basement but struggled to get in the door. Surprisingly, Mrs. Burris showed up. She opened the door for me and explained how each lock worked.

I looked at her, puzzled, and wondered how she knew I was there. Mrs. Burris explained. "I waited around to make sure you knew how to get in and would be able to lock up."

"Thank you, Mrs. Burris, you have done so much."

She shrugged her shoulders and followed me into the office. "Please, call me Anita."

I sat my evidence box on a table and went to get the box with the evidence from the first case.

"Jara, is there anything else I can help you with? I'd be more than happy to. I owe Granny May so much. It's the least I can do."

"Thank you for that. You have done a lot already. Oh, by the way, Victoria says hi and that you should come to the house soon. She would love to see you."

I went about my business of getting an empty box to place the items I needed into it and didn't pay attention to whether Mrs. Burris had left or not. When I came back to the table, Mrs. Burris was still standing there.

"Anita, is there anything else I can help you with, or is there something I need to know?"

"Oh no, no, no my dear. I just smelled something that took me back. I guess you caught me daydreaming."

"Really?" I noticed she was by the box of evidence from the first murder. "May I ask what you smelled?"

"I know it can't be, but I smelled the perfume my husband bought me while we were honeymooning in France." She must have seen the shocked look on my face. "Oh, my dear, I'm so sorry. I'll leave you to it."

"No, no, please wait. Can I ask you a couple questions?"

"Sure."

"Do you work for this building or for the FBI?"

"Oh, the FBI. Of course. You don't think I could be down here or have access to everything if I didn't?" She let out a hardy laugh and winked at me.

Makes sense, never really thought about it that way. Now I have even more questions but for another time. "Anita, do you remember the name of the perfume that you smelled?"

"Well, it smells a lot like L'Interdit. I love that perfume. You can't get it anymore, at least not the original. My husband got it for me in 1965, I believe. We were in France, and he knew I absolutely adored Audrey Hepburn. So he bought me the perfume that was made exclusively for her."

"Audrey Hepburn's perfume. Seriously? How did you get ahold of that?"

"Well, initially it was made just for her, like I said. The creator, Givenchy I believe, wanted to market it. She refused, told him she forbade it. Later, she allowed its release and Givenchy named it L'Interdit. The word *l'interdit* is translated to forbidden in French."

My jaw dropped to the floor. I yelled out loud—"FORBIDDEN! Of course!"—and hugged Mrs. Burris.

"Oh, my dear, are you okay?"

"Mrs. Burris, I mean Anita, you just gave me a huge break in this case. Thank you so much. I'll explain later. Thank you again. If you'll excuse me, I have some calls to make."

"Glad I could help," she said, with a confused look on her face. "Let me know if there's anything else I can do."

I nodded and excitedly dialed Tess's number. I didn't even let her say hello before I began. "Tess, I got it," I said with excitement. “Mr. Branson *was* telling you the name of the perfume.”

“What? Huh? Jara? What do you mean?”

“Yes, it’s Jara. Sorry. When Mr. Branson told you the name of the perfume was forbidden and laughed, he was really telling you its name, L’Interdit. In French it means forbidden.”

“That son of a bitch.” Tess growled. “He knew this all along and tried to trick us, play it off. By the way, how do you know this?”

I went into the long explanation about Katerina smelling the perfume on me last night and her naming some of the ingredients, plus Victoria knowing about the French bag and the handkerchief. Then about Mrs. Burris’s honeymoon perfume and the story behind that.

“I’m still going to take it to New York to confirm it all, but if we need, we’ll have corroborating witnesses.”

We talked a while longer, trying to figure out what French bags, perfume, and a classy handkerchief had to do with these murders. It definitely meant something since they were present at all the crime scenes. We hung up, and all I could think was, *Mr. Branson, we got you on this one.*

Travis came into the room and bellowed, “What in the hell is that smell?”

“That’s the smell of knowledge and winning, my friend!”

I spent the rest of the day comparing all the purses, the handkerchiefs, and the smells. The perfume smell was lost on me, but the purses were an exact match except for the wear and tear. The handkerchiefs also matched. Well, almost. Each was silk with the same embroidery pattern, but the stitches were not identical. So they were definitely hand-stitched.

I looked through the murder books to see if there was any significant mention of the purse and handkerchiefs. Interestingly enough, I saw that the parents used to live in France in the 1960s. What a coincidence. I looked through all the interviews of the Branson family. I couldn’t find any with the Branson mother before she passed. I decided to do a deep dive into the family to figure out what they were all about. My first search brought up Andrew Branson and the murder trial, of course. Andrew was a single male, one of three triplets. He and his brother, Alan, both worked for the insurance company their grandfather had started in Hartford, Connecticut. Antoinette, their sister, didn't follow in the family footsteps. She graduated magna cum laude from Harvard, but I wasn't able to learn what she did after her graduation, other than move to Europe. Her last known address was near Gimont, France.

France. Why does France keep coming up in all of this? Family having lived there, Antoinette currently living there, and evidence coming from there. What the hell? Plus, Katerina and I were just there. What a small world.

I decided to go with my gut to contact André Garnier, a peer from Interpol. Katerina and I met up with him while we were in France. I took a chance on the time difference and gave him a call. Surprisingly, he answered on the first ring.

"André, how are you? Jara here."

"*Bonjour*, Jara, long time no hear."

"Funny. Katerina and I were just talking about how we wish were still there, but that's not what I'm calling about. I need to pick your brain about a case, if you don't mind."

"Sure, what can I do for you?"

"I need a deep dive into a family that used to live in France, probably in the '80s maybe '90s. Mr. and Mrs. James Branson Jr., parents of Andrew, Alan, and Antoinette Branson. She goes by Toni. She allegedly lives in Gimont, France, but I'm not sure."

"Are they living or deceased?"

"The father passed in 2014 and the mother in 2020, both here in the States. Also, I need to know a current address for Toni."

"Sounds easy enough. So how is it back in the States with my lovely Katerina?" André asked with a lilt in his voice.

"Good and bad. Love being home, but I've been so busy working I am barely able to enjoy my house and my lovely Katerina."

"So you're having issues with a case and not seeing Katerina," André said deviously. "I can help with both of those issues."

"You are always the flirt. Thank you for the offer, but doing the lookup is enough. I'll talk with you later."

"Send Katerina my love."

"I will."

I hung up, shaking my head. *What a wonderful guy and such a flirt.* I must have been daydreaming when Travis walked in.

"So where are you, Quinn? I've been talking to you for five minutes. Where did you drift off to?"

"France, actually. I spoke with André from Interpol. He's based in France. I'm working on a hunch." I explained the details to Travis.

"Double-checking everything again, I see," Travis laughed.

"Hey, we said we're going to start at the beginning. This is the beginning. I need to know about the parents, what type of upbringing the triplets had. Did something happen to cause this behavior? Did they even commit the crimes?"

While we were talking, my phone rang, a French number.

"Hello."

"Jara, are you sure about the names you gave me?" André asked.

"André, I read them directly from my file." I looked it up again and reread all the family information to him.

"Well Jara, there is no Antoinette or Toni Branson in all of France with this birthdate. There is, however, an Anthony Branson with this birthday in Gimont."

"André, is there any way you could get me a photo of this Anthony Branson?"

"Past or present?"

"Both, if you can. That would be perfect. I owe you. So what about the parents?"

"Still working on that. I'm looking in a few other places for them," he said, as he tapped on a keyboard. "I'll call you after I get more information."

I had another hunch I wanted to explore and figured this was as good a time as any. "André, I have one more favor to ask of you, if you don't mind."

"Another so soon, *ma chérie*?"

"Could you look up in your database any homicides with a cross-dressing element and exsanguination?"

"No blood, *chérie*?" André asked, curiosity in his voice. "That should be easy enough to look up. Anything else?"

"I'm hoping that's all. Thank you again."

We disconnected, and I went back and pulled everything out, lining up the items on a table. By this time Travis was staring at me.

"What are you up to?" he asked, as circled the table and me.

"I have this gut feeling that won't go away. I want to see what this family is all about. Something isn't sitting well with me, and I know it's right here, right in front of me."

"As I always say, go with your gut, girl. But I'm packing up for the day. You coming?"

I looked at the clock. Man it was late. "Yeah, yeah, leaving soon. I promise." I called Katerina and apologized profusely before I told her I had spoken to André.

"Ahh, sweet André. Come home soon, please, and be safe."

I packed up my stuff and put away all the evidence. I was on my way out, when I saw Mrs. Burris again. "Mrs. uh...Anita, hi. I'm on my way out. Hope you have a good night."

"Good night, Jara. Hope you are making some headway."

"Honestly, I don't know. I never know 'til it's over."

"Good luck then, my dear."

"Thank you. Yes, luck, going to need a lot of it. Good night."

It was late when I finally made it home. All the lights were off except one. I slipped into the house and made my way to the kitchen, grabbed a beer, and saw a wrapped up sandwich with my name on it. I started toward the den to do some more work when I heard a voice.

"Oh no you don't. No more working tonight. Remember, the nights are mine, even if there is only a little left of this one. You need to eat and go to bed so you are fresh in the morning." Katerina had come in from the back porch with a glass of wine in her hand.

“Oh, I was, uh…just going to eat a sandwich and have a beer.” I was caught, red-handed, walking into the den with a file in my hand.

“Eat the sandwich, but the file needs to be put away,” Katerina said sternly.

I didn’t have a good argument to stay up and read the file I had already read over one hundred times. At least, that was what it felt like. Plus, looking at the seriousness on Katerina’s beautiful face, I knew it would be an argument I had no chance of winning. I finished the sandwich and put away the file. “All yours, my love. Time to get some sleep.”

“Sleep?” Katerina laughed wickedly. “Who said anything about sleep? I said you needed to go to bed. It’s my turn for attention.”

Again, an argument I would not win, nor did I want to.

Chapter Thirteen

I woke refreshed the next morning, even though I didn't get much sleep. I wasn't complaining. Some things were worth it. I gathered my things and packed a small bag for New York. Katerina came in with some coffee and a smile.

"My bags are already in the car. I can't wait to get to New York City," Katerina said excitedly.

"You know this is a work trip for me, right?"

"Not the whole time." She kissed my neck. It was very distracting. "The rules apply there too. The nights are mine."

"Okay, you have me there. Maybe we can have dinner with Chase and Abby?"

"No, they left for the weekend to see Abby's folks in Maine, so we'll have the place all to ourselves."

I gave Katerina a questioning look. "Why do I think you had something to do with Chase and Abby not being home?"

Katerina gave a mischievous grin. "I'll never tell, but I get you all to myself at the apartment. We can have a romantic dinner with a beautiful view of Central Park."

Granny May left each of her grandchildren property in her will. They'd all decided which one they wanted but shared access with each other. It was amazing, not a single disagreement between them. Katerina took the properties in France. Chase took the New York City apartment, and CJ took the horse ranch in Virginia. It was as if Granny knew all along which child should get which property.

"Remember, my love, I am going on business." I tried to act serious but couldn't resist the grin. "But any fringe benefits are most welcome."

"Wonderful." Katerina pulled me to her. "Best business trip ever."

I walked into the kitchen to get some more coffee, as Katerina went upstairs for some last-minute items. Victoria was sitting at the kitchen island with a smirk on her face. "It looks like you two are going to have fun in the city. While you are gone, I have decided to have a small dinner party with some old friends. I hope that is okay. I invited Anita Burris and Susan Hatfield, among others. Have you made any progress in Mr. Hatfield's murder case?"

"I'm sorry, Victoria. It seems like we have a lot of leads but not a lot of progress. I wish I had better news for you. I'm happy you're having a party though. Please give Mrs. Hatfield my best and tell her we are working very hard. Heck, Anita knows how hard we're working." I felt bad that I couldn't say more, but honestly, what was there to say?

"Keep working on it, dear. I have faith in you. You'll figure out something." Victoria made her way around the island and hugged me. "If anyone can solve this, it's you."

"Thanks Victoria, I needed that vote of confidence."

Katerina bounded into the kitchen. I had actually never seen her with this much pep in her step.

"It looks like someone is excited to go into the city." Victoria let me go and gave her daughter a quick hug.

I wasn't one for big cities, let alone New York, but Katerina fit right into the hustle and bustle of city life.

"C'mon, slow poke," she teased. "We're going to be late. My nose hounds will be waiting for us, and they are very excited about this."

I rolled my eyes and grabbed a to-go coffee. "I don't think they're the only ones excited," I said, as I headed for the car. I heard whispering between Katerina and Victoria. *Lord knows what they're up to*. I figured I would find out on the way.

Chapter Fourteen

We hit good traffic for the trip and made it to the Manhattan apartment in about an hour. Katerina had called ahead and made an appointment at an establishment called The Nose Knows. We headed to the Cobble Hill area of Brooklyn a bit early to grab something to eat, and we found a little café in a beautiful, brick, historic building. We sat at an outside table, and I felt as if we were in a quaint little village and not New York City at all. Granted there were more people than I was used to, but it was surprisingly quiet. After lunch, we walked down Smith Street to a small storefront with a large nose painted on the window. You didn't have to be a detective to know this had to be the place. Inside were sparkling glass cases with small, intricate bottles. A few ladies were helping a handful of customers, pulling out bottle after bottle. In the back of the store was a statuesque brunette, her hair pulled up and back, wearing librarian type glasses. She was different than the other women, beyond the lab coat and clipboard. An air of confidence exuded from her.

"Elly!" Katerina exclaimed. Everyone in the store turned to her as she ran to the elegant woman.

Putting down her clipboard, Elly opened her arms to greet Katerina. "Kat! I am so glad to see you. I have been looking forward to this since you called."

I walked up to them as they embraced and noticed people still staring.

Katerina turned to me after a minute. "Jara, this is Eleanor Stovall, the best chemist and nose in the country, maybe even the world."

The lady laughed and held out her hand to me. "Call me Elly, please, and don't listen to her. I'm not the best, but I will admit I have a good nose for things."

Taking her hand, I said, "Then you, Elly, are exactly the person I need. If you'll excuse me, let me go get the items I need help with."

I shook my head and went out the door. Of course Katerina knew this person. I bet that was what she and Victoria were whispering about. I got to my Rover and, after unlocking the vault in the back, I retrieved four of each item, purses and handkerchiefs. There were two from the old cases and one from a recent one. Plus, I'd bought an unrelated purse and handkerchief at a vintage store as a control. I brought in the boxes, and Elly's eyes lit up as if she were about to open a Christmas gift.

Without moving her eyes off the boxes, she unlocked a side door and disappeared behind the brightly lit storefront. It was like a whole different world back there, microscopes, lab coats, beakers...You name it, it was there. A fully functioning lab for what exactly, I didn't know. I felt as if I had stepped into the Batcave.

"Jara, welcome to my magic kingdom." Elly made a sweeping gesture, indicating the entire room. "This is where it all happens, making personal fragrances, discovering new mixtures and blends, and hopefully creating the next new perfume sensation. Nothing can beat Chanel No. 5 in my opinion though."

I could smell all kinds of scents, flowery, woodsy, musky, citrusy...but to actually name them? There was no way I could. I thought it would be overwhelming, like a department store perfume section or a funeral home with tons of flowers, but this wasn't bad. To be honest, I was lucky to figure out a few of those scents. No way could I mix them without it probably smelling like bug spray.

"Can we go somewhere private, as in without all these other amazing smells?" I asked, looking around.

"Of course. Upstairs I have an area especially for this." Elly led us over to a door with an elevator behind it.

Katerina was grinning from ear to ear. "I just love all of this."

We rode to the fifth floor and entered what looked like a grand parlor of sorts, decorated in plush, royal reds and deep purples, with tables alongside comfortable couches.

"This is where we bring our most exclusive clients, people who want their own personal fragrance. May we get started? I am very excited about this."

I set the boxes on a table. “Before we start, Elly, how much has Katerina told you about what I have?”

Elly turned to Katerina. I had just noticed they were holding hands. “All she has told me is that you have an old scent, possibly perfume, you need identified. She knows I love a good mystery.”

“Nothing else?”

“Jara! I wouldn’t compromise your case, I promise. Jesus.” Katerina scoffed and sat in a nearby chair.

I could tell she was pouting. “Honey, I’m sorry. I have to keep the integrity of the case at all costs. I’m not accusing you of anything.” I turned to the boxes on the table and opened them. “Elly, you don’t mind if I record all of this, do you? I need it for documentation.”

“Of course not. Let’s begin.”

Elly went into a small room next to the one we were in. She took off her lab coat, washed her face, arms and hands, and put on a fresh lab coat and white gloves. She returned and set three more pair of gloves on the table. She then took out index cards and put them in front of each box. I had already set up the video camera. After recording her preparation, I narrowed the focus to the work area. I sat at the table with the camera remote and asked if Elly was ready. She nodded.

I said my name, the date, and the name of the store. I rechecked the camera to make sure it was recording and continued. “I am sitting here with Dr. Eleanor Stovall, biochemist and perfumer. Am I correct with that doctor?”

“Yes, Ms., I mean Agent Quinn, you are.”

I smiled. “Can you tell me your background and training, please, for the record?”

“Yes, of course. I graduated summa cum laude from MIT with a degree in chemistry and molecular biology. I also hold an MBA from Harvard. I then went to Versailles, France, and attended ISIPCA, completing a multitude of graduate courses on fragrance development, advanced composition, and regulatory affairs management of fragrance and cosmetics. I interned with some of the best perfumers in the world. I worked for perfumers in France and Thailand before opening my business, The Nose Knows, here in Brooklyn. My business makes personal fragrances and cosmetics and, on occasion, separates and identifies scents for law enforcement agencies."

I was blown away. She was more than qualified for this project. I could feel my heart pounding throughout my body and hoped the audio didn't pick that up. I looked over to Katerina, who had a Cheshire grin on her face. Of course she knew all this about Elly. Katerina mouthed *I love you* to me, and I started to calm down and focus back on Elly. She was still detailing her background. I smiled at her, cueing that what she had said was more than enough.

"May I begin? I will try to explain my process as I go if you would like," Elly said. I nodded. Elly took the first box and pulled out the purse and the handkerchief. She lifted each to her nose and took a deep breath and held it for a few moments. She began writing things down on the index cards and kept smelling each again, over and over. "Do you want me to tell you my findings now or after the last one?"

"At the end of each box please, and then we can discuss them all as a whole."

"Very well." She took each item again and wrote more notes on the cards. "Okay, box one. Both the handkerchief and the purse had the same smell to them. Some of the top notes were citrus, possibly a blend of lemon and lime, with a floral scent of lavender. Not very unusual or unique. The heart notes are definitely jasmine and cinnamon. I could smell a base note of vanilla and sandalwood. I can't place the perfume, but it seems very generic."

"Thank you. Can you repeat the same process with each of the others please?"

"Of course."

She put away box one. I zoomed the camera focus out, as she stood up and walked across the room to take a few deep breaths. She returned, changed her gloves, and opened box two. She took the handkerchief and lifted it to her nose. Her eyes widened like saucers, and a smile came over her face. She inhaled again, deeper this time. "Oh my, this can't be." She breathed in again and began writing furiously on the index cards. She lifted the purse out of the box and again inhaled deeply. "Oh my, wow, oh my" she kept repeating. "May I place the handkerchief on my skin?"

I figured it wouldn't hurt since she'd cleaned her arms, and we were in the process of determining this scent. It wasn't like doing so would make it go away. I nodded my head and said yes.

She gently took the handkerchief from the evidence bag and laid it on her left arm. She bent over and inhaled as if she was smelling a pie at Christmas. Again, she smiled and appeared to drift off in a daydream. "Ahhhh...L'Interdit. I haven't smelled the original in years. This is amazing. The spring-like smell is fruity, like peach, orange, and strawberry. So fresh, with heart notes of jasmine, lily of the valley, narcissus and powdery scents of iris and roses. There is a musky base note, sandalwood, and a grassy smell. This is unbelievable. Oh, this takes me back." Elly's eyes were still closed. She was talking as if she were back in France.

"I met the perfumer, Francis Fabron, before he passed in 2005. Hubert Givenchy requested Fabron to create this fragrance for his client, Audrey Hepburn. Givenchy was her personal dresser. When Givenchy gave this fragrance to Hepburn in the '50s, Fabron asked if he could mass produce it. Her alleged reply was *"Je vous l'interdis."* Later, when she allowed its distribution, Givenchy named the scent L'Interdit, French for forbidden. This is so remarkable." She opened her eyes. "Sorry for the history lesson, but this perfume is so unique. It is the first one ever backed by a celebrity. In my opinion, it made the business what it is today. People wanting their own fragrance. I can't believe this is the original."

I smiled, knowing she had confirmed what others guessed at. "Okay, ready for the others?"

"Of course, but let me clear my palate again." Elly got up, shaking her head and repeating, "I can't believe it." Elly went back to the adjacent room, washed her hands and arms again, then returned. She put on the third set of gloves and reached for box number three. She gently pulled out the evidence bag with the handkerchief, opened it, inhaled deeply and laughed. "You're trying to trick me, aren't you?"

"Excuse me?"

"This is also L'Interdit, but it's the Les Mythiques version, the remix from around 2007. It is very close to the original, but a little spicier." She wrote down a lot of things and looked at me. "Number four?"

Elly repeated what she did with the first three boxes. She inhaled deeply, got a puzzled look on her face, and inhaled again. "Wow, this is again L'Interdit but different. I smell vetiver, and there are hints of patchouli and orange blossom, a lot of flowery hints also." She pointed to a wall of books. "May I?"

"Sure."

She got up and skimmed through the books. "Here it is." She pulled out a large notebook and started flipping through its pages. "Gotcha! This last one is again L'Interdit, but the 2018 version. So we have god only knows what with number one, the original L'Interdit in number two, my personal favorite, the 2007 version in number three, and the 2018 version in number four. I am 100 percent certain. Here are my notes on each one, and I'll also include my prior research."

I wanted to make sure there weren't any questions on this. "So Dr. Stovall, again you stated box number two had the original L'Interdit fragrance, correct?"

"Yes, I am 100 percent certain."

"Thank you, Doctor, for your time and work. I will have the audio of this meeting transcribed. Could we meet later for you to sign for its authenticity?"

"Of course."

"Time is 3:48 p.m., this is the video of myself, Agent Jara Quinn, and perfumer, Dr. Eleanor Stovall. End tape."

I turned off the camera and exclaimed, "Oh my god, Elly, thank you so much. You are amazing. I can't fathom how you do this."

"I guess I got the gift of the nose," she said with a chuckle. "I am so glad to finally meet you. Katerina has spoken of you for years and years."

"Years and years?" I looked over to Katerina. She had joined us by this time.

"I have known Elly since high school. She was going to MIT when I went to Notre Dame and met you. She finished school here in the States, then went off to France, as you know from her résumé. We got together every chance we could and wrote nonstop."

Looking back and forth between Katerina and Elly, I asked "How is it then I never met you?"

"It never worked out for us all to get together." Katerina shrugged. "But she knows all about you. Even had the insight back in college that we should be together as a couple."

"Well, Elly, thank you for that. I needed all the help I could get with her."

Katerina giggled. "You know you had me the whole time."

We decided to get an early dinner at a nearby bistro. I let Katerina and Elly go ahead while I secured the evidence in my car vault, and then I caught up to them. As we walked down the sidewalk, I touched Elly's elbow and stopped her. "Thank you for helping me with this. I hope you understand you may be called as an expert witness in this case."

"It may be fun and enlightening to let people know what I do."

I looked at Elly a little closer. With her beautiful brown eyes, high cheek bones, long neck, and square shoulders, I would have guessed she had been a model in France, not a genius. To say the least, I was impressed. The bistro was a quiet, trendy little spot with bright colors, comfy chairs, and an all over great vibe.

"This is a new spot," Elly said. "They are still in the process of restoring the area. The great part is the people who were not displaced. They were given the opportunity to be in a new area with housing and job opportunities." Elly's pride was reflected in her voice as she spoke.

Katerina smiled. "I have a feeling you had something to do with all this, didn't you?"

"I couldn't take over a building and kick out over one hundred people, now, could I?" Elly said, with a glint in her eye. "I had to do something or at least try and help."

"It looks like you and others went above and beyond," I said, as I looked around the area.

A waiter approached. "Elly, your usual?"

"But of course, and whatever they want."

Katerina and I ordered and sat back on the couch. Katerina reached for my hand, and I flinched.

Elly chuckled. "Oh it's okay. This is a very diverse place."

I loosened up, took Katerina's hand, and mouthed *sorry*.

Soon the food and wine came. Katerina and Elly began busily chatting about high school and Katerina's trips to France. Elly brought up their high school prom. "Do you still have pictures of us at prom? What a hoot!"

"Actually, I do." Katerina pulled out an envelope. "One of the best memories of high school. You were so handsome."

I thought handsome was a strange way to describe Elly. I must have had a puzzled look on my face.

Elly guffawed. "I see you caught the wording, Jara. I was very handsome in high school and for a few years after that, if I say so myself."

My face must have still showed confusion.

Katerina spoke up. "Honey, do you remember me talking about Larry, my high school boyfriend, and how I would go to Europe sometimes to see him?"

"Yes, I was jealous as hell when you would leave. I knew you were close, but damn, that was high school. Why?"

Both Elly and Katerina were laughing. "Jara, meet Larry."

Elly reached out her hand. "Glad to finally meet you, Jara. Like I said earlier, I did a lot in Europe. It was life-changing, you could say."

At first, I was in shock, but then my face brightened as I looked back and forth at each of them. "Larry?! You are the high school boyfriend? Seriously? Well, that explains some things. I have seen people who have gone through the transition, but Elly, I had no idea. You look magnificent."

They were both chortling and pointing at me. Katerina snuggled up to me once they calmed down. "I can't believe you didn't know, you the detective and all."

"But she," I sputtered, turning toward Elly, "I mean, you are beautiful. More than just beautiful."

"It's amazing what money can buy."

Elly told me her story of always feeling out of sorts, not feeling like herself. "I realized, late in high school, I felt more like one of the girls than one of the guys. Katerina was my saving grace. She allowed me to explore my feelings and eccentricities. She was even there during all my surgeries. I couldn't have made it without her. The best girlfriend ever."

I was looking at Katerina with even more love and admiration. "Yes, best girlfriend ever."

Katerina grabbed both of our hands and squeezed them. She then reached for her drink and raised her glass. "I love you both so much. I'm the luckiest girl in the world."

More drinks came, and we discussed old times and new adventures. As we were talking, Elly turned to me. "Okay, it's been killing me, no pun intended, but what was all this smelling about?"

"I can't really discuss many of the details of the case, but I will say some of the items you tested for me were found at crime scenes."

"Crime scenes? As in more than one?"

"I'm afraid so. This is a long and complicated case. I'm far from figuring it out."

Elly's voice took on a serious tone. "Well, I hope I helped at least a little."

"You did in many ways. A lot of mysteries were cleared up today. Thank you."

We gathered our things and headed for the door. As we all said our goodbyes, Katerina and Elly lingered in their hug a bit.

"Stay in touch, please," Katerina said, as she grabbed Elly's hands. "It's been too long. You know you are always welcome at the house."

Elly smiled and nodded. "I promise I will stay in touch. Tell your mother hi for me."

We left Elly and walked to where the car was parked. I looked at Katerina and said, "That dinner explained a lot. I wondered why I never heard of Larry anymore."

"I didn't feel it was my story to tell. I figured you'd find out sooner or later. I'm so happy you know now and have met my friend. I hope she can be yours also."

"Is this what you and your mother were whispering about before we left?"

Katerina smiled and nodded her head. "Mom has known since the beginning. She was the one who recommended Elly as your 'nose' for this case."

We reached my Rover. Something was different. I looked around at the key locks and saw scratches. "Someone has tried to get in here. What the hell?" I found even more scratches by the windows and even a small pry mark by the back door.

"It's New York," Katerina said. "Someone saw a nice ride and tried to break in."

"Kat, I think it was more than that. Someone really wanted in here."

I opened the vault. All the contents were safe and secure. I resecured the vault and shut the back door, making sure it locked. "I'm going to need to get this fixed as soon as possible." I tried to think of who knew I was coming to New York and for what reason, other than my team. Something was eating at me again. "Kat, I know you want to stay the weekend in the city, but would you consider going home tonight instead of staying here?" I could see her starting to pout. "Okay, okay, we'll spend tonight in the city, but we go home tomorrow. I'm not feeling safe, and I don't want you to be hurt."

"Sweetheart, I'll be fine. I'm not afraid of what's out there. You should know that by now."

I looked at her beautiful face. She was serious, not bothered at all. We made it to the apartment in decent time, even though there was heavy traffic. I decided to bring my evidence upstairs, just to make sure it was safe. Maybe Katerina was right. My car was a good target to hit, but I was still not taking a chance.

I hadn't been to the East Side apartment before. It was huge, as in any city huge, but for New York, it was massive. Two floors encompassed three-thousand square feet and offered multiple views of Central Park and the skyline. The sun was dipping behind the park as stars started popping out. Actually, there were no stars, just the lights of the city, shining brightly in the newly dark sky.

Katerina came up behind me and wrapped her arms around my waist. "So what do you think of the view?"

"The view is amazing! Seems massive and busy but still has a beauty to it. Not sure I'd want to live here though. No place to sail. Buildings and traffic are everywhere."

She swung me around. "Like I said, how do you like the view?"

I started to repeat myself, but no words came out. All I saw was a gorgeous silhouette of a woman with long, wavy, red hair, an emerald necklace, and nothing else. This view I could live with forever. I pulled her to me and began kissing and touching her everywhere I could. She grabbed my hands and backed me up. “We have all night,” she said breathily as she undressed me.

We made love all over that apartment, taking short breaks to snack and drink a little. I could feel the excitement in her body. Then I whispered to her, “You like it here, don’t you? The hum of the city, the sparkle of the lights.”

“Yes, I guess I do. I loved coming to the city with Granny. Always something new to see and do. I wouldn’t want to live here, though, I don’t think. Too much is never a good thing.”

“Oh really? Guess I’ll go to sleep now,” I said with a teasing voice.

She laughed and jumped on me. “You know what I mean.”

Chapter Fifteen

We decided to stay in the city one more day. There were a couple of shops and exhibits Katerina wanted to see before we left. I found Granny May's safe in the apartment and stored the evidence there. I checked it again and finished getting dressed. Katerina walked in as she saw me strapping on my ankle holster.

Annoyed, she shook her head. "Seriously, I know this is New York, but do you have to be armed everywhere we go?"

"Actually, yes, especially when I'm working on a case. I can never be too careful."

Katerina rolled her eyes and walked out. I felt silly wearing both my guns. But after being shot, I never went anywhere without at least one. I made sure neither gun was obvious and joined Katerina in the living room. I saw her standing stiffly. Figuring she was mad, I started apologizing. She put up her hand to stop me, and I saw she was on the phone.

"She is where?" Katerina said to the person on the phone. "Yes, sir. I understand. I'll tell her. We'll be right there."

Katerina hung up the phone with tears in her eyes. "Elly has been attacked. It happened last night when she left her building. She's at the hospital and asking for us, you in particular."

We rushed to the hospital and were taken to Elly's room. Two policemen were at the door, and the doctor was at her bedside. I asked the police why they were still there, and one of the officers said the detective that was assigned was looking at this as a hate crime and wanted guards posted. I identified myself as FBI and got the detective's name and card, Noel Gregory. When we stepped inside the room, Elly motioned us closer to her bed. "Doctor, please tell my friends, Katerina and FBI Special Agent Jara Quinn, what you just told me."

"Well, the good news is Ms. Stovall will be physically okay. She has a concussion and some bruises on her arms and legs.

What worried me was a cut on her right femoral artery. She is very lucky it wasn't too deep. Thank God she's a fighter."

What he said hit me like a ton of bricks. "Cut on her right femoral artery? Doctor, are you sure?"

"Positive. Ms. Stovall made it about five blocks before collapsing. She lost a lot of blood, but a cabbie saw her and called 911. She is very lucky."

I tried to keep my voice calm. "Thank you, Doctor. Thank you very much. If Ms. Stovall doesn't mind, may I have a copy of her injuries report?"

Elly nodded her approval.

"Agent Quinn, I'll make a copy for you immediately. I take it this is important?"

"Yes, Doctor, it is. Again, thank you."

I had so many questions, but I knew I couldn't interview Elly here or like this. I looked at Katerina and mouthed, *my case*, and pointed to my phone. I asked the doctor for somewhere private so I could go to use my phone. He showed me a door down the hall, and I left to make some calls. My first was to Travis, and I explained the whole situation to him.

"Holy shit, you really think this attack is related to our case? You said it was a woman. I mean, a man to a woman already. Doesn't the unsub only hit men, then make them women?"

"I don't know, but Elly had her femoral artery cut. Everything about this is odd. My Rover was tampered with, now this. It has to be connected. Please call SSA Stewart and let him know. I need to call Tess now. I'll talk to you later."

I rang up Tess.

"Tess, things are crazy here in New York."

"What do you mean? Things are happening here also. Someone tried to break into the evidence locker here at CSP, no idea how yet. Was just notified. It really pisses me off."

"What the hell is going on? Why is somebody trying to steal all the evidence? It's not like it's new or anything. They could have tried this years ago."

"Well, actually it did happen once during the trial, but nothing of importance was taken except a ring that was found near the body of number four. We never figured out a connection."

“Are you kidding me? Evidence was stolen. You never told me. What the hell, Tess? Don’t you think that might have been something I needed to know? Jesus!”

“I’m sorry, I should have told you, but Jacob said it was no big deal.”

“Jacob said. Since when do you listen to Jacob? So was this ring removed from the evidence log also? I caught some discrepancies.”

“Wow. Um, I don’t know.” I could hear concern in her voice. “Never really paid attention since they shut the case down after the confession.”

“We may be coming back to town after today. Might have some back and forth to here for a while. I’m going to treat this incident as part of the case until we find out differently.”

I hung up, frustrated and angry. I walked back to Elly’s room. My mind was racing. I asked the officers to call the lead detective at once. When I entered the room, Elly was asleep, but lights and beeps were everywhere. How anyone could sleep through that I didn’t know. I remembered back to when I was shot and all the time we spent in the hospital with Victoria. It gave me the creeps. Katerina was sitting by the bed, holding Elly’s hand. I put my hand on her shoulder, and she turned her head to me, tears in her eyes.

“Did we do this? Did we bring her trouble?” she asked, her eyes pleading behind the tears.

I exhaled and shrugged my shoulders. “Honey, I don’t know, but I’m going to find out.”

Elly started to stir in her bed. She was slowly waking up, a slight grin on her face. “Hey ladies, long time no see.”

“Hey, girl,” Kat said, “you could have just asked us to stay in New York. You didn’t have to go and do all this.”

Elly looked at me with very serious eyes. “Jara, I have to talk with you on the record, I mean on video.”

“Okay, I guess. You want to do this now? I mean if you feel this is that important.”

“Not sure, but I need to tell you what happened, what I smelled, and what was said. I want to help. I have no idea if it’s related to your case or not, but it might be.”

“Okay, if you insist. I’ll run down and get my equipment. Just give me a second.”

While I was downstairs, I texted SSA Stewart, telling him I was going to interview Ms. Stovall. "Did Travis call you and explain what was going on? I want to treat this as part of my case, and the victim wants to give a statement. Am I allowed jurisdiction? Also, can you call the lead detective and let them know we're involved?"

SSA Stewart agreed, "Treat it like ours until we learn differently. I'll start making the calls."

I gave him the borough we were in and Elly's information. I grabbed my stuff that I'd locked up in the Rover and headed back upstairs. A large man was hurrying into the hospital at the same time I was. I could tell he was law enforcement due to the badge and the gun. He was a tall, handsome, muscular black man with an air of a detective, notebook in hand, worn shoes, and a distinct badge on his belt. But no way this was Noel.

Taking a chance, I called out, "Detective!"

He turned around and looked at me, face serious and determined. "So you must be the FBI agent I was just told to turn my case over to. Thanks for that."

"Oh sir, I'm sorry. I'm working on a huge case and strongly believe this is related. I promise you, I want to work with you, not cut you out. I honestly need your help."

"You have a serious case, huh? Well, I have a big case also. A lot of hate crimes are happening. I believe this is one of them. I'm really happy this one is actually alive."

"Alive? How many do you have?"

"Well, with this one," he said, seven. At least five dead, one in a coma, and her. That's why this is important to me."

I let out a large sigh. Could this case and the others be related to mine? It really didn't fit the MO, but I'd learned that not everything came in patterns.

"Sir, Ms. Stovall has requested to give me a video statement right away. I would like to video the statement from her before an official interview takes place, if you don't mind."

"You're asking my permission?" he asked, in disbelief. "Well, that's new. Sure, go ahead, as long as I can ask questions afterward."

"Thank you, sir. By the way, I'm Jara Quinn." I reached out my hand.

"Hi, Miss Quinn. I'm Detective Noel Gregory, NYPD." He let out a large breath. "To be honest, I'm glad for the help. This case is killing me."

"You're Noel?" I shook my head. "I would love to know all about your case, but not now. I don't want to taint my interview."

Detective Gregory nodded his head. "Yes, and it's pronounced like I said it, Nole, not No-el. Let's get up there."

"Whatever you say, Detective Gregory." It seemed I'd offended him with my mispronunciation. When we walked into Elly's room, she was still awake and talking with Katerina. Both were crying.

"Hi, Elly," I said "This. is Detective Noel Gregory, NYPD. If you don't mind, he would like to sit in on your statement and ask you some questions afterward if you're feeling up to it?"

"Nice to meet you Detective Gregory. Sorry I don't have my best face on at the moment, but this needs to be done."

I set up my equipment and gently asked Katerina to step out of the room. God knows I didn't want her any more involved than she had to be. I turned on the camera and tested it, then we started.

"My name is Special Agent Jara Quinn. It is 10:15 a.m. With me is Detective Noel Gregory, NYPD, and the victim, Eleanor Stovall. Could each of you say your names and spell them please, for the record." Both did, and I continued. "Ms. Stovall, can you go through the events from last night, please?"

Elly's voice trembled as she tried to speak.

"Elly, it's okay. Do your best. We're here for you." I reached out and touched her hand.

"Well, after dinner I went back to work to close up. I had finished a few things upstairs and went down to the first floor to see if the shop was ready to close. There were three employees left and one customer. Two of my employees were cleaning up, and the third was waiting on a customer."

I cut in. "How long have these employees been with you?"

"Oh, since I opened the building years ago."

"Go on. Can you describe the customer?"

"Of course. She was stunning. She had dark hair swept up on the top of her head, dark eyes, thin face, but prominent features like high cheekbones, thick eyebrows, and very red lips. She had a brown bag but wore black shoes, which I thought was odd. You always need the shoes to match the purse. Well anyway, my employee called out to me and said the customer wanted to speak with me if possible. I agreed and walked over. She seemed nice enough. Quiet, soft-spoken. I introduced myself and told her I was leaving and didn't have much time. I was supposed to have a date last night. I told her, if she needed more time, she could make an appointment for another day. But she refused, saying that she could just speak with me now, that it wouldn't take long. She offered to walk out with me and talk as we walked for a bit. I only live a few blocks away but didn't want her to know where I live, so I decided to walk in the opposite direction. She never introduced herself but started asking me about my business and what different perfumes I have made. She then asked me for directions, which I thought odd. She could have asked anyone in the store for those. We had walked about a block and parted ways. I decided to go home by way of the park but started feeling odd. I was so dizzy I fell to the ground, and I believe I passed out. The next thing I knew, I was in an alley being lifted into a vehicle before I passed out again. I woke up later in a Brownstone basement, tied to a bed type thing. I didn't recognize who was in the room with me or how many there were. All I know is I wanted to get out of there. I felt a hand on my leg. They must have thought I was still passed out, because they weren't really paying attention to me. I knocked something metal out of their hand and heard it clink when it hit the floor. Before they reacted, I was able to get loose and I ran. Not sure how far. I don't know much after that other than waking up here. Jara, I mean Agent Quinn, the reason I wanted you here so badly was I swear to God I thought I heard her mumbling over and over the word forbidden, and I smelled L'Interdit. After smelling it earlier, I'm positive she was wearing L'Interdit, the original."

I sat back in my chair, my mind racing. *What the hell? Did Elly get attacked by my perp?* It didn't make sense. She wasn't a man. She had already made the transition. I looked over at Detective Gregory. I could tell he was confused about the perfume, but I decided not to address it yet. "Detective, if you have questions, please go ahead."

The detective took his cue and began. “Miss Stovall, I’m Detective Gregory. We spoke briefly last night when they brought you in. I only have a few questions for you today. Did the perp say anything else to you? Anything negative in nature? Other than forbidden?”

“Sir, we were talking about perfumes, then she asked me for directions prior to shoving me in the alley. No negative talk other than the word forbidden being mumbled.”

“I hate to ask this, but was there anything sexual about the attack?” Detective Gregory’s tone softened. “Were you violated in any way?”

“Come to think of it, she did grab my breasts as I was passing out. And she put her hand on my crotch, but I didn’t feel penetrated, if that is what you’re asking.”

“Yes, thank you Miss Stovall, that was what I was asking. Do you know where you were taken? Did she have help moving you?”

“Once I fell, I was pretty out of it. I could feel a person pulling me up and walking me toward a car. It sounded like a man, but I can’t be sure. I also don’t know the type of car other than it had a back door, and I was rolled into it. It had to be a large car, because I easily fit into it. Couldn’t tell you where I was taken. I was in and out a lot. I heard both a man and a woman having a conversation in the car, but I only saw the woman.”

The detective and I looked at each other. We both had more questions than answers.

“So, Ms. Stovall, are you saying there were two people who abducted you?” Detective Gregory asked.

“No. Yes. Well, no,” Elly said. “I heard two voices. I didn’t see two people.”

“Well, that doesn’t make a lick of sense,” blurted out Detective Gregory. “Two voices, one person. Are you sure about this?”

“I am only telling you what I know, Detective,” Elly said sternly. “If you don’t believe me, then leave me alone.”

I stood up and said, “Let’s take a break, please,” before it got confrontational. “This is Agent Quinn and Detective Gregory. I’m pausing the interview with Eleanor Stovall. It is 10:45 a.m.” I shut off the video.

"Detective, we aren't here to grill the witness. Just get her story. What is your deal?"

Detective Gregory scoffed. "Fine. Miss Stovall, I am sorry. I didn't mean to come on so strong, but this case is very important to me."

"Thank you, Detective. I accept your apology. I am grateful for your enthusiasm, but honestly, I'm telling you all I know and it's important to me also."

Elly coughed, and I suggested we stop and let her rest. "The doctor said she'd be here for a couple days and not to push her." I guided the detective out of the room and motioned to Katerina to return to Elly's bedside. By this time, Detective Gregory was talking to himself and pacing in the hall.

"Detective?"

"Call me Noel."

"Okay, Noel, are you okay?"

"Five dead bodies, one in a coma and one finally alive. But I still have no answers, no idea how many perps. Are they women? Are they men? How many are there? I'm at a loss." He stopped and glared at me. "By the way, why are you here? You know her? What about your case?" He pointed at me. "How did the FBI get into this?"

"Well, sir, I interviewed Ms. Stovall yesterday for my case. I was informed this morning that she was attacked last night, and she asked me to come."

"So FBI isn't officially involved even though we received a phone call. Jesus, I'm asking more questions." He started back into the room.

I stepped in front of him and took a deep breath, trying to figure out what I could say at this point. "Listen, we are both on the same side here. The victim's side. Luckily, we both want to solve this case. People have died. Can't we work together? I'm positive Ms. Stovall's attack is related to my cases, and maybe I can help you with yours. If you want me to make this an official FBI case, I will."

Detective Gregory was pacing again. He grabbed a toothpick out of his pocket and shoved it in his mouth. You could tell he was craving a cigarette, but there was nowhere near to smoke.

"I don't see how some Fed can help me with my case. I got this," he said angrily.

"Do you? Do you really? How many suspects do you have, any? I doubt it. And I don't see any solved cases on your docket either."

Katerina shot me a look from inside of Elly's room. Guess I was getting too loud.

"I'm sorry, Detective. Let's go somewhere I can get more coffee and maybe you can get a cigarette."

Detective Gregory smiled. "You got me. I actually need a cigar. All these damn rules, but I know a place."

I went in and told Kat I was leaving and would be back. Elly forced a smile and mouthed, *Thank you.*

He and I went outside to his car. He pulled out a couple of cigars and files. "I have a favorite cigar bar around here, about fifteen minutes walking distance. You game?"

"Sure. Doubt if I'll partake, but please be my guest."

We walked a while and came to another old, brick building. We took a few steps down to a large, heavy door with a polished gold handle. Inside was smoky and spicy, with red leather booths, plush couches, and small cocktail tables. The bar itself was highly polished oak and about the length of the room, with high-backed, brass stools. The wall behind the bar was impressive, bottle after bottle of high-end spirits. I shook my head and laughed.

"What's so funny?" Acting as if I was laughing at him.

"Oh, I'm sorry, I'm not laughing at you. I was just kicking myself that I'm sort of on the clock right now. This is my kind of place."

"Well hell then, Fed, we have something in common."

He waved at a waitress and pointed over to a corner couch area with a large coffee table. We walked over and he made himself quite at home. I had a feeling he had used this area as an office before. He sat back, plopped his files on the table, and lit up one of his cigars.

"Now this is more like it." He leaned back on the couch. I was waiting for him to unbutton some buttons. Thank God, he didn't.

"So, Agent Quinn."

"Jara, please."

"Okay, Jara. You think our cases are related? Why?"

I explained to him the cross-dressing aspect.

“That don’t mean shit,” he said. “Miss Stovall is already a woman. This is a pure hate crime.”

“On that sir, I will agree with you. There is definitely hate involved, but a very controlled hate.” I explained to him about the word forbidden and the perfume, L’Interdit.

“Okay, you got me on that. I guess I’d better tell you my victims also had a weird smell and one had forbidden carved on her chest.”

That got my attention. I sat straight up, which was very hard to do on that couch. “What? Forbidden carved on her? What victim? When?”

Detective Gregory leaned forward and shuffled through his files. “Here.” He handed me a folder. “Amy Vincent, age thirty-two, was the first victim. She had just changed over to female two weeks prior. It was in 2000, my very first case. It was brutal. Cut off her breasts and violated her. No semen was found though. Just a hell of a lot of blood.”

“There was blood at this scene?”

“Blood. Hell yes. I told you this was brutal!” He was almost shouting. “Blood was everywhere. We have boxes and boxes of blood-covered stuff. We ran it back then, but DNA wasn’t as up to date as it is now. At that time, it only came up as her blood, but we know there had to be some from the perpetrator. My others weren't like that. There was almost no blood at all. Actually, the very last one had no blood. Even in the victim.”

“Detective, on your last one, any of them actually, was there an incision on the femoral artery by chance?”

He looked at me with shock. “How did you know that? We kept that one out of the papers. No one was to know that. All of the victims had a cut there, but only the last one had no blood. My lady in a coma lost so much blood she got brain damage, among other things.”

“Sir, we are working a total of nine murders, eight in Connecticut and one body here in New York. In each of them, all of their blood was drained via a puncture on the femoral artery. I do believe, Detective, our cases are related.”

The detective’s cigar had gone out by now, and he was aggressively chewing the end of it.

“Detective, may I look through these files now? It may help both of our cases.”

He motioned his hand for me to pick them up. I felt as if I was opening a Pandora's box, a bloody one. I took the folders and took a deep breath, then sat back on the couch. I skimmed through each of the files. All the victims were transvestites or transsexuals. Most had genitalia mutilation, and there was mention of a distinct smell on each of the bodies. Like the detective said, all were mutilated except for the last one in 2020.

Wait, I thought, Andrew Branson was caught and confessed to five murders from 2013 to 2019. He was allegedly locked up during the last one in 2020. I had to call Tess. "Noel, could you excuse me for a moment? I need to make a very important call."

He waved me off and continued to chew on a cigar. I made my way out to the street and dialed Tess.

"Where the hell are you? How's Miss Stovall? Is she okay? Are these connected?"

"Slow down, Tess. Yes, I think these are all connected."

"These, as in more than one?"

"Yeah, hate to tell you, but Detective Gregory's murders date back to the year 2000."

"What the hell? The bastard started in 2000 in New York? Damn." Sounding frustrated she asked, "And do we have one more player on our team now?"

I chuckled. "Not wanting to play well with others, I see."

"As long as he actually works. Tired of pouty men. Jacob's being his typical non-helpful self, and Travis is pouting around, wondering where you are and when you will be back."

"Really, Travis is pouting? Tell them what we have here and have Travis call Stewart again. We need to know how to work this. At least now we have a knowledgeable, motivated contact in the NYPD."

"The NYPD borough captain called me yesterday and said it was all ours since the FBI is involved. Said they had plenty to do. He sent all of his extra evidence to us yesterday."

"Extra evidence?"

"Yes, officer notes, and etcetera."

"Remind me again which borough this was?"

"Lower Manhattan."

"Okay, this happened in Brooklyn. Do you think you might want to road trip here and see all this New York stuff?"

"If you don't mind, yes." Excitement rose in her voice. "I'll be on my way and see if Travis wants to join."

"Not Jacob?"

"Hell no. Pure dead weight. Don't even know where he is right now. I'll call when we're on our way."

After Tess and I hung up, I called Katerina. "How's Elly?"

"Sleeping right now. The doctor thinks Elly will be here for at least a few days. They want to make sure the femoral artery is fully sealed. They are going to do some more tests and a CAT scan regarding the concussion, just to rule anything out. She still has a huge headache."

"Speaking of headaches, do you think you would be up for company tonight and tomorrow at the apartment?"

"What do you mean company? I'm staying here."

"Well, Tess and Travis are coming up, and the NYPD detective will be coming over. We have some work we need to get done."

"At the apartment? I guess that's okay. I'll call Chase, tell him to extend his trip."

"Thanks, Kat. I love you."

"Love you too. I'll see you soon. Pick me up, and I'll go with you to the apartment. I'll fix dinner for you all, change clothes, then come back here."

I knew Katerina wanted to help, but her fixing dinner scared me. I wasn't going to refuse her though. I figured she was trying to keep busy and do something for the case. "Thanks, love. Tell Elly we're working hard on this and send her my best."

I went back into the smoky room. Noel was right where I'd left him, but he had started another cigar and bought himself a drink.

"Wasn't sure if you were a Scotch girl or not, so I've left the tab open."

I smiled. What the hell, even at this hour, I thought. The waitress came over, and I made my order. "Dirty vodka martini, please. Extra olives." The waitress walked away, and I explained to Noel that my partners, Tess and Travis, were coming to New York.

"Humph. Well, can't really work at the station, too many questions and eyes and ears. Work here?"

"I doubt if the other clientele would appreciate our conversation. You know, murder and all. I have a place where we can all fit and stay over if need be."

"Well, look at you Fed, a place in New York and Connecticut. FBI must be paying you well."

"If you must know, the NYC apartment was an inheritance gift to my girlfriend. We don't get here very often. Anything else you need to know?" I said gruffly.

"Hey, I was just being friendly and asking about you. You don't have to bust my chops for it."

Noel acted offended, but I was positive he wasn't. I had a feeling the tough guy was also a huge teddy bear. Why else would he still be on these cases and working them so hard since 2000? My turn for questions. "Why are you so dogged on this case? I'm sure you have others to work."

Noel got very serious, removed the cigar from his mouth, and took a swig of Scotch. "Years ago, I was a patrol officer taking my detective's exam. I was lucky and got to work with the homicide division. Then this case came along. I responded to it as patrol. Soon after I passed my detective's exam, and since no one else wanted the case, they assigned it to me. My partner and I couldn't solve it, and no one else seemed to care. Only the LGBTQ community seemed concerned. All I could think of was my victim and her family. Someone had to care."

There was a sadness about him. His shoulders were slumped, and he was chewing extra hard on his cigar. "There's something else, isn't there?"

"Like I said, I thought her family had to care. Well, they didn't," he said angrily. "She was dead to them even before he went through the transition to be a she. In their eyes, she was already dead for years. My brother, Scotty," Noel paused a bit, appearing a little choked up. He took another swig of his drink and continued. "My brother, Scotty, was gay and had a lot of transexual and transvestite friends. He was killed in the village by a lunatic out to kill as many transvestites, transsexuals, gays, and lesbians as he could. The asshole was never caught after killing at least seven people and injuring many others. Even though my family is Catholic, my parents loved Scotty. Didn't quite understand him but loved him anyway. His dying broke my mother's heart. She was still waiting for his killer to be caught when she passed away in 2011. My dad is still alive, but he doesn't talk about it anymore. I have two other brothers and three sisters. You know, the typical Catholic family. We're close but not like we used to be. Something about Amy's family not caring made me care more. I thought of Scotty. What if he had been alone before he died?" Noel choked up, swallowed hard, and started again. "I have to be there for Amy and all the others. Someone has to care."

"And the department allows you to work on these all the time?"

"Well, some of the other murders were assigned to me because of the first one, but they all went cold. So I said fuck it and transferred to the cold case unit. Now I get to pick and choose what I work on. As long as I have some results, they pretty much leave me alone."

Things started coming into focus for me. His passion stemmed from his family and his brother, so he was going to be the family that cared for those that didn't. Elly happened to be a huge piece in the puzzle that could help us solve this mess. I took a large drink of my martini. Perfect. I caught Noel staring at me.

"A girl after my own heart, even if you are a Fed. Cheers." Noel raised his glass.

We clinked glasses. "I always love a perfect martini. Are there any more files we should see that you need to get from the office? I also want you to look at our file of the body that was dropped in New York."

"Everything I have is copied right here." He pulled out a flash drive. "In this day and age everything seems to be digital. I have to stay up with the times, though I do like the feel of paper and being able to go page by page through a murder book. That's why I still hold on to hard copies of things."

I nodded my head in agreement as my phone rang. It was Katerina.

"Hey honey, is everything okay?"

"Yeah, I guess so. Still waiting on CAT scan results, but overall, it's good. When are you going to the apartment?"

I looked at Noel and mouthed *When?*

"Anytime, as long as you have beverages and a smoking area."

"Always," I said to him, then returned to my phone call. "Honey, I'll be there in about thirty minutes to pick you up."

We finished our drinks and walked back to the hospital. I went up to Elly's room and gave Katerina a hug. Elly was sound asleep through all the beeps and noises. It was weird having a friend who was also a victim. I hoped I hadn't brought this on her. I told the nurse how to reach me and to call anytime. Katerina also asked permission to come back and stay through the night. The nursing staff had been wonderful and a godsend.

We were silent as Katerina and I walked to the car. I put my arm around her. "Are you okay?"

"I can't believe you came here, we came here, to interview my friend, and now she is in the ICU. What have we done?" Katerina was crying and repeating, "What have we done?"

"Honey, I don't know. I have racked my brain, trying to figure that out, but you aren't responsible for this. I feel bad, too, but we didn't attack her, a lunatic did."

Katerina turned and faced me. "But we put her in this position! We came here. We put her in this case. I'm not saying we did it, but damn, at some point we're responsible."

"I'm sorry. I can't think that way. I have a job to do. I can't be responsible for every person I interview."

"Can't be responsible?! Seriously?! This is my friend we are talking about. Damn it! We brought her into this! It's our fault! Jesus Christ!" Katerina was wildly gesturing and shouting.

I stopped still in the parking lot. "FINE!" I yelled. "I brought her into this. I'm sorry. If I thought she would be in danger in any way, I would have either taken precautions or not done the interview. Elly was to confirm a perfume, not identify a killer. This is the last thing I would think would happen. I'm sorry."

We walked to the car, not touching. It was a tense, silent car ride to the apartment, Katerina staring out the window. We pulled into the underground parking and sat in silence for what seemed like forever. I reached my hand over and touched Katerina's leg. "I don't want to fight with you. I'm sorry. I do feel very guilty about what happened, but I can't let it stop me from focusing on solving this case. Especially now. I also don't want to put you out. We can go somewhere else to work."

Katerina turned to me. Her face had softened, and there were tears in her eyes. "I don't want to fight either. I feel so guilty. I want you here in the apartment, solving this. Whatever it takes." Her face changed back to anger. "You catch this motherfucker! If you don't..." she started crying.

"And if I don't?"

"I don't know. I can't even think about that."

"Kat, you know I'll do everything I can to solve Elly's attack and the rest of these murders. But I can't focus on work if I feel it will jeopardize us in any way."

"I feel so responsible. What if she had died?"

"But she didn't die. Elly is a fighter, like the doctor said, and maybe she is the key to help solve all of these. Helping the families of all the other victims. Please, Kat, I need your support in this. It's what I do."

Katerina pulled me to her and kissed me. "I know, I know. You know you have my support...in everything. If anyone can solve this, it is you. I know that."

I thought to myself, *God, I hope she is right. Can I solve this?* She must have seen the doubt in my face.

"Honey, I love you. I know in my heart this is not your fault, and I know you can solve this. I'm just worried, and scared, and taking it out on you."

I smiled slightly. "I will do everything I can to solve this and keep the people I love out of harm's way."

We got out of the Rover, and I grabbed the evidence I'd gathered at the hospital. Tess and Travis had pulled up, and I saw Noel in the distance. I directed them all where to park, and we met them at the building's door. I introduced Katerina. The only person she hadn't met was Tess. Katerina gave her the once over, then looked at me. The message was loud and clear. Look but don't touch. Travis saw the look and laughed. He quickly stopped when Katerina turned her glare to him, and we made our way upstairs in silence.

Breaking the tension Noel whistled. "Damn, Fed, this is your apartment?"

"Noel, I told you it's a family inheritance to Katerina. It's no big deal."

"No big deal! My apartment could fit in here about ten times. This is amazing."

"I'm glad you like it, but remember, we are here to work."

Travis turned to Noel. "I'm impressed, too, brother."

"I don't suppose you got a computer around here?" Noel asked.

Katerina rolled her eyes and went to the den. I followed her. I could tell she was tired and not wanting to socialize. She pointed to a closet door, which I opened. Inside was a computer and monitors that looked like they should be at NASA. "Great, I'll never hear the end of this."

"Use it or not, I don't care," Katerina said dryly, as she turned to leave the den. I stepped in front of her. I pulled her in tight and held her. At first, she started to pull away, but she grabbed ahold of me tightly and started crying. Not a small cry, but a heaving cry of agony. I held her until she stopped shaking and pulled back to wipe her tears.

With as much determination as I could muster, I told her "My love, we'll get this bastard, I promise."

Katerina gave a faint smile and nodded her head. Katerina went upstairs to our room, and I called the others into the den. "Let's set up in here." Noel started to open his mouth, but I stopped him. "I know, I know. Can we just get on with it, please? If you can't handle it, I can always find an FBI office to work in."

Noel plopped down on the couch. Tess sat beside him, and Travis sat at the desk chair. I looked at all of them. "So it's settled. We're staying here?"

All voiced agreement. Noel handed me his flash drive, and I booted the computer. Travis gathered paper and pens so we could take notes. I logged in with the password Katerina had told me. I inserted the flash drive, and *boom,* on the huge monitor a photo of Amy Vincent's crime scene appeared. Noel was right. It was brutal and gruesome.

"Damn, Noel, you could have warned me this would be the first thing we would see." I was so glad Katerina wasn't in there.

"Sorry, that was the last thing I was looking at before Miss Stovall was attacked."

Noel went through each of his cases. I was impressed by the detail he gave about each of them. We learned each crime scene got cleaner and more ritualistic. We found similarities. Each had a distinct odor. I would guess L'Interdit. His victims were transexuals or transvestites. Ours were cross-dressed by the killer. All appeared staged in one way or another. Noel's murders started in 2000, and ours in 2014, at least the ones we knew about.

"Since the Branson murders allegedly started in 2014, and we have overlap," Tess said, "could we have two killers, or did Andrew move around?"

"I guess we have to be open to that, the way this is looking." Travis replied. "We all feel they are related, right?"

Everyone agreed. "So where do we go from here?" I asked. "Do we call our bosses and make this a new official task force? I think we have enough evidence to prove these are related."

Travis grumbled. "Stewart is not going to like this. He wanted this over with already."

"Well, SSA Stewart will have to get over it," I said. "I probably should call and give him the bad news. What's the worst that could happen?"

There was a collective groan in the room.

Chapter Sixteen

I went to our bedroom. Thankfully, Katerina had fallen into the sleep she desperately needed. I love watching her sleep. I kissed her forehead and quietly left the room, closing the door behind me. I decided to call SSA Stewart from the balcony. If the call went too bad, I could jump. He answered in a stern voice, "What now?!"

"SSA Stewart, this is Jara."

"I know who it is. Get on with it."

"Yes, sir, I have some news on our cases."

"I am hoping you are going to tell me this case is almost over."

"Well uh, no, sir. I'm calling to tell you there are more victims in New York than we first knew."

"What the hell! More?" I heard a loud thunk over the phone. Was he throwing things? "How many has this nutbag killed?"

"It looks like at least five more dead, one in a coma, and this latest attack on Ms. Stovall." I eased into the next part. "The cases aren't exactly the same, but we can't ignore the similarities between the ones here in New York City and ours. There is a NYPD detective who has been working these since 2000."

"Damn, since 2000? Why hasn't anyone put these together?" I knew this was a rhetorical question, but his silence was deafening, and the question begged to be answered.

"Sir, I don't know. The detective seems to have a handle on the New York cases but has minimal leads since they happened in different boroughs. I really think..."

Stewart cut me off. "I don't need excuses, Quinn. I want a plan now!"

I hadn't really thought that far ahead. Crimes by the same suspected perpetrator, in multiple states, were usually turned over to the FBI. I didn't want to cut Noel out of this, so we needed a place to work where it was accessible to all of us. "Well sir, right now, all of us are here in New York at Katerina's family apartment. But I feel the FBI building would be best suited if we are to take the lead."

"Good idea. Give me all the people I need to inform and get the names I need clearance for."

I gave him Noel's name and his boss's contact information, silently hoping this group wouldn't grow.

"Okay, Quinn, make this happen. We need to know as soon as possible if Mr. Branson is actually guilty. His lawyer has filed a petition with the court claiming alleged pressure by the prosecution on his plea agreement. I don't think it will stand up to scrutiny, but you know how it is with these rich folks who believe they are above the law." Frustration edged his voice.

"But sir, his Alford plea is functionally the same as a guilty plea and should have waived his rights to any appeal."

"Don't you think I know that, Quinn?" Anger replaced the frustration. "I'm not the one in charge of those things. But these fancy lawyer types still think they have a shot, especially with all these new cases."

Yeah, no pressure. "Has the judge said when there would be a ruling on this?"

"No, they are reviewing it. I'll let you know when I know."

"All right. We'll be back on Monday, working here until then. I have an interview with Mr. Branson on Wednesday. I hope it isn't canceled."

"I doubt it. That egotistical psychopath will love the attention. He'll keep the appointment."

"Thank you, sir. I'll be in touch."

I went in and told the others what Stewart said. Noel groaned.

"What?" I asked, glaring at Noel. "You said you wanted help, and now you got it. So suck it up."

Everyone turned and looked at me.

"Damn, I'm sorry, but my patience is running thin, and I'm frustrated as hell. Again, I'm sorry. Now let's get back to work."

Katerina woke up and went back to the hospital. That nap did wonders for her. The rest of us began sorting out all of the similarities of the cases and making a timeline. We ordered food and worked through the night. Katerina stayed at the hospital, which was probably for the best.

The next morning, we decided we had done all that we could with what we had. I told Noel he was welcome to stay at our house in Connecticut.

"If it's anything like this, hell yeah."

Travis shook his head. "Just you wait, buddy. Just you wait."

Everyone laughed, packed up their things, and headed home. I lay down on the couch to try to think and relax. I woke up three hours later with Katerina stroking my hair.

"How long have you been here?"

"Only a little while. I think we need to go home. Elly is insisting I leave and get some rest. Her room is still guarded, so she feels safe at the moment."

I told Katerina I had invited Noel to stay with us and she giggled. "I told Elly the same thing. I guess as long as everyone is safe, we could fill up the house."

I didn't think of that. All of us could stay at the house and commute to work from there. The house was definitely big enough. I told my idea to Katerina. "Do you think Victoria would mind?"

"No, she is going to the apartment in Bridgeport. She said she still has a lot of Foundation work to do. Plus, she wouldn't want to be in our way. I need to go with her part of the time to get some work done anyway."

I was about to call SSA Stewart, when my phone rang. It was him calling me. "Sir, I was just about to call you."

"Quinn, I'm glad I reached you. Have you by chance seen the news?"

"No sir, did something happen?"

"You could say that. Our building had a breach. Someone broke in to the evidence lock up. We're unsure if anything is missing. We're in the process of inventorying what remains."

"Remains, sir?"

"Yeah, when the bastards hit the lockup, they used an incendiary device to torch the rest to cover their tracks. One of your teammates was slightly injured, along with a few others."

"My teammate? Oh, Jacob. Why was he there?"

"Hell if I know. I thought he was with you."

"No sir, we couldn't get a hold of him, so he didn't join us in New York."

"Well, that sure as hell don't make a goddamn bit of sense. Quinn, get your shit together, and get your people squared away."

"Yes, sir. Do you know if we are able to work in the office?"

"Not at this time. They are still checking out the structural integrity of the building."

"Well, sir, the team will be staying at the Lansing house. There are multiple vaults and extra rooms we could set up in, so if you don't mind, we could work there also. I'm sure Mrs. Burris could set something up. Plus, we have most of the evidence with us already."

"Fine, I'll talk to Anita about it. Call me when you get back."

Then I heard nothing.

Chapter Seventeen

I told Katerina about the FBI building and the possibility of the team not only staying but working from the house. I couldn't wrap my head around why Jacob was at HQ when we weren't there and how he was close enough to the blast to get hurt. We cleaned up the apartment, gathered all of our things, and headed back home. I was looking forward to sleeping in my own bed tonight. Hell, just to sleep.

Victoria had dinner ready for us. Katerina had already told her mother about Elly, so when we came into the kitchen, we all held each other and cried. We ate quietly and went to bed. Both of us were asleep within minutes. Morning came and I jumped into the shower. Katerina joined me. She put her arms around me and kissed my neck. "We aren't going to have much time over the next few weeks, so I need some love from you now."

I laughed but agreed. "I love you."

Instead of making love, we held each other tightly and cried some more. After our shower, Katerina kissed me again and left to get dressed. I couldn't help but wonder how I got so lucky. I finished getting dressed and heard the doorbell ring. I'm not sure if I'd ever heard the doorbell before. Usually people just walked right in. I heard Victoria laughing and talking, so I figured it was one of her friends. In a way, I was right. Mrs. Burris had arrived with two large trucks, now parked in the drive. Wow, she was efficient.

Once I made my way downstairs, I overheard Victoria and Anita talking about this past weekend's dinner. I walked up to them but waited quietly. Victoria turned and saw me. "Oh, there you are. I'm trying to tell Anita here what's been going on and where we might have all this set up. I was thinking about the theater room and the two rooms adjacent. Sound good?"

I nodded my head. "Perfect. I will also be cleaning up a couple of rooms for guests, if you don't mind."

I had a feeling Anita knew more about this case than Victoria, but she didn't let on. I showed Anita the theater and the two rooms on either side. In no time, she was setting up the rooms and directing movers where to put boxes. I called SSA Stewart and asked if I should stay here or come in.

"Hell, might as well stay there. That's where the party's going to be, plus we're still not back in the building yet."

Party. I think not, but if he says so. I called Travis and asked him to swing by the office to see if he could get in and grab any evidence that survived.

"Nothing there," he said. "I helped Anita secure it all in the trucks. Everything should be with her. I'll call Tess and Jacob."

I called Noel. "Everything is set up now at the house, so you are welcome to grab everything and come on up."

"Damn, Fed. You work fast. How about I get there this evening? I still have a few things to get together."

I gave him the address and went to check on Anita. She had already transformed the two adjoining rooms to work areas, a section of the theater to a media area, and another small room as a secure area for the evidence to be stored.

She saw me walk in and ask, "Do you need any part of this to be a SCIF or a Faraday cage?"

I thought for a moment. "Do you think we should? I have never set up a mobile office before. Depending on how long this takes, we may need to run a couple of secure lines out of here."

"Oh, sorry if I overstepped, but I already have those ordered for the computers, faxes, and phones. I think, after what has happened, a SCIF would be necessary."

"Mrs. Burris, I mean Anita, may I clone you?" I smiled. "You are the most efficient person I have ever met."

Katerina came down to tell me she was off with Victoria to the Foundation. "Aunt Anita, I heard you were here." They gave each other a big hug and looked each other over. "Looking good, Aunt Anita."

"Same to you, dear, but I do worry about your taste in partners," she said. "I told you never to get with a Fed."

"I know, I know. Couldn't help it though. It was fate."

"Well, you can't argue with fate. We'll have to catch up later. Lots of work to do for this one." She nodded her head toward me.

"She's always a lot of work."

"Hey, I'm standing right here."

They both laughed. Katerina kissed me goodbye, and I was soon left standing in the hall alone. I figured I'd put myself to use and call a catering company to cover some lunches and dinners for the week. After ordering, I remembered Tess and I had the interview with Mr. Branson on Wednesday, and I called her.

"En route to you now. What the hell happened?"

I explained what I knew. "Have you spoken with Jacob? He was at the building when it happened. Not sure of the extent of his injuries."

"Yeah, I called him. He didn't tell me he got hurt. Just like him to be secretive. Why was he there anyway?" Tess asked.

"That's the million-dollar question. We'll ask him when we see him. Is the interview still on for Wednesday?" I asked hopefully.

"As far as I know." Tess said she still had some things to box up. "Be there soon."

Chapter Eighteen

Travis, Tess, and Jacob all arrived at the same time. I saw Jacob had driven separately. I wasn't sure if he was on board with our set up or not. Honestly, I didn't care. Each of them brought in a bag, so that was at least a good sign all were willing to work as much as it took. I put Jacob and Tess at opposite ends of the hall, Travis by Jacob, and Noel by Tess. We fixed up Granny May's room in case Elly came to stay with us. Tess and Jacob unloaded their vehicles of boxes and boxes of evidence. Travis only had a few.

"Girl, is this a good idea? Everything here in one place?" Travis asked.

"Only thing I could think of was to get it all together and get the most work out of everyone. Mrs. Burris has seen to everything and secured it all."

Travis made a low whistle and shook his head. "She is one mysterious, efficient woman."

We started putting everything into the rooms and made sure each case was separate. I had Travis and Jacob go through and inventory everything we had. I heard a few grumblings, but I ignored them. I needed to work on interview questions. I had asked Tess for a copy of all the interview notes she had for Mr. Branson. She handed me another box.

Shit, here we go. I read through all the interviews. He definitely was a cagey one. I was in deep in thought, reading the last interview, when I saw I was getting a call from France.

"*Bonjour*, André. I thought you had forgotten about me?"

"*Bonjour chérie*, never. I wanted to make sure the information I was getting was correct."

"So I take it you found something?"

"*Oui.* I hope you are sitting down. I will send you all of this, but I figured you would want to know things sooner rather than later."

I grabbed a couple pens and some paper and told him to shoot.

"First, I am told Toni Branson is living as Anthony Branson in Gimont, a small commune in the Southwest. The neighbors say the person who stays in this eighteenth-century home comes and goes often. They have only seen a female there a time or two."

I wondered if this was Toni trying to hide. There had been a lot of publicity about her brother's case.

André continued. "Toni or Anthony, whichever, has not been seen in a few months. Nobody seems to know where she or he is. I checked, and there have been many flights back and forth to New York on passports for both of them, both Anthony, as male, and Toni, as female."

"Am I missing something here? Both have passports?"

"*Oui.*"

"Can you get me those dates and maybe even a copy of each passport?"

"Oh *chérie*, you take me as inefficient. The dates have already been sent. It is going to take me some time for the passports. Now on to the parents. Mr. and Mrs. Branson are both deceased. Although James Branson passed in 2014 in the United States, Nancy Branson died in 1975 in Northern France. She was murdered by a man named Pierre Formet. From what I saw of the crime photos, it was a bloody mess."

"Mrs. Branson died in France?" I asked as I fumbled through my notes. "I have Mrs. Branson dying here in the US in 2020. Are you sure?"

"*Oui, chérie,* Nancy Branson, born 1945, murdered April of 1975."

I kept looking through the stack of papers and finally found it. "Shit, it was Mrs. Nicolette Branson who died here. Someone just put the initial N instead of the whole name. So do you have a list of what was found at Mrs. Nancy Branson's crime scene with you?"

"*Oui*. What are you wondering?"

"Did Mrs. Branson have her purse, a handkerchief, or any other items with her when she was found?"

I heard flipping of papers. "No ma'am. It says here, her child, Alan, had the purse when he was found. It says Mrs. Branson was abducted from her car and taken elsewhere."

"Wait a minute, back up, her child?"

"Yes, all three children were with her when Mr. Formet grabbed her, leaving them in the car."

"Did any of them witness the murder?"

"Not that it is written. It says she was taken to another location and was found by a dumpster in an alley. Alan was found wandering around the parking lot where the car was parked. Someone called the police and said they thought he was lost. He was eight years old at the time."

"Where were his siblings?"

More paper flipping. "They were still in the car when the police found them. It was only Alan who wandered away. The car was parked in the parking lot of a market."

"Anything else?"

"The little girl had a handkerchief with her but wasn't crying. They even noted she didn't cry the entire time she was around the police. The father picked up the children from the station over three hours later. He said he was out of town on business. It doesn't say if that was ever confirmed."

"Let me get this straight. You said this was Nancy Branson, correct?"

"*Oui,* Nancy. Mr. Formet was caught in the fall of 1975. He had kidnapped a thirty-year-old female prostitute and tortured her. She managed to escape and was able to identify Mr. Formet as her abductor. He was suspected of at least four other abductions and murders between 1970 and when he was caught. Although he kept saying he didn't kill Mrs. Branson, he had no alibi. There was no trial. From what I gather, they charged him with all the murders and abductions in one case. He pled guilty and was sentenced. The father moved to Connecticut to be near his family shortly after the plea was agreed upon. I assume he married Nicolette there."

"Would it be possible for me to talk with Formet?"

"*Non, chérie,* he died in prison in 1992."

"Thank you so much, André. You have been a godsend."

"Tell *mon amour,* Katerina, I'm still waiting for her."

I chuckled. "André, you do dream, don't you?"

Chapter Nineteen

I couldn't believe what André had just told me. Mrs. Branson, at least the first Mrs. Branson, had been murdered. Plus, the children had witnessed her abduction. I went into the theater room where Tess and Travis were still arranging the evidence. I had no idea where Jacob was. I told Travis and Tess what André had told me.

"No fucking way. What the hell? I knew none of that." Tess slammed the folders she was holding onto the table. "No one has ever mentioned a mother named Nancy Branson. I only knew of Nicolette Branson."

"And she is dead, correct?"

"Dead, definitely. She passed away during COVID-19 in 2020. Nicolette said she was their mother, and they called her mother, so I guess I just assumed. Plus, she was French. Well, son of a bitch."

"Tess, by the way, where is Jacob?"

Tess looked around and shrugged her shoulders. "Hell if I know. He was just here."

Travis stood up. "I'll go find him. He snoops."

As if he heard us, Jacob appeared. I gave him a real shitty stare. "And you have been somewhere working, I hope?"

"Why is everyone on my ass? Yes, I was working. I was arranging the boxes in the other room, but I'm still sore from the explosion." Jacob was rubbing his right arm.

Tess rolled her eyes. "Whatever, Jacob. We're learning new things here that we should have known years ago. We fucked up, and now we have to play catch up. Why don't you make yourself useful and check on the Branson family history. Again!"

Jacob saluted Tess. "Yes, ma'am. Whatever you say, ma'am."

Travis threw down a box. "Listen, all of you, we are here to work together. And we are lucky enough to have a place to work. So put your bullshit aside and let's solve this damn thing. We aren't at a country club."

"Aren't we?" Jacob said with a sneer.

I stepped directly in front of him, our noses almost touching, my eyes locked on him. "No, Jacob, you are in my home, and you will treat it as such. Understand?"

Katerina walked in with Noel right after I had yelled at Jacob. "Are we all good here? I found this one wandering about," she said, her arm through his.

"Damn, Fed, now this is what I call an office. And the scenery is amazing too." He playfully pulled Katerina closer to him.

Katerina laughed. "Yes, I come with the house. But sorry, I'm taken. I'll drop you off here. She looked at me and smiled. "I'll be in our room if you need me. See you, Noel."

"Okay, looks like the gang is all here. Noel, you brought your stuff, right?"

"Yeah, have it in the next room. Did I interrupt something?" Noel locked his gaze on Jacob, who had backed away from me and was leaning against the wall.

Everyone seemed tired and overwhelmed. "How about tonight we just relax and get our bearings? Dinner should be here shortly, and we can start fresh tomorrow. Tess, would you show Noel where your rooms are? There is also an indoor and outdoor pool, a garden, and an exercise area. Plus, you know where these three rooms are. Any room on the east end of the house is off limits, clear?"

Everyone nodded their head, and I left to see Katerina. She was changing clothes when I walked into our room. I always loved to watch her body move, even while doing the smallest things.

"You going to stand there and watch or help me?" Katerina whispered with her back to me. She didn't have to ask me twice. I came up behind her and slipped my arms around her, feeling the tightness of her stomach and her back against me. I slid off her pants and let her step out of them. She turned around and faced me in her bra and panties. I reached around and unhooked her bra. "Hey now," she said, "I'm supposed to be getting redressed."

I went ahead and took her bra off and let it drop to the floor, then I bent and gently kissed each breast. I was backing her up to the bed when I heard Travis bellow, "Food's here!"

We both giggled, as she reached for a T-shirt and a hoodie. I handed her a pair of sweatpants and quickly changed my clothes. “Guess we’d better eat. With a house full of detectives, they’ll be searching for us soon.”

Katerina and I came downstairs to a counter full of food and everyone standing around. “What the hell? Are you going to just stare at it or eat it? I’m not serving you,” I said, as I grabbed a plate.

Noel patted his stomach. “This keeps getting better and better.”

Everyone grabbed plates and utensils and dug in. Katerina and I grabbed wine and a beer and headed for the back porch. We were just getting settled when Tess and Noel came out to join us.

“May we join you? It’s so pretty out here,” Tess said.

Katerina smiled. “Of course, and thank you. We love it out here. One of our favorite spots.”

“I can see why.” Noel gestured toward the water. “This is amazing. And the sailboats, they’re magnificent. If I lived here, I’d never leave.”

“Yes, it is definitely hard to leave this,” Katerina agreed, “but it’s good to get away. Makes you appreciate coming back home.”

I looked around the porch and garden. “Where are Travis and Jacob?”

Tess nodded her head toward the house. “I think Travis is having a heart-to-heart with Jacob about work ethics and being a team player. I’m hoping it doesn’t fall on deaf ears.”

“Uh, Travis has a way of getting his point across and being heard loud and clear,” I said.

We silently sat and ate for a while, taking in the quiet evening and the beautiful view. Katerina and I excused ourselves to turn in for the night, hoping for a fresh start in the morning.

After we slid under the covers, Katerina rolled over to me and put her head on my shoulder. “You’re going to solve this soon, I hope? I know it’s early, but I didn’t realize just how much I like my privacy.”

"Soon, baby, soon. I promise. If we aren't getting anywhere here, I'll move us to another federal building, I promise. Thank you, for being such a gracious host with your house."

Katerina smiled and kissed me. "How was I to say no? Plus, it's your house now, too, you know."

We had just drifted off to sleep when my phone rang. I answered groggily. "Quinn."

"*Chérie*, I hate to bother you at this late hour, but I was just informed Toni Branson arrived in Paris from the United States a few hours ago. Would you like me to have her picked up? If I did, though, I could only hold her for a short while."

I sat straight up in bed and tried to clear my head. "Toni is there? But she was here? Am I getting that right?"

"*Oui*, flew in from New York early this morning."

"Any idea when she came to New York?" I wondered if she was in the city at the time of Elly's attack.

"I can check flight records now that I know she used the passport for this trip in Toni's name and not Anthony's."

"Please do. I would greatly appreciate it. Is there any way she could be followed and not picked up yet? And please let me know when or if she changes to Anthony. Oh, one more thing. Photos, please, even if you think they are worthless."

"For you, anything. I woke you, no?"

"*Oui*," I said, in a terrible French accent.

"Then tell the beautiful one beside you *bonjour* for me."

I chuckled. I couldn't argue with the beautiful part. "I will, I promise."

"Goodnight and pleasant dreams," he said as he hung up.

"So Toni Branson was in New York City," I said out loud. How interesting.

Chapter Twenty

I tossed and turned the rest of the night, finally falling asleep right before Katerina's alarm went off. I was awakened by kisses on my neck and her hands rubbing my body. My favorite way to be awakened.

"I heard your phone ring last night. Was it about the case?" Katerina asked.

"*Oui.*" My French accent was not improving.

Katerina howled with laughter. "So my French boyfriend is calling you now in the middle of the night. Should I be jealous?"

"Hell no, all he does is ask about you. He only talks to me because I have an interesting case."

"Is there anything interesting that you can tell me, or is it all secret?"

"I can say André found the third triplet. She flew into Paris from none other than New York City."

The pleasant rubbing on my body stopped, and Katerina sat up in bed. "Oh my god! Do you think she attacked Elly?"

"Honey, I don't know, and I'm not going to jump to conclusions." Although in my head I already was.

"Well, it seems fishy to me. Too coincidental." Katerina got out of bed and started to pace.

All I could do was lie there and watch. She was in her own little world. I let her pace and mumble, as I got out of bed. I brushed my teeth and hair, threw on some jeans, a t-shirt, and a hoodie. Now this was the way to get ready for work. I was reaching for the door knob, when I heard a voice behind me.

"Haven't you been listening to anything I was saying?"

I stopped dead and turned around. "Honestly, Kat, no I haven't. You know I can't discuss this with you. You probably know more than you should."

"Fine! I'll keep my ideas to myself then." She stormed away from me.

Well great, this day is going to be fun. I made my way downstairs and started a large pot of coffee. It looked like breakfast had been dropped off. Bagels, fruit, and the like were now on the counters. I helped myself to a bagel, as others started showing up in the kitchen.

"Help yourself. Coffee is being made. One who empties it makes the next pot. Oh, and clean up your after yourselves. When everyone is ready, let's meet in the theater. I have more news."

I collected a few things from the vault and walked to the theater to look them over. I was coming out again for a coffee refill and saw Katerina standing at the door. She threw her arms around me. "I knew not to come in, so I waited. I know you can't talk to me about any of this, so I won't ask. But do you think Elly is in any more danger?"

"Honestly Kat, I don't know. I feel stupid she was hurt in the first place. Someone has to be watching this investigation to know she was involved. I would love to have her here, but I don't know how I could explain her being in the place with all the investigators."

"I'm going to go up and see her today after work at the Foundation. Probably spend the night. I'll let you know how she is. Please, call me if there's anything I should know." Katerina hugged me harder and kissed me goodbye.

"Kat, please call me when you get there. I don't want to worry."

She smiled that beautiful smile. "Okay, I love you."

"Love you too."

Chapter Twenty-One

I grabbed another bagel and cup of coffee and went back to the theater. Everyone was there, even Jacob.

"I have some news. André, my Interpol contact in France, called last night and informed me Toni Branson was just in New York City and flew back to Paris last night. They are going to watch her and try to send us photos. They will also let us know if she begins to live as Anthony again or returns to the States."

Jacob spoke up. "So are we really thinking a girl is doing all of this? Attacking and moving victims?"

Tess gave him a shitty look. "Seriously, Jacob? You don't think women are capable of murder? Or have the brains or brawn enough to do what has been happening? You are so close-minded. Everyone is a suspect until they aren't, male or female."

Travis and I gave each other the knowing look that things were not good in CSP land. Noel looked at all of us. His look said it all, but he voiced it anyway.

He had been standing in the doorway, listening to everything. His voice boomed as he looked around the room, his eyes shooting lasers at Jacob and Tess. "Are we going to argue or solve this thing? You two need to get your shit together! If you can't work together, then one or both of you needs to go home. I agree with Tess though. Everyone is a suspect until they aren't. Believe me, a woman can do anything a man can, sometimes better. And in this case, worse, if you know what I mean."

"Aren't you the feminist in a man's body?" Travis teased.

"I try to keep up with the times. Have to know what's going on around you. I have seen some really ugly murders committed by women. I put nothing past them." Noel was pacing, looking like he was going to give us a full lecture.

"Please," Tess said, "no lessons on the feminist movement. Jacob may run out crying with his insecurity."

Noel laughed and looked over to Jacob, who was glaring at us. "No worries, Tess, I'll grab him and give him a big ole man hug."

We all laughed except Jacob. He grabbed a file and snapped back at us. "Let's stop this nonsense and get back to work."

"Jacob, are you pouting? You never want to work," Tess teased.

"Fuck you, Tess. I want to solve this thing like all of you, so keep preaching." Jacob slammed the file on table.

I stood up and raised my voice. "Can we shut the fuck up and focus on this case? Tess, where are we on your end?"

Both Tess and Jacob ran down their progress, which was almost nothing. Noel said he wanted to reinterview Elly. "Maybe she has remembered something she couldn't when in the hospital."

I hesitated but said I would bring it up to Elly to see if it was okay. I got a strange look from Noel. He started to open his mouth to speak but said nothing. "Tess, you and I need to work on our interview questions for tomorrow. You good with that?" I asked.

She nodded, and we went to the room with the evidence from the first five cases. We gathered items and information I felt I could use while talking to Andrew Branson. I wanted to ask him new questions and maybe even surprise him. At least, that was my goal. I was confident that I had my game plan all worked out and hoped Tess would go along with it. I checked my email for anything from André. Yes, what I wanted was there.

Chapter Twenty-Two

Katerina picked up Elly from the hospital and helped her get settled back into her home. I spoke with Katerina once they reached the apartment. Elly refused police protection but knew danger was still out there. Katerina said Elly was holding up very well, or at least was putting up a good front.

I worked most of the night. No matter how much preparation I did, or even if felt I had the suspect dead to rights, I was always very nervous. I was bound and determined not to let Branson get the better of me. In the morning, I got cleaned up and dressed. I definitely didn't look like a Fed now. I was going for a particular look, but I sure as hell wasn't going to wear a dress. I walked downstairs to the foyer, where Tess was waiting for me.

"What in the hell do you have on?" She barely held back a snicker.

"I decided to try and take him back to his childhood. Too much?"

"It's definitely not of this decade, but if it works, I'm all for it." Tess finally let out the laughter she was holding in.

I explained my plan to her. "André called last night and sent some pictures of the original Mrs. Branson and family. In one of the photos, Mrs. Branson had on flared pants and a flowered shirt, with what looked like a Hermes scarf. I knew Victoria had some vintage clothing in a spare closet, so I rummaged through and found the perfect outfit, including a Hermes scarf. I am hoping this will bring back some memories."

Travis tromped down the stairs. "Oh my god! I need a picture of this. Jara Quinn, FBI agent, guardian of the homeland, possible Mod Squad member, looking as if she is going to a love in." He laughed, taking pictures with his phone. "Jara, the '70s called, they want their clothes back."

"Shut up, Travis. There is method to my madness."

He kept walking around and snapping pictures. Noel came around the corner and his eyes widened. He opened his mouth, but I cut him off.

"One word," I said, "one word and I'll shoot you where you stand."

Before we were even out the door, I was getting notifications about the pictures Travis was sending out. He even sent them to Katerina. I grabbed Tess by the arm. "Let's get out of here before I shoot them all."

We walked out to my Rover and locked up our evidence and interview materials in the back compartment.

"I hope this get up does what I intend, or this interview will be all for naught."

We rode in silence most of the way, each of us sensing the other's nervousness. As we pulled into the institution's parking lot, Tess looked over at me. "No matter what happens, we have at least tried. Who knows what we will get this time. I have faith in you."

I smiled a nervously. "Thanks. Here goes nothing."

I put my game face on as we entered the building with two boxes and a few loose folders. I carried the Dofan purse from the first crime scene. I had told SSA Stewart my plan and received permission to use it as a prop. The handkerchief was inside the purse in a bag. I was very grateful both items still had the L'Interdit smell, since I didn't want to wear the perfume. I received some strange looks from the staff as we entered, but no one said a word. Heck, it was an insane asylum. They would have seen weirder.

We met Mr. Branson's lawyer, William Payne, outside the interview room. He kept looking at his watch. Tess blurted out, "You got somewhere else to be?"

"Oh, Detective Goodwin, hello. I'm still not sure what this interview is for, but I am sure it is a waste of time."

Tess reached for the door. "We'll judge whether it's a waste or not." She never bothered to introduce me. Nor did Mr. Payne even look twice at me, other than as an annoyance.

We walked in, put our stuff on the table, and took our seats. We could hear shuffling down the hall and knew Andrew was being escorted to the room in cuffs. I kept my back to the door and didn't turn my head when they entered. Tess stood and stared him down until he took his seat. Two guards stood behind him, and his lawyer sat beside him.

"Are these cuffs necessary?" Mr. Payne asked, looking over to Tess.

The guards' faces showed no emotion and gave no hint on if the cuffs should remain. I was sitting across from Mr. Branson and decided to take a chance. I stood up, pushing my chair out with such force it almost fell backward. I stared at Mr. Branson, as I spoke to the guards.

"Andrew here is going to be a good boy, aren't you, Andy? He doesn't need the cuffs with us."

Andrew's eyes grew big as saucers when he saw my entire outfit. I even dramatically dropped my purse on the table in his line of sight. I thought I saw a bit of a tremble from him but couldn't be sure.

"Sirs, please, if you will." I nodded to Mr. Branson. "He'll be good. Right, Andy?"

Andrew nodded his head like a young child.

"Very good. Now that is settled, let's get started."

The guards removed the cuffs and moved back to the wall. I was brave, but not stupid. The guards could definitely stay.

"Andrew, or may I call you Andy?" He nodded his head again. "Thank you, Andy. I'm Jara. Can I ask you some questions today? I am so confused about your case, you know, female brains and all. I would like you to help me get it straightened out."

Andrew had not moved a muscle since the cuffs came off, except to nod his head.

"So, Andrew, uh...Andy." I was pushing it trying to get him back to his childhood. I ventured a guess he wasn't called Andrew until he was older. "You confessed to what, four murders, maybe five?"

Andrew raised his hand like a child showing the number five.

"Okay, good, five then. Wow, that's a lot. And you did this all by yourself? That must have been a lot of work." Andrew stared at me. "I am so impressed on how clean each of the scenes were. I bet, growing up, you stayed out of trouble by keeping things clean. I know my mother was a stickler on that. Were you yelled at or punished for being messy?" I was going on a hunch, and Tess let me go. Andrew nodded his head up and down as in yes, his eyes darting back and forth from me to the purse on the table. "Andy, did you like living in France?"

His eyes got big again. "*Oui*, I was born there."

Damn, I wished I spoke French, but oh well, I'd give it a go. "I bet you went to all sorts of places with your family."

Andrew replied after a few seconds. "Father never went."

"Oh, okay, so just your mother, your siblings, and you went places together. What were your favorite places?"

"The beach, the museums. I liked to see the mimes in Paris. They would perform all day in Montmartre. One day we had our picture drawn by one of the artists there."

I knew of the area. Katerina and I had visited this district in Paris. Mimes were everywhere, and artists with their easels were painting and drawing. I could tell he was back there in his mind. "Andy, was there a favorite place, or safe place you went to?"

Tess glanced over at me but said nothing. Mr. Payne spoke up, "What do these questions have to do with anything? This is a waste of time." Before I could respond, Andrew started talking.

"We would go to the café. Mother liked the café. She would talk to the owner, and we would get all the cakes and cookies we wanted. But we couldn't tell Father. He didn't like us eating desserts all the time. Philippe was really nice. He let us play in the back area with the pots and pans, while he and Mother went upstairs to talk."

"Andy, that sounds wonderful. I would love to go to this café. I love desserts."

He smiled. "I don't think it is there anymore. There was a fire. Father said a place like that shouldn't continue in business. My father would know. He was a good businessman."

"Yes, Andy, he was. Would he get mad at your mother for going there with you?" Andrew nodded his head yes.

"Andy, can we talk about your mother a bit more?" Andrew smiled and nodded yes again. "She was a good person, wasn't she? Sweet and kind..."

"Yes, she was wonderful. She would sing us songs and buy us toys and clothes. One day, we all got to dress alike, even Toni. We had so much fun." His face changed to either sadness or anger.

"Andy," I said softly, "did your Father get mad about this?"

Andrew stared at my purse and started crying. "That's when he took her from us."

I could tell whatever sadness Andrew had was turning to anger. I tried to reassure him that he was safe.

"Andrew, it's okay, you're safe here. No one is going to hurt you here. Did he take Toni?" He wasn't calming down, so I decided to swing for the fences. I pushed the purse over to him. He grabbed it like a drowning man going for a life preserver and wrapped it in his arms.

"He took her from us. Mother, not Toni. He told us she had to go away and for us to stay in the car. I heard him yelling at her for dressing us alike and her going to the café. Mother pushed him away and told us we were going to the store. Father came to the store after us. He pulled her out of the car and slapped her. Father took Mother away, and she never came back. We left the car and looked for her. We wanted to help her."

Now this was new. This whole time Mrs. Branson's murder was credited to a Pierre Formet, a confessed serial killer from Northern France. If what Andrew was saying were true, his father killed his mother. That would definitely mess a kid up. And to keep it a secret all these years...I wondered what hold the father had over the kids to keep them quiet.

"Andy, I know you looked for her. You were a good boy. Did you ever find your mother?"

Andrew appeared confused for a moment. "It was really messy. Mother wouldn't have liked that. She was on the ground and very dirty."

"Did you go near your mother or see your father around there?"

"Father told us to stay in the car, but after a while we couldn't. We went to the alley and saw, but we ran back to the car. I had Mother's purse and I ran. I don't know what happened after that."

Holy shit! Andrew and his siblings witnessed his mother not only being abducted but also being murdered by their father. "Thank you, Andy, for telling me about that. It seems like your mother was a really nice lady and a good mom." Andrew held tight to the purse and nodded his head yes.

"When we were first talking, you said you committed five murders." I held up my hand counting off five. "Correct?" Andrew nodded his head yes. I pulled out Mrs. Branson's crime-scene photos and photos of Amy Vincent's crime scene, Noel's first murder in 2000. I spread the photos in front of him. He started trembling so much I thought he might fall out of his chair. His eyes darted back and forth between the photos, and he clutched the purse tighter. The similarities between these two crime scenes were remarkable.

"Mother didn't like to be messy. Father made her messy, so now he is messy."

"Who is messy, Andy, your father?"

"No," he shouted, HIM!" He was pointing to the photo of a dead Amy Vincent. "Now he is messy. Father made us sad, now Father is sad."

"Andy, who is this person?" I pointed to the photo of Ms. Vincent.

"That was my new mother. She was mean. She was our age, but Father said she was our mother."

Tess and I looked at each other, our heads screaming. "Your new mother, can you explain?"

"It was our new mother. Father said so. Father had been seeing him for years, always made him dress like our mother. Like he did with Toni. We didn't like our new mother, so I took him away." Andrew's face scrunched up. "But he was a she when she died. I checked."

I remembered Noel said Ms. Vincent had recently finished her transition around two weeks prior to her death.

"These others are so clean. Were these about your mother too?"

"She liked to be clean. I'm not talking anymore. I'm done. Can I keep the purse?"

I reached across the table and took hold of the purse. "No, Andrew," I said sternly. "That's forbidden."

His eyes blazed like fire. Palpable anger spread from every pore. I nodded to the guards who immediately came over and cuffed him. I took the purse back.

"Yes, Andrew. I know about Forbidden, L'Interdit, your mother's perfume."

His eyes began to soften as he looked at the purse again. "Mother was a good woman." The guards lifted him from his chair and started to take him back to his room. He turned to me. "We can talk again, I hope."

"I hope so too, Andrew. I would like that."

When the guards led Andrew from the room, a collective sigh was let out.

Mr. Payne remained still and started to grumble. "You already knew he committed those murders. He confessed. So what he said here doesn't mean much."

I ignored him, as I packed up my things and motioned to Tess I was ready to go. But I couldn't help myself. I turned back to Mr. Payne. "Sir, the photos I showed him were crime-scene photos of his mother's murder and of a woman named Amy Vincent. She was a recently transitioned transgender woman who was murdered in 2000 in New York. Mr. Branson just confessed to witnessing his mother's murder and committing the one in 2000."

We walked out, leaving the lawyer with his mouth gaped open. I'd say my outfit worked wonders.

Chapter Twenty-Three

I was shocked by all the information we had learned. I turned to look at Tess. I thought she'd been walking beside me, but she was still standing at the door of the hospital. She was staring into space, with her hand over her mouth. I walked back to her and touched her shoulder. "We did good today."

She flinched. "Oh yes, I'm sorry, you startled me. I am so blown away right now." She gave her head a little shake. "Do we call the boys now and tell them what we learned?"

I thought about it for a moment and told her she should call her prosecuting attorney. I said I would call Noel and André. Noel could then tell the rest of the guys if he wanted to. She agreed and we made our respective calls.

I left a message for André on his phone. "I solved a murder of yours. You owe me. Call me back." I then called Noel and asked him to go somewhere private. He was gruff initially and told me he would explain later.

"Noel, I showed Mr. Branson a crime-scene photo of Amy Vincent. He admitted to killing her, saying she had been his new mother."

Noel became very quiet.

"Noel, are you okay?"

"I knew she had an older boyfriend, but she kept him away from everyone. She dated him even before the transition. We could never find him. No pictures or anything, and no one seemed to know his name."

I heard a gasp and choking noises on the other end of the call. I knew Noel was trying his best to keep from crying on the phone.

"I thought you should know before we got back."

He whispered a thank you and hung up.

I then called Katerina and learned that Elly had settled in and was taking a nap.

"I think being at home is helping her," Katerina said. "She is more relaxed, and the color is returning to her face. She was so pale in the hospital. I might come home tonight, if that's okay. How was your interview? Loved the outfit, by the way. Elly loved it, too, although she commented about the purse and the shoes again."

"Oh, course she did." I laughed. "I was going for the 1970s Mod Squad/Fed look. I think I pulled it off. The interview went great. I'll tell you about it later."

"Speaking of later, you keeping the outfit on for a while? We could play dress up when I get home. Do a 70s love in."

I let out a large belly laugh. Tess whipped her head and looked at me, wide-eyed. Heck, I was shocked I had such a reaction.

"Sweetheart, when you get home, we can do whatever you want." We said our good byes and hung up. I turned to Tess. "I think it's time we headed back. Ready?"

"Definitely! I haven't felt this good about this case in quite a while. Thank you. You know you did good today."

"Tess, we did good today." I said, repeating my earlier words.

We rode home with such large smiles on our faces, it almost hurt. Excitement filled the car. I wanted to scream with joy and jump and pump my fist in the air. How in the hell did we pull this off? I felt the purse had even more significance than we'd thought, but I wasn't sure how. I was going to use it again. Maybe even as a reward.

When we were almost home, Tess asked, "Now we have Andrew's confession on the Amy Vincent murder, do you think he is responsible for Noel's other cases?"

"I have a hunch about something and a weird feeling in my gut. There was something odd in the way he confessed to the Vincent murder. Not only Andrew, but his siblings also saw their mother's body. I don't think Andrew is the only murderer here."

Tess's phone beeped, and she looked at her message. Her mouth gaped open. "No way! Oh my god, no way."

I was busting with curiosity and hit my hand on the steering wheel. "What, more news?"

"They found DNA on my last victim's body, on his forehead. It matched the DNA on Elly and the fifth murder Andrew confessed to." Tess scrolled to read more. "There is also an unknown trace bit of DNA on Elly we haven't seen before. We need to do more DNA tests on everything, the old cases, the new ones, and even Noel's."

"Did the DNA match anyone, I mean any of the Branson's?"

Tess kept reading her message and shaking her head. "No way in hell, it can't be."

I pulled the car over and turned off the engine. "Tess, please read me all of it."

Tess put her phone on her lap, her face white with disbelief. "It can't be, it just can't be."

"Damn it, Tess, tell me!"

"Here goes. I hope you are ready for this. The DNA on Elly and on my last victim is a partial match to Andrew Branson."

I furrowed my brow and shook my head. "Andrew? But we just saw him. He's locked up. Wait, you said a partial match to Andrew, not a full match."

"There was only a small amount of DNA tested, but it is Andrew's. It matched the fifth crime scene. The only one with DNA found."

"You said there was other DNA found on Elly? Did it match anyone?"

"Yes, there is more, but it matches nothing in the database. We need to test more stuff. There had to be DNA left behind on something."

"Looks like long days ahead with forensics. We are going to have to run and rerun everything from each case." I was shaking my head, knowing what a pain in the ass this was going to be, not to mention the cost.

Chapter Twenty-Four

We made record time back to the house. The excitement was palpable. So much had happened. Where should we even start? We carried in our boxes and folders, setting them on the table in the theater. "Where is everyone?" I heard a noise around the corner.

"Oh, hello dears." Mrs. Burris greeted us warmly.

"Mrs. Burris...Anita, hi, what are you doing here? Where is everyone?"

"I'm here doing a security check and making sure there wasn't anything else you needed. Every off-site facility needs routine checks. I figured why not today?"

Puzzled, Tess looked at me and asked, "Mrs. Burris, that answers why you're here, but where is everyone else?"

"Oh dear, I have no idea. No one was here when I arrived. I thought it strange but figured you all had things you were doing."

Multiple thoughts were zipping through my head. "How did you get in here if no one was here?"

Mrs. Burris laughed loudly. "Oh my dear girl, I work for the FBI, and I set up this facility. A regular door lock is not going to keep me out."

I heard grumbling in the foyer and heavy footsteps. Travis burst into the room. "Of all the stupid things. After you called Noel, all of us were summoned to headquarters so Noel could be checked out. When we got there, the boss wasn't even around." He looked over at Mrs. Burris. "And the head of security is standing right here! What a clusterfuck waste of time."

Travis threw down his coat. Jacob walked over and flopped in a theater seat, and Noel rocked from one foot to the other. This made no sense.

"Travis, who called you to come to HQ?"

He pointed over to Jacob. Jacob shrugged his shoulders and pulled out his phone. “Here. I got a text from SSA Stewart to come to HQ. See.”

I looked at his phone, and sure enough there was a message. I took the phone from his hand and did a return text. *Undeliverable*. Son of a bitch.

Things were not adding up, too many coincidences. “Mrs. Burris, may I ask why you picked today to come here? Today of all days.”

“Oh my, well like I said before, all off-site facilities need to be checked. I had a reminder on my phone to come out today.”

“May I ask if your calendar reminder is electronic or a hang on your wall kind?”

“Electronic of course. See, it is right here on my phone.”

Sure enough there was a reminder to tour this off-site facility today, but it hadn’t even been a month yet, only a few weeks.

“Somebody has to be messing with us. Mrs. Burris, when did you get here and have you finished your inspection?”

Mrs. Burris looked a bit taken aback. “What are you asking, Jara? That I finagled a way so I could be alone here? Why on earth for? And yes, I am done with my inspection. All things are locked and secured as they should be.”

My head was swirling. There was no way we could have a breach. If we did, the whole case would go to shit. Someone knew Tess and I would be gone, Victoria would be at the Foundation, Katerina in NYC with Elly, but the guys...They had no plans to go anywhere. At this point I trusted no one. I was so angry. I wanted to down a beer and scream in the yard. *Think, Jara. Think.*

“Everyone,” I said a bit too loudly, “everyone, grab a pad of paper and pen and write down everything, I mean everything you have done since you woke up this morning. When you are done, please put the sheets in this folder.”

Mrs. Burris started to turn and leave. “Anita, please, you too. If you have anything on yours that my security clearance shouldn’t see, don’t worry, I’m sealing the folder and giving it to SSA Stewart.”

She heaved a sigh, pursed her lips, and put down her coat. She picked up a pad of paper and started writing. I sat at one of the tables and wrote down my day in detail. *This is crazy. Who is trying to sabotage us and how are they doing it?*

We all finished and put the pads in a large folder. I sealed it, and we all wrote our names across the seal.

"I think we have had enough excitement for the day. I'm going to secure our evidence, then I need some alone time. We'll debrief tomorrow. All good?"

I put the boxes in the vault and took another look around. Nothing seemed disturbed, but then again how in the hell would I know? I logged everything in, including the folder with the day's activities, and locked up the vault. When I turned to go to the kitchen, I almost jumped out of my skin. Mrs. Burris was right behind me.

"My god, you scared the shit out of me!"

"I'm sorry, dear. I wanted to make sure you were okay. I know today shook you up a bit, but you handled it beautifully."

My face scrunched. "Please don't tell me this was a security drill. I may lose it."

"No, dear, but if it was, you would have passed. We'll get to the bottom of this, I promise."

"Glad you can be so sure. Myself, I'll have to wait and see."

"Yes, we will," she said slowly and deliberately.

I went to the kitchen, grabbed a six-pack of beer, and headed for my boat. Granny May left the sailboat to me when she passed. She knew how much I loved it. The teak trim still gleamed like new. It had been a while since I went sailing. I missed it so much, and Granny too. I'd renamed the boat *The Penthouse* after an old house Katerina and I shared when we were in college, our oasis away from the world. I climbed on board, sat on the bow, and leaned against the cabin. I let the rocking of the boat relax me, as I downed my first beer and started on the second.

"Permission to come aboard, Captain?" It was Katerina.

"How could I ever deny my first officer? I thought you were staying in the city another night?"

"Elly said she was fine. I think she needed some time alone, and I think my presence reminded her of the attack. Travis told me you'd probably be out here when I couldn't find you upstairs or working. He said you wanted to be alone."

God, it was good to see her. I knew I couldn't tell her everything about my day, but she would know something happened. "Yes, but that doesn't apply to you. I am very glad to see you. I have really missed you. You're sure Elly is okay?"

"How sweet, I missed you too. Elly is good, hardheaded but good. She wants to go to her shop and check on things. I told her I didn't think it was a good idea, but she wouldn't listen. She absolutely refuses any protection."

I nodded my head and took another long drink of my beer.

"Bad day?"

"Good and bad." I shrugged. "Or should I say it was a typical day."

Katerina sat down beside me. She took a beer and leaned into me. I squeezed her hand, hoping she knew how much her presence without questions meant to me. I hated not telling her things. The boat rocked a bit harder when a large schooner entered the harbor. I watched her glide effortlessly to her dock.

"We need a trip," I exclaimed.

Katerina laughed. "We just got back."

"Okay, then maybe just a sail, even for a day."

Katerina's emerald eyes glowed. "Just the two of us?"

"Most definitely, my love."

We cuddled in closer, thinking about what could be, as the orange sky turned dark and the stars popped out, one by one. Katerina stood up, took my hand, and led me to the cabin. She locked the door behind us and started unbuttoning her top. I sat back on the cabin bed and watched, as she slowly wiggled out of her pants. She took her hair down and walked over to me. My eyes were glued to her. She put her hands on my shoulders and pushed me back, straddling my body. I could feel her body heat radiate over me. I moved my hand to touch her, but she took it and held it to the bed.

"No, it is my turn to have you. You have worked hard enough today. Let me do everything," she whispered, as she began kissing my neck and removing my clothes. She kissed me so deeply I thought I'd lose my mind. Then she made love to me, and I wasn't sure if I wanted my mind back. She was amazing, her moans and noises were making me crazy. We made love over and over, as our bodies moved to the rocking of the boat. We collapsed into each other and finally fell asleep.

I woke up as the sun peeked around the curtains in the cabin. I looked over at this gorgeous woman beside me, the woman who called me her partner in life, and I realized again how lucky I was. She was my friend, my backbone, my conscience, and my lover. I never knew I could love someone this much. I traced the curve of her body with my finger, following it with kisses. I felt her hand in my hair, as her body started to move to my touch. We made love again, not seeming to get enough of each other.

Katerina moaned. She whispered, "I miss those times in the Penthouse."

I knew what she meant, those college days filled with young love and desires, fumbling around but loving every minute of it.

"I'd say we have gotten a little better at this. At least no more Lucy and Ethel shenanigans."

We both burst out laughing, remembering when we broke a pull-out couch while trying to make love.

"Can't say we were boring!" she replied.

As much as we didn't want to, we got out of bed and dressed. *Guess it's time to go back to reality.*

We made our way back to the house. Holding hands and laughing, we followed the heavenly aroma of coffee into the kitchen. Everyone was standing by the island. No one said a word, as Katerina and I each grabbed a cup of coffee and headed upstairs. Travis walked to the base of the staircase and yelled, "One at a time in the shower, please. We have to work sometime."

We giggled like schoolgirls caught staying up too late. Of course, we didn't listen to him and showered together. It was nice to have a night and a morning like this. Made it feel life was good and all was well with the world, even though we knew it wasn't. We both had long days ahead.

I dressed casually, hoping I didn't have to go to HQ or anywhere else for that matter. Katerina, on the other hand, stepped out, dressed to the nines. She wore a Veronese green dress, with black buttons all the way down the back. Her emerald necklace and earrings accented her eyes perfectly, making them even more vibrant. She was stunning.

"Wow! You are dressed to impress. Anyone I know?"

"Funny, and yes, I need to impress. I am presenting our findings to the Foundation board today. Mom and I are hoping they see this as a good start with getting the money back. And since green is the color of money, I am hoping this brings us luck."

"Well, you look like a trillion bucks. I'm impressed."

We walked downstairs to the foyer, where I kissed Katerina goodbye and wished her luck. Her mother was waiting in the car. As Katerina went out the door, she turned and blew Travis a kiss. He and Noel had been standing in the doorway watching. As I walked over to them, Travis sighed. "How someone like you got a woman like that, I'll never know."

I grinned and smacked him on the arm. Noel started to say something, but no words came out, which made me laugh. "She makes you speechless, doesn't she?"

Travis and I started to walk toward the theater to meet with the others, but then I pointed him to the den instead.

"Travis, what went on yesterday? Do you have any idea?"

He shook his head. "Not a damn clue. We were all making fun of you, then we went to work. We were doing a new whiteboard, listing all the things each of the scenes had in common, including Noel's. He and Jacob began arguing about what we should be considering. After a while, you spoke with Noel to tell him about the interview. He came in and told us what was going on. A few minutes later, Jacob stood up and said he got a text from the boss and showed it to us. We all climbed in my vehicle and drove to HQ, just to find out the boss wasn't there. Heck, hardly anyone was, except for construction workers. He's been gone to Quantico for two days and is only due back today."

"Then what the fuck? Who is messing with us?"

"Jara, do you still have those cameras we set up from when we had that thing with Senator Lansing last year?"

"Oh my god, Travis, sometimes you're a genius. Yes. I never took them down. We have to get to them before yesterday is taped over."

We both ran back upstairs and headed for the small room off Granny May's. Yes, the cameras were still functioning.

"How do we do this?" I asked, looking around the machines. "I know we can't use it as evidence, but we can at least see what everyone was doing."

Travis knew technology way better than I did, so I told him the passwords and he logged in.

"Travis, can you tell if anyone has messed with these? Other than us."

He shook his head. "Doesn't look like it. Looks like it hasn't been touched for at least six months. That is, if I'm reading the logs right."

He downloaded all the captured material from the past two weeks. We had arrived just in time because it was on a two-week loop. We decided to keep taping and not tell anyone. It was, of course, a private home, and private homes did have camera systems, so we didn't need to announce it.

"Hey, can we look at yesterday real quick?" I was anxious to see what was captured.

"Sure." He loaded it up and we fast forwarded through the night part. It showed nothing unusual until we saw Jacob in the garden. "Okay, that's weird," Travis mumbled. "He never said he was outside."

We saw all the guys walk through the foyer, go outside, and leave. Nothing else was on the cameras. Most of them were motion-sensors. About an hour after the guys left, the camera showed Mrs. Burris pulling in. Travis and I shared a look of astonishment, as we watched Mrs. Burris pick the lock with ease. I was watching her as she moved through the house, when Travis yelled, "Whoa, what was that?"

He rewound the footage and slowed it down. A dark, black sedan had slowly pulled in the driveway, then turned around and sped off. We got a plate number but didn't recognize the people in the car. It looked like four people, but the windows had a tint to them, so I wasn't sure. Travis took still shots of the car and tried to zoom in closer. I continued to watch Mrs. Burris move through the house, checking locks but never entering the vault. She walked into the dining room, and I heard a voice. Holy shit, I forgot we had mic'ed up the room for the meeting with the senator. I put on headphones and listened more closely. Travis saw what I was doing and saw the screen with Mrs. Burris on a phone. I felt Travis shaking me, asking if I was okay. I stopped the recording and took off the headphones. "Travis, Mrs. Burris is speaking French."

Travis made copies of everything on two thumb drives. He put one in his pocket and handed the other to me. I considered putting it in my pocket, also, but thought better of it. Knowing me, it would go through the next washer cycle. I decided to put it in Granny's bedroom safe but remembered I didn't have the combination. I pulled out my phone to call Katerina, but Travis stopped me.

"What? I'm just calling Kat."

"Exactly, for combinations. If someone is messing with our electronics, then I'm not using them. Call her on this." He handed me a burner phone.

"A burner? Where did you get this and when?"

"I ran into town last night and got a couple. Here's yours. I'm not making it widely known that we have these."

"Good idea. Can't be too careful." I called Katerina and it went straight to voicemail, probably because she didn't recognize the number or she was still in her meeting. I left a message and told her to call back on a different line.

"What's with this new number? Spy games again?"

"I can't explain right now, but what is the combination to Granny's safe?"

She gave it to me without any questions. I put the drive in the safe and locked it. I then told Kat I loved her and hung up. Not the time for small talk.

"We need to get downstairs soon, before they come looking for us."

Travis and I were whispering as we walked down the staircase. Noel's voice boomed, "Where the hell have you two been? We have been waiting for over an hour."

Travis started laughing. "Oh, just having a quickie between friends. Don't mind us. You could have gone ahead and started."

"No, we couldn't. The vault combination has changed."

"Oh shit," I said. "I'm so sorry." I rushed down the stairs. "I changed everything last night to be on the safe side."

"Really? You don't trust us?" Noel got louder.

"It's not that I don't trust you. I'm trying to protect all of us and protect our case, yours included. You got a problem with that, city boy?"

By this time, we were toe-to-toe. Noel grunted and walked away. I went to the vault and unlocked it.

"We need to know what we are working on, and what our plan is. Travis and I are going to gather what we want to have retested from the old cases. I have a feeling we may hit a wall trying to get the money for all this retesting, so we need to be picky. Tess, how about you?"

"Jacob and I are going to do the same. I need to contact NYPD to see if they have anything else from their case. Noel, can you help me with that?"

"Sure, I'd still like to interview Elly again, but I want to go over these DNA results first and see how they match up. Jara, your guy from France have any other information?"

Wow, he had slipped my mind. "Thanks Noel. I forgot I was going to call him."

We all got on our phones and the business began. I slipped off to another room and called André.

"*Chérie*, my sweet, to what do I owe this pleasure? My Katerina leaving you for me?"

He always made me laugh. "In your wildest dreams, André."

"*Oui, chérie, oui.* So now what can I help you with?"

I told him all that we learned in our interview with Andrew and that I would be sending him the transcripts of the meeting.

"So now I have solved one of yours and another here, and I'm needing more information on Toni. She's still being surveilled?"

"*Oui.* Is it time to gather the DNA yet?"

"Working on a warrant right now, but can you either ask her or covertly get it so I can test a theory?"

"Another gut pain, *chérie*?"

"Gut feeling, André. Gut feeling, but then again, this is beginning to be a pain to me. Just let me know what you can get."

Call to André done, I called SSA Stewart. He picked up on the first ring.

"Jara, hello. I was just going to call you. Anita told me of the clusterfuck that happened yesterday. Do you need to bring everything back here?"

In my head I was kicking myself. I should have called him last night. Of course, Mrs. Burris was the first to tell him. "No, sir. All safety precautions have been taken. Did Mrs. Burris say we should come back there?"

"No, no, no. On the contrary, she said all was secure. So what can I do for you, Jara?"

"Well, sir, I'd like to meet with you as soon as possible, get you up to date where we are and what we need to go forward." I had made a quick sidestep and didn't tell him everything over the phone. I thought it best to do it in person.

"Very well. Meet me at my office at nine a.m. tomorrow. Don't be late."

I informed everyone Tess and I would be going to HQ in the morning to do a debrief with the boss. I gathered all my notes on the interview and outlined what evidence we wanted retested. I decided to call Quantico and spoke with a friend I had in the lab. We had actually graduated Academy together, even went on a couple dates. We ended as friends though.

"Jara, hello. How have you been? I'm sure this isn't a social call. What can I do for you?"

"I'm fine, Amelia, how are you doing? And you're right, sorry, this isn't a social call. I was wondering if you had any of the evidence from the Branson case stored in your lab. I know the state sent some there to be tested, but I'm not sure if it ever was. I was told the state shut the case down pretty quickly after the confession."

I heard tapping of keys in the background. "Good news, Jara, I have a lot in inventory that was never tested. It's all under the state case number."

"Amelia, what do I need to do to have it changed to an FBI case number and have it all run?"

"All of it?"

"Yes, all of it. Even things that seem unimportant. I also have a few things that need to be entered as new evidence."

"Let me check into all of this. I'm not sure what paperwork I'll need. It's not going to be cheap either way."

"I figured that. I'm meeting with the SSA tomorrow morning to fill him in. Anything special I need to tell him?"

"I'll send you my inventory list and what has and hasn't been done. Do you want any results if I have them?"

"Please, Amelia. Thank you so much. I owe you."

Travis had started going through our evidence when the fax machine started to chirp. Damn, Amelia was efficient. I walked over to the machine and grabbed the first page. I dropped it as if it were on fire.

LEAVE IT ALONE

Ten pages carried the same message. Someone wanted the case to go away, badly. I bent over and collected the pages.

. "What's that?" Jacob was standing right behind me.

"Oh, just some things I asked for. It's nothing, really." I walked away before he could see or ask anything more.

I quietly slid the warnings to Travis, then turned my back to the others and put my finger over my lips. Travis picked up the pages and looked at each one. He has such a poker face.

"Yep," he said, "glad these came in. The boss probably wants to have these." He placed them into a folder and handed them back to me. I put them on the bottom of my ever-growing pile to take to HQ. The fax machine beeped again, and my phone went off at the same time. Tess saw me almost jump out of my skin.

"You okay? What has gotten into you?"

"Oh, it's nothing." I tried to play it off. "Just a bit tired, I guess." I had no poker face. I looked at my phone. Amelia texted to make sure the fax had plenty of paper. She was sending hard copies of inventory and results by fax and by email. I went back to the fax machine. Jacob was already there.

"Hey, this is the evidence we sent to be tested years ago. What's going on?" Jacob grumbled.

"We're having everything tested and retested, remember? I needed a list of what was already there, so we didn't duplicate."

"Well, did you get the list from the state lab too?"

"There's still stuff at the state lab that wasn't sent?"

"I think so. I'm not sure, but I think we should see. I'll call them right now."

If my face appeared shocked, that's because it was. This is the first time Jacob had initiated anything regarding this case. He went into the other room to call the lab.

"Where is Jacob going?" Tess asked.

"He's calling the state lab for a list of anything that is still there from the old cases," I replied.

Tess walked over to a table that had stacks of folders and started going through them. "See, that's funny. I called for this last week. Here it is." She handed me the folder. Sure enough, beneath a letterhead that said *Connecticut State Police Lab* was an inventory of what was left. I took the folder and walked into the room where Jacob was talking. He saw me enter but kept talking.

"Oh, you did? Okay, my bad. I'll look for it." He looked over at me. "They say they sent it."

I held up the folder Tess gave me. "You mean this list?"

Jacob grabbed the folder and stormed past me. "God damn it, Tess, anything else you're not gonna tell me or leave me out of? You're making me look like a fool."

"You're doing that all on your own, Jacob. I told you I called the lab, but of course you probably weren't listening, as usual."

"I listen to what I'm included in. You have shut me out from day one. You couldn't handle they closed down your precious career case. Somehow you had to blame me."

"I never blamed you. I blamed me and the court system that wanted it to be over. You took me not sleeping with you as a sign I blamed you? You didn't want to admit we had run our course."

"Oh, get over it. I know I have. You aren't the only woman out there. I can still be your partner and not sleep with you."

"Oh, for the love of God, you two," I yelled. "Get over it. Can you work together or not?"

"Well, don't stop it now. It's just getting good." Noel seemed amused. We all glared at him. "Fine, fine, I'll butt out."

"Thank you." I turned back to Tess and Jacob. "I'm not asking this again. Can you two work together or not?"

They nodded their heads and sat down.

"Tess, do you have your stuff ready for tomorrow?"

"Yep, all of it."

"Okay, same here. I'm taking all of mine and locking it in the Rover. You could lock yours up here or out there."

Tess followed me out to the car. "You're not going to tell me what's going on, are you? You and Travis are being so secretive."

"Honestly, Tess, I would love to. But we have to figure out what we have first. It may be nothing."

"You didn't jump like it was nothing."

"Oh that. Too much coffee and lack of sleep, I guess. No worries."

"If you say so. Sorry for blowing up at Jacob again. I'm thin on patience too."

"Again, no worries. But it has to stop. He's your partner, and you have to work with him."

"Yes, I guess I do."

Everything was securely locked up, and we went back in to the others. "Tomorrow, Tess and I are going to HQ. Jacob, could you go to the state lab and take what's there to Quantico? And Noel, you go reinterview Elly. Travis, you figure out if you're going to go with Jacob or with Noel. As for me, I'm going to the back porch to wait for a call. We all good?"

Everyone nodded or said yes. I was hoping André would call with news about Toni. I was hoping for a miracle.

While having a beer on the back porch and watching the water, I saw Jacob in the garden again. Curiosity got the better of me, and I walked down to where he was.

"Hey, Jacob."

"Oh, hi. I'm sorry. Am I not to be down here?"

He had on a pair of shorts and a T-shirt, and for the first time, I noticed how in shape he was.

"You're allowed. Feel free to be here. It's one of my favorite places. It's so calming and beautiful."

"Yes, it is. I have been coming down here to do my meditation and yoga. I didn't want to make a big deal out of it. It's something I do for me. My new girlfriend taught me."

"Well, this is the perfect place for focus and relaxation. A new girlfriend, huh? Does Tess know?"

"Nah, didn't want to throw it in her face. My girlfriend is a stewardess, so I don't get to see much of her, with her schedule and mine."

"Well, good luck to you both. Enjoy the garden."

"Thank you. I will."

Tess was taking a walk with Noel down by the water. They seemed to be getting along well. Travis was sitting next to my chair.

"Has Mother Hen checked on all of her chicks?"

"Oh, shut up, Travis. You know, it's hard for me to work with other people, especially if they are not getting along."

"I know, Lone Ranger, this must be tough, but it seems to be all working out."

"So who are you going with tomorrow, Jacob or Noel?"

"I think I'll go with Noel. Give Jake some autonomy, see what he does with it."

Wise as usual.

Chapter Twenty-Five

The morning came fast. I'm not sure why I was so nervous about this meeting with SSA Stewart, but I was. I snuck off to Granny's room to get the flash drive out of her vault and put it in my pocket. I was contemplating telling Tess about it but decided not to. I met her at the Rover and made sure all of my files were still locked up where they should be. Everything was safe and sound. The guys were also getting ready to leave. Victoria had stayed at the Foundation, and Katerina was with Elly. I wondered how we were going to secure the house. I went back through it and checked the locks on all the doors and the vault. I then made a phone call to a friend of mine in local law enforcement, Sgt. Mike Cooper, to ask for a favor. I explained to Mike the situation of the house being an off-site workspace. He immediately agreed to have a couple of off-duty officers sit in front of the house, and I breathed a sigh of relief. I went back outside and told them the house would be guarded. We all climbed in our respective vehicles and left. On our way down the drive, the first officer pulled in and waved. *Wow, that was quick.*

Tess and I rode in silence until we reached HQ, then she asked, "So now do I get to know everything?"

I let out a big sigh. "Tess, let me talk to the SSA first. I promise, if he says it's okay I will tell you everything."

Tess got out of the car and slammed the door. She went to the back to get her papers. "So you still don't trust me?"

I made it to the back of the Rover, not happy my door was slammed. "Listen, be mad at me, but don't take it out on my car. Honestly, I barely trust anyone anymore. I don't work with others well, but I have shared with you everything that I can. When I get the okay, you'll know everything, I promise. Anyway, aren't we supposed to keep our cases separate?"

"You're right, but I still don't like it. I feel it's not just about the case."

I said nothing, but she had good instincts. I grabbed everything and, after going through security, I went to SSA Stewart's office. Tess followed along. SSA Stewart was waiting in the front office with Mrs. Burris.

"Anita, uh, Mrs. Burris. Hello." I looked back and forth between her and SSA Stewart.

"Jara, I'm just leaving." Mrs. Burris nodded to my boss. "Jack, we'll talk later."

I was sure I had a shocked look on my face, not knowing what to say or where to go, as I watched her walk out of the office. Would SSA Stewart believe my doubts regarding Mrs. Burris? Should I even show him the flash drive?

"Sir, may I speak with you privately? Detective Goodwin can join us later if you don't mind."

"Of course, of course. Let's talk. We have a lot to go over."

I turned to Tess and mouthed, *I promise*. She shrugged and sat down in one of the oversized chairs in the front office.

I followed the SSA into his office, went to the couch, and set all my files down.

"Leave those over there and come to my desk," he ordered.

"Okay, uh, so formal?"

"Yes and no. We both have a lot of information to share with each other, and my stuff is here. So who goes first?"

"Sir, may I speak freely?"

"Of course, Jara."

"Sir, there have been some, well, things about this case that have me baffled."

"Well, Jara, it is an investigation. You can't have all the answers immediately."

"I know that, sir, but there were some inconsistencies initially on the evidence records from CSP. We have all the evidence now, I think, and it is intact, but I can't figure out why everything wouldn't have been listed on the copy given to us."

"What does CSP say about this?" SSA Stewart's face started turning red and developed a look of concern.

"They have no answers, so Travis and I are double-checking everything."

"Good idea. Anything else?"

"Well sir, I appreciate all that Mrs. Burris has done for us, but I wonder what her role is here. She's never given me a straight answer."

"Is this a concern that will affect this case?"

"Yes, sir, it may be."

"I'm surprised your girlfriend's mother hasn't told you about Mrs. Burris."

"Victoria? I know they're acquainted, but that's about it."

"I can tell you this. Mrs. Burris is one of the biggest assets we have. She was friends with Granny May for years. Mrs. Burris attended the Naval Academy and was recruited by, well no one knows for certain, to do special missions for our country. Her family helped Granny's family bring over many people during World War II and during the Cold War. Mrs. Burris has continued that work."

"So she's a spy? For who?"

The SSA started laughing. "Like I said before, no one knows for certain. I know she has worked for all the alphabet agencies, CIA, NSA, Homeland, and even some agencies people don't know about. She is an expert in security systems, forgery, and espionage. It is rumored her family worked closely with Varian Fry at the Emergency Rescue Committee in France. It is also rumored she is the unknown daughter of Wilhelm (Bill) and Mina Spira, but that isn't confirmed."

"Wait, I know who they are. Katerina and I just returned from France. We learned Bill Spira was a cartoonist who got arrested. He and Adolfo Kaminsky saved thousands of people by forging paperwork to get them out of occupied France. And well, the ERC did amazing work. You said her family is from France?"

"No, not from France initially, but later settled there. Why?"

"Part of this case is spilling over into France. One of the Branson triplets, Toni, lives there. Through my Interpol contact, we learned of the abduction and murder of the triplets' mother in France. Pierre Formet was arrested for those crimes. During our interview with Andrew, he stated his father abducted the mother in front of the children, then killed the mother. Andrew inferred he saw the crime scene and saw his father with his mother's body. I have notified Interpol in France." I took a deep breath and continued. "The other day, after Tess and I interviewed Mr. Branson, the guys were all called here to meet with you, but you were at Quantico. Mrs. Burris showed up at the house unexpectedly, picked the lock, and walked around the house. She also made a call in French. Now knowing her background, that is not that surprising."

"How do you know all this?"

"Sir, back during the investigation of Senator Lansing, I had surveillance equipment installed on the grounds and in the house. Mrs. Burris admitted to picking the lock, but I didn't ask her about the phone call. If she still has family in France, that would make sense. But it is all so coincidental."

"That is odd. She does have family there, a granddaughter named Quinn, like your last name. She is a singer in Paris. And why the guys were called here, I don't know. I am still trying to figure that out. Who received the call?"

"Tess's partner Jacob."

"Well then that's bullshit! If I wanted you here, I'd call you or Travis, not a CSP detective."

Holy shit, I thought, *he's right*. Why didn't that dawn on me? "You're right sir. That makes no sense. I have a couple of other things to show you." I pulled out the flash drive and plugged it in. "Soon after Mrs. Burris arrived, a dark sedan pulled into the drive. No one got out, and they sped away. Again, another coincidence."

"I don't believe in coincidences. Did you have Jacob's phone traced?"

"We did a reverse number search, but it was undeliverable. To do more than that, I would need your permission."

"Well, you have it. You want him off the case?"

"No sir, not yet. I want him near."

"Okay, talk to Mrs. Burris. I bet you know more about her than you think. Want to bring the detective in now?"

"One more thing, sir, I called the Quantico lab for evidence information. While I was waiting for them to fax it, another fax came in." I pulled out the folder with the papers saying *LEAVE IT ALONE.*

"And this came over the fax?"

"Yes sir."

SSA Stewart pulled out his phone and texted someone. "If you don't mind, I am going to have Anita investigate this. Keep this between us."

I nodded, as I got up and motioned for Tess to come in. We moved over to the couch, and I started in on what we had learned, the interview, and what we were currently working. Tess went through her investigations, then announced, "I just received a call from NYPD. They have uncovered more evidence in that murder. I think we need to go there and meet with them again. I am going to ask Det. Gregory to be a liaison with them."

The SSA sat back. "I agree. Any new suspects in New York, or are we still looking at the Branson family?"

I explained how new DNA was found on Elly that had some of the same DNA markers as one of the earlier cases and a set of unknown DNA. I also told him Det. Gregory and Travis were reinterviewing Elly today.

SSA Stewart nodded his head. "At least we have one live victim. This may help. So what else do you need?"

I tried to explain my hunch about Andrew Branson not committing all of the murders. "We now know he killed Amy Vincent in New York in 2000, and he confessed to the fifth murder he was charged with, but he couldn't have been involved with the new murders or the attack on Elly."

"I'm sure there is more. Out with it."

"Well, sir, we'd like the lab to test all the evidence from Det. Gregory's cases, including Amy Vincent, plus retest the evidence we have from before the conviction and after."

A strange whistle came out of SSA Stewart. He stood up and started pacing. "That is a helluva lot of money, Quinn. How do we justify redoing some of these? Especially since we have someone locked up for at least five of the crimes. You need it all retested?"

"Sir, we are going through all the evidence the lab already has and will be sure not to duplicate any of the confirmed tests. But there is something about Andrew's confession to CSP's five crimes that isn't sitting with me. It was too vague and matter of fact. When he confessed to Amy Vincent he had more detail. When discussing Ms. Vincent's case and his mother's, it was like he was reliving them. In everything I read about his earlier confession, he was totally unemotional."

Tess was nodding her head in agreement. “Sir, my confessions really were cut and dry, unlike the reaction Jara got from him at the hospital.”

After a few minutes of awkward silence, the boss gave his approval. “Keep me posted on these tests. If things start looking as if Andrew Branson is the only suspect, we cut it off. Got it? Plus, go interview him some more. I hear he likes your, uh, look.”

“So you heard about that?” I grinned and heard Tess chuckle.

“Yes, I think all of the FBI knows, pictures even.”

I mumbled, “Damn it, Travis.”

“From the first day I met you, you showed flair.” He looked down at his phone, “This may be one picture I put on my wall. Next time, though, wear the socks too.” He let out a large guttural laugh and walked to the door. “Is there anything else?”

“One more thing, sir, I am working with Interpol on retrieving DNA from Antoinette, Toni Branson. I may need a warrant at some point for that.”

“It never ends with you, does it Quinn?” He opened the door. We were being dismissed.

“Thank you, sir, and the black car?”

Tess gave me a look.

“I’ll look into it and get back to you.”

We gathered our things and headed to the car.

“Black car?” Tess asked.

I explained a dark sedan was seen at the house the day we were all gone. “I’m having the Bureau look into it.”

“And you couldn’t tell me this? What else aren’t you telling me? Who saw this car?”

“Tess, I am sorry. I’m not the kind of person to share information until I know more about it. I have a camera at the house that picked up this car, so we have a still shot of it and the plate. Sorry I didn’t tell you.”

“Whatever. Probably good Jacob and I will be gone tomorrow. Give you time to think about what this task force and teammates mean.”

I gave Tess a shitty look. “Seriously? You are going to lecture me about sharing and teammates? Might want to look at your own house and clean that up first before lecturing me.”

We both got in the car, shutting our doors a bit too heavily. We rode in silence most of the way home. This was getting old.

"Tess, I'm sorry. I didn't mean to attack you or cut you out of this investigation. I'm not a very trusting person, especially when it comes to situations where coincidences take place. I know I should have told you, but to be honest I'm not sure if I can trust Jacob. And until today, I even had questions about Mrs. Burris. I don't think it was a coincidence that no one was home when...A...Mrs. Burris showed up, and...B...a dark sedan showed up. Plus, why did Jacob get a call from FBI HQ and not Travis or I? Makes no sense. I learned today, per the FBI, Mrs. Burris is on the up and up. But the car and Jacob's call I'm still not sure about."

Tess waited quietly until I finished rambling on. "I wondered why Jacob got that text and not you or Travis. I have been trying to check that out myself."

"Thanks Tess, I appreciate that, but I don't want to strain your partnership even more than it already is."

"Strain it!" She scoffed. "Can't strain a partnership that is already broken. I'll let you know what I find out. Please let me know if you learn anything."

I agreed. Thank God, we got that in the open. Sure made the ride a lot less tense.

Chapter Twenty-Six

While Tess and Jara were at their meeting, Noel and Travis met with Elly and Katerina.

Elly greeted them at the door of her brownstone and showed them to a beautiful living room. Rich colors surrounded the room, deep reds on the walls, with a chocolate couch and pops of purple, blue, and gold accents. A sleek, baby grand piano sat in a corner, surrounded by other musical instruments. Colorful art hung on the walls, and a plush, gold rug partially covered exquisite hardwood floors.

"Gentlemen, welcome to my home," Elly said, as she ushered them in. "You all know Katerina by now, I assume."

Katerina stood, smiled at Noel and gave Travis a hug. "I'm so glad you are looking into this some more. I fear for Elly's safety."

Noel turned to Katerina "Well, ma'am, so am I. Has something happened that we don't know about?"

"No, no, it's only a fear I have." Katerina reached over to Elly, who sat quietly but nodded her head.

Noel looked straight at Elly. "Until I catch this son of a bitch, pardon my language...but until this sicko is off the streets, I fear for everyone's safety."

"Gentlemen, please sit," Elly said. "Relax. Would either of you like something to drink? Tea, coffee, soda...?"

Each accepted ice tea and sat down. Noel sat on the couch but kept moving about, not seeming to get comfortable.

"Det. Gregory, you can move if you like," Elly said with a laugh in her voice. "I know my couch can sometimes swallow a person up."

"I'm fine, ma'am. I'll figure it out."

Noel finally got settled with his briefcase on his lap and pulled out a couple of folders. "I don't want to drudge on about this and make you keep repeating your story, but I really need you to go over it again with me in case I missed something."

Travis noted Noel was smart to put it on himself, instead of accusing the victim of changing stories.

"I'd be happy to, Detective. I will do my best," Elly said. "Well, Katerina and Jara had left after our dinner, and I was finishing some things at the office. I had been so excited to smell what they brought me that I was still on cloud nine. I went downstairs to check on my employees and secure things before closing. A lady was in the showroom with one of my employees. My employee motioned me over and said this customer wanted to speak to me. I agreed. She asked if I was leaving for the night. I said yes, and she wanted to know if she could walk with me. I thought it a bit odd at the time, but she seemed harmless enough."

Noel interrupted. "Can you describe her for me, please?"

"I can try. I'm better with smells than with faces. Hmm...she was tall, maybe 5'10" or 5'11", white, short dark hair, dark eyes, nothing really stood out. She had an athletic or muscular build, almost manly, and she carried a brown purse. I noticed that because she also had on black heels. No one carries a brown purse with black shoes," Elly said with disdain. "I also smelled a familiar fragrance on her. I couldn't tell if it was her who was wearing L'Interdit, or if I was still smelling it from earlier."

"Do you know what she wanted in your store?"

"Hmmm...no, I don't remember. But all we do is work with fragrances, so I assumed she had a question about or wanted a perfume."

"Anything else?"

"Well when we were outside, she asked me a question...uh, what was it...Oh, she wanted to know where Paisano's butcher shop was. I pointed down the street, and told her it was probably closed at that hour. Without asking anything else, she said thank you and started walking down the street. I thought it was strange for her to ask for me specifically in the store, and only ask for directions. I watched her for a moment, then started walking home. I was a bit on edge and didn't want a customer to know where I live, so I decided to walk in the park for a bit and soak up the night air. Next thing I remember, I was lying in an alley with a huge, pounding headache. I felt someone lift me up and put me in a car or SUV. I knew it had to be big, because I fit in the backseat easily. I passed out and woke up in the basement of a brownstone."

"A brownstone. How do you know it was a brownstone? Did you see it?"

"Sir, no I didn't see the outside, but I live in a brownstone, grew up in a brownstone, and own six brownstones. It was definitely a brownstone. A basement in a brownstone. I was still groggy, but I looked around and saw I was tied up. Soft ties actually, like men's neckties. I was getting out of them when someone came in the room. I couldn't tell if it was the same woman I had spoken with earlier or someone else. They were coming toward me with a small knife. I was almost free but pretended I was still passed out. They came near me with the knife and tried to cut my thigh. We started fighting. I guess I knocked the stuff out of their hands, and we fell to the ground. I was able to move away, and I kicked to keep them off me. All I could think about was getting the hell out of there. I made it up the basement stairs and the back door was right there, so I rushed out. I didn't see anything on the first floor. I stumbled down the alley and saw a lamppost and crawled to it. I don't remember much after that."

"Is this where the EMTs found you?"

"I believe so. As I said, I don't remember much else. I know I crawled as far as I could. I don't remember anything else from the street or alley, only seeing flashing lights and waking up in the hospital."

Noel shook his head. He knew where Elly was picked up and the area. The police at the scene had assumed she was dumped there, so no one went in depth to look around the alley. There were brownstones all up and down that street. Their concern had been to get Elly medical help. Noel knew an opportunity was missed.

"Do you know who all was with you? In the car or the brownstone perhaps?"

"I didn't see anyone else at the brownstone but like I told you before, I thought I heard a male and a female talking in the vehicle. I never saw two people at the same time though."

Noel seemed to have an *Aha* moment. "Elly, when you heard the voices, were they talking, fighting, yelling at each other or over each other?"

"They were talking, discussing, I guess. No voices were raised. Why?"

"I need to know if they ever talked over the other, spoke at the same time," he said.

Elly sat back in her chair and closed her eyes, as if going back to that time. "No, Detective, they spoke one at a time. Actually, now that I think of it, the conversation didn't make much sense. I was really out of it, but it was like each of them were talking to themselves rather than to each other. I figured it was my head injury."

"Thank you, that is very helpful."

Elly leaned forward. "Detective, what are you thinking?"

"I'd rather not say at this moment. It's just a hunch, and I don't want to put anything in your head that isn't true. But if I learn anything, I promise, I will let you know."

Noel sat up from the couch the best he could. He looked directly at Elly showing a softness and kindness rare for a police officer. "So, Elly, how are you feeling? Really, I mean both physically and mentally?"

She seemed caught off guard by this change in tone and concern. So was Travis. Elly sat back in her chair again, tears filling her eyes.

"Detective, I'm fine...I'm..." Elly choked up, struggling for words. Katerina reached her hand over, then stood behind Elly and put her hands on Elly's shoulders. Elly began to shake, as tears poured from her eyes. Noel stood up and walked over to Elly and bent on one knee. He took her hand gently and softly said, "Ma'am, I promise you, I will do everything in my power to keep you safe and catch the person or persons responsible for hurting you."

Katerina and Travis exchanged looks, even though both had known Noel for only a little while, his actions seemed so foreign to them. Elly appeared comforted and her trembling lessened. Noel gave her a tissue. He stayed on his knee until Elly smiled and nodded her head. He clumsily got up and returned to the sofa.

"Thank you, Detective. I appreciate all you are doing. Any more questions?" Elly asked between sniffles.

"I think I have bothered you enough for one day, ma'am. But please, Elly, if you remember anything else, no matter how small, please call me." He handed her his card. "My cell phone number is on the back."

Katerina, who was still standing behind Elly, said, "Elly, can you tell the detective what you thought you heard your abductor say?"

"Elly, did you hear something?"

"Oh yes, I had forgotten. I'm not sure, but I think the female said the word forbidden, which is the English translation of the perfume I identified for Jara and Kat, L'Interdit. Then one voice said, 'It's not their fault. This is how they were born.' The other voice said, 'It's wrong! It's forbidden. Daddy said it isn't allowed.' That's all I could make out, talk about Daddy and forbidden."

Travis spoke up. "Elly, do you think you were targeted because of your transition? We know there have been hate crimes, and we also know there are some gender-identity issues within the Branson family."

"I thought Andrew Branson was locked up?" Elly sounded surprised.

"He is, but we are looking at everything now. With what you said about forbidden, Daddy, and L'Interdit, we can't ignore the possibility a Branson family member was involved."

Noel scrunched up his face and gave a stern look to Travis, letting it be known he hadn't wanted to give Elly this information. He let out a large sigh and turned back to Elly. "Ma'am, I mean no offense, but I can't say I totally understand being a transexual, or transvestitism, or whatever, or being gay, or whatever they are calling it now..."

Katerina giggled a little bit but stopped after seeing how sincere Noel was.

He continued. "Ma'am, did you ever feel you were two different people in one body? And if so, were you straight or gay?"

Elly chuckled. "I'm sorry, Detective. I'm not laughing at you, but a lot of misconceptions are out there. Even people in transition are confused by things. For example, when I was a man, I preferred men as my sexual partners, even though I did sleep with some women. But I knew, deep inside, I was always a woman. So was I gay or doing what was natural for me as a woman? Now that I have transitioned, I still love men, so does that mean I am straight now? Honestly, I don't know. All I do know is this is who I am supposed to be."

Noel shook his head. "Honestly, ma'am, does it matter who you love? We're all human, love should be love."

Elly smiled. "You are 100 percent right Detective, but I think it makes others feel more comfortable when a label is attached. Seriously, with all the labels out there, even I'm confused!"

Noel smiled and nodded his head. "I understand. What we can't label or understand we start fearing or hating. Maybe that is a bit extreme, but that is what I have seen in my years as a police officer."

Noel looked over at Travis and back at Elly. "We'll be getting out of your hair now. I want to go over to where you were found and look around a little bit. See if I can find this brownstone."

Travis nodded in agreement. Katerina walked over and gave him another hug, then turned to Noel. He offered a handshake, but Katerina pushed it away and hugged him also. Noel seemed taken aback at first, but then he hugged her back.

Elly joined in. "If this is a hug fest, I want in on it!" She gave Travis and Noel each a quick hug and stepped back. "Thank you both, again, for all you are doing."

Katerina showed them to the door and thanked them. "I'll see you both later. I am going to stay here for a bit and head home after dinner."

Travis and Noel waved goodbye and headed for the car. Both were energized and excited. "Is the killing and staging area right under our noses?" Noel asked. "Do you think it's a brownstone near where they found Elly?"

Travis shrugged his shoulders. "I don't know, but let's find out!"

They couldn't get there fast enough.

Chapter Twenty-Seven

Noel wasted no time driving them to the area where Elly had been found. Everything to the north were businesses, so he and Travis walked south.

"Travis, I know the crime-scene techs went through here and officers scoured the block, but let's go farther down the alley. Maybe Elly ran farther than we thought. She is a fighter."

Travis agreed and they began walking the alley. About two blocks down, Noel saw a moving truck at one of the brownstones. The crew was at the back door. Travis walked to the back of the truck, and Noel went to talk with the movers. Travis started looking in the back of the cargo area.

"Hey, what are your two doing?" A sweaty, burly many yelled at Travis. Both Noel and Travis showed their badges. "Oh, sorry officers, what do you want? I have a job to get finished."

Noel touched the man's elbow and turned him back toward the door. "Sir, we are investigating an assault that happened near here."

"It wasn't me. I have never been here before. I got this moving job yesterday."

Noel followed the mover into the home while Travis called HQ and asked for ownership records of the property The mover said the place had been vacant for almost a year, except for a few odds and ends he was clearing out. Noel looked around the place and saw the mover was right. Not much by means of furniture, but he did notice food trash in the wastebasket. So someone had been there. He couldn't retrieve any of the food until the trash was put outside.

"Need to get my guys to finish up, not getting paid by the hour."

"So where are you taking this stuff?" Noel asked, while still looking around.

"Some storage unit on the other side of Brooklyn. Don't know why someone would keep this crap, but hey, who am I to judge? It's a job."

Noel thanked the mover for his time and walked back outside. Travis had been looking in the moving truck and the surrounding dumpsters. Travis shook his head when he saw Noel.

"The property is owned by a company that filed bankruptcy and isn't from the area. It's so weird. I mean, it's a three-story brownstone with a basement, and there's not even enough stuff to fill this truck."

. "See anything suspicious?"

"Depends on what you call suspicious. Bags of dirty linen, a table, a few lights...What is suspicious is what is not here. No TV, bed, couch, stereo...nothing."

About that time, the mover came running out the back door. "Hey you! You're a cop, right?"

Noel turned around. "Yeah, NYPD, why?"

"Then you need to see this."

The mover took Noel and Travis to the basement. The overhead lights were extremely bright. "Over here." The mover pointed to a table and the floor. "You won't believe what's in the next room. I'm not moving that stuff."

Both Travis and Noel moved past the man and closer to the room. "Holy shit!" Noel said with a gasp once he opened the door.

I got a call from Travis that they were at a brownstone near where Elly was found and were in the process of securing the area as a crime scene.

"Jara, man, wow, uh...You need to get here and see this. This has to be the place where some of the victims were brought before they were killed and staged."

"Travis, tell me, what is it? Tell me!"

"No Jara, I can't explain it. You and Tess need to get here quick, please."

"On our way. You two take it easy. Who is in charge of the scene, you or Noel?"

"Noel right now. He had quicker access to get backup to secure the area. We'll figure it all out later."

"Travis, where is Katerina? Is she still with Elly?"

"Not sure. She said she was coming home after dinner."

Tess gave me a strange look. I hung up and started walking to the car. "We have to go. Now! I'll explain on the way."

We both got on our phones en route. Tess called Jacob, and I called SSA Stewart. Tess told Jacob we were going to NYC, that we might have found the crime scene. He said he was still at Quantico, but he would leave right away. I filled in the SSA on what I knew. He informed me the FBI would need to take over the scene, but all NYPD would assist. I called Travis and informed him and told him we were about thirty minutes out.

"Hey Jara, be careful. It's pouring down rain here."

Katerina and Elly had ordered dinner and were finishing up. "Elly love, I need to be getting back home. Are you going to be okay? I can stay."

"Kat, I'm going to be fine. Thanks so much for being with me. You don't know how much I appreciate all your support. But please, get back to your family."

"Elly, you are family. You are welcome at the house anytime."

Elly smiled and hugged Katerina. "I know. I love you."

When Katerina got to the door, she stopped. "Oh my, Elly, it's raining cats and dogs. May I borrow an umbrella and a coat? I'll never make it to the garage without getting soaked."

Elly pulled out a tan Max Mara trench coat. "Here, this should fit you perfectly."

Katerina's eyes widened "Oh, Elly, I couldn't. This is one of your favorites."

"I know, I haven't been able to wear it since my attack. I'm not sure why. I hate for it to go to waste. I'll go back to SAKS and get something different. Keep it. It's yours. Here is the matching umbrella."

"Elly, thank you so much. This will save my run to my car. Love you."

"Call me when you get home. You know I worry."

"No problem, love. I'll ring you."

Katerina pulled her hair up, popped up the collar, and opened the umbrella once outside. It was at least five blocks to get to the garage where her car was parked, so she moved quickly, keeping her head down. It was really pouring. Katerina felt a twinge in her back, but kept moving, thinking it was the way she was holding her head under the umbrella. *Why are my feet so heavy?* She slowed down, changing the umbrella to her other hand. It slipped, and she started feeling nauseous and dizzy, almost dropping the umbrella. “What the hell is happening to me?”

Katerina felt a hand touch her elbow and guide her to the alley before the garage. She started vomiting uncontrollably. Someone was holding her up. “What the hell?” Next thing she knew, she heard a door slam above her. *I’m in a trunk!* Before she could panic, she passed out.

Chapter Twenty-Eight

Tess and I arrived at the brownstone. It was still pouring rain. We ran in the back door from the alley. Travis grabbed me as soon as I got inside.

"Tess, you go on down. Jara, I need to talk to you."

"Later, Travis, I need to see this basement." I tried to push past him.

"Jara, please, stop! I have to talk with you, now."

I'd never heard Travis raise his voice to me like that. "Travis, what? I don't have time for this."

"Jara, it's Kat. We think she's been taken."

"Taken? What do you mean taken? She's with Elly just a few miles from here."

"Jara, Kat decided to drive back home. Elly just called me. She noticed that Kat forgot her purse. She ran after her and saw someone push her into the alley. When Elly reached the alley, Kat was gone. She saw her umbrella and a bunch of vomit. Jara, I'm sorry. I'm on my way over there."

I stood there not believing what I heard. Tess was walking up the stairs, her face white as a sheet. I started to push past her to go down to the basement. Travis grabbed me again.

"Jara, please don't go down there. We have to find Kat first. I can't have you seeing that and having your imagination run wild."

"God damn it, Travis. I need to see the basement. I'll meet you at Elly's."

Travis knew arguing was useless. "Do what the hell you want. I'm going to find Katerina."

I looked down the basement stairs, then looked over at Tess. The color still hadn't returned to her face. "Fine, Travis, I'll ride with you. Tess, call me if you find anything." I threw her my Rover keys.

The ride to Elly's seemed like it took hours. Travis was silent the entire ride. What did he mean Katerina was taken? It was still pouring when we arrived. Officers were already present, walking up and down the route Elly said Katerina took to her car. Elly ran to me and gave me a huge hug.

"I am so sorry, Jara!"

"It's not your fault, Elly. What happened?"

Elly explained about Katerina borrowing her raincoat and umbrella.

"She left her purse on the bench by the door. With all the rain, she was a bit frazzled. I saw her purse sitting there after she left, so I grabbed a coat and went after her. I saw her start to stumble. Someone came up behind her and guided her to the alley."

"Someone pushed her into the alley?"

"No, it was like they saw her stumble and helped her, directed her into the alley. I called out to her, but she didn't acknowledge me. When I got there, neither Katerina, nor this other person were there. I saw the umbrella on the ground and fresh vomit. I'm not sure why, but I put the umbrella over the vomit pile."

I heard Travis call my name, and he motioned me over. I hugged Elly and told her I'd be right back.

"Jara, the officers are saying there is no sign of Katerina and allegedly no witnesses."

"Travis, Elly said fresh vomit was in the alley. We need to preserve this scene and collect the vomit to have it tested immediately. The way Elly described it was almost exactly how she was abducted. We know she was drugged. We need to know what they used on Katerina."

Travis looked over to Elly, who started crying again.

"Elly that was very smart," Travis told her. "If Katerina was drugged, we might find out what it was. Thank you."

I put my arm around Elly, trying to comfort her.

"Jara, this is all my fault. In my coat, she looked like me when she left here. They took her because they thought she was me."

It hit me then. Someone wanted to silence Elly. Since she got away, whoever this was had loose ends to tie up. That's why Travis didn't want me to see the basement, because Katerina was probably heading to a place just like it. Son of a bitch!

Travis looked at me, knowing I had put it all together and realized the danger Katerina was in. He tried to grab my arm as

I ran back to the alley. I walked the alley, scouring every inch. Who were they really after, Elly or Katerina? If they were after Elly and realized they made a mistake, would they immediately kill Kat? Horrible thoughts were racing through my mind. I couldn't lose her, not this way. Travis had caught up to me.

"We'll find her. I promise."

Tears streaming down my face, I collapsed against a dumpster. All I could think was yes, we'll find her, but in what shape? I put my hand down to steady myself and felt a sharp pain shoot through my fingers.

"What the..."

My hand had landed on a piece of red, reflector plastic, possibly a taillight cover. I showed Travis the piece.

"Looks recent. It would be crushed or dirtier if it had been in this alley long. Here's hoping Katerina got a good kick in and knocked this thing out."

Travis gave the piece to an officer to bag into evidence and told him to add a possible missing taillight to the BOLO.

"Travis, I need to know more about the brownstone. I have to figure out who owns it and why they were moving the stuff inside it. That may be where they are taking Katerina."

Travis let me know what he had learned about the owners and the storage unit. He called Noel, asking for a place we could work. Noel gave us an address and said he would meet us there. We all arrived at a small building on Manhattan's Lower East Side. I looked over to Noel and asked, "What is this? This isn't an NYPD precinct."

"Well, Fed, it used to be. Now, some of us use it as a quieter place to work. I have all my cold cases here. Looks can be deceiving, Jara."

The only thing brightening up the dingy, two-story, concrete building was a collection of graffiti tags strewn across the front. It looked almost abandoned, except the windows were still intact. Noel unlocked the front door and hit a button, illuminating the foyer and another door. This second door was steel and had a top-notch security mechanism.

"Greatest little secret in the area," Noel said proudly, as he swiped a card, punched in a code, and turned another key. We walked in and the whole floor lit up.

"Welcome to NYPDX, or Xanadu, as we call it. We have a top-of-the-line computer system that can connect to any law enforcement agency in the US. We're working on extending it to Interpol and other international agencies, but that may take a while."

"Geez, Noel, I never knew NYPD had this." I gawped at all the technology.

"Exactly, most don't know about this, and that is exactly how we want to keep it. Some of us who work out of here have put our own money into this. We'd hate to see it shut down."

"I don't blame you. This is like the Batcave," Travis exclaimed.

"So, Noel," I said, "where can we set up? I want to run the owner of the brownstone, see if we can narrow down who really owns it."

Noel brought out his notepad. "Okay, the company that hired the movers was Global Services Inc., pretty generic. The head guy talked to a man named...uh, Edward, didn't give a last name, only an address where this stuff was being moved to."

Noel logged me into the computer, and I punched in the address he'd given. I yelled out to the guys, "Yep, it was a storage facility all right, but it has been closed for over five years. Then where were these guys going to unload this stuff? Noel, what was the mover's name and company again?"

He flipped a few pages of his notebook. "That's odd, I thought I got his name. It's Gus something. Travis, did you see any markings on the truck?"

Travis thought a moment. "I think it said Elite Movers."

I punched that into the computer. "Uh, guys, I think we have been played. There is no Elite Movers in New York City, nor in the state. Where is Gus now?"

"I left him with the officers collecting evidence, still at the brownstone." Noel pulled out his phone. I couldn't hear what he was saying until he got louder and louder. "You dumbasses, you let him go? Well did you at least get a last name and address?" Noel hung up abruptly.

"Gus Edwards, Elite Movers, 853 Broadway, NY, NY 10003. Son of a bitch, that is an office building at Union Square in Manhattan. I know there are a lot of companies in the buildings there, but no moving companies. He duped us. The officer said this Gus guy just left and was picked up in an old Cadillac."

"Did the officer give a description of the car or a plate number?"

"No plate, just said an old Caddy, probably from the '70s since it was so big. The officer noticed it because large cars don't do well in the city. He also noticed a broken taillight and told Gus to tell the driver to get it fixed."

Travis and I looked at each other, then Travis yelled at Noel, "Get that officer back on the phone."

All of our searches into Gus and the moving company were dead ends. We got the VIN off the moving truck and learned it had been stolen a couple of weeks ago. Noel had gotten more information about the Cadillac and added a description of Gus to the BOLO. He contacted DOT and had them connect a feed to us so we could search for the car in real time. I looked up the brownstone address and found the corresponding cameras. I rewound the films, and I was able to find a large, goldish-brown Cadillac heading down 7th after it exited the alley. I kept switching cameras and found the car again a couple of blocks away, heading for 9th Street. I had taken a still shot of the car and given it to Noel and Travis. Noel attached it to the BOLO, and Travis pulled up the cameras near the alley where Katerina was abducted.

"Holy shit! It's the same one. We got it. Jara, you still following that car?"

I had lost the car and was searching for it, when the cameras flipped to where 9th Street turns into Hamilton and exits heading toward the Battery. If they hit that tunnel, we could lose them going into Manhattan. I yelled at Noel to get cars to the end of the tunnel quickly. But instead of going to the tunnel, the Cadillac stayed on 278 heading to the waterfront district. It exited off 278 onto Atlantic Ave and headed west to Columbia St. Then I lost them again.

"Noel, help me. I lost them at Atlantic and Columbia. I have no idea which way they went. They could be anywhere."

Noel put his hand on my shoulder gently. "We'll find them, Fed. They can't be far."

He radioed another officer and told them where the car was last seen. It seemed like an eternity before the radio crackled, and the officer said they had found the car and were approaching.

I stood and headed for the door. "I have to go. Where are they?"

Noel had the officer repeat the location.

"Seriously? Okay we are enroute." Noel looked over at me, "This makes no sense, they are in line for the ferry off Pier 6."

I grabbed my stuff and headed to the car. "I'll drive," yelled Noel. "You are in no shape to drive. Plus, this is my city."

Chapter Twenty-Nine

We arrived at the pier in what seemed record time for NYC traffic. The officers had two men out of the car and lying face down on the ground. I ran to the car. They were opening the trunk. I held my breath...No Katerina. I ran to the men on the ground and kicked one of them in the side as hard as I could.

"Where is the woman you took?!" I screamed as I kicked him again. Travis grabbed me and pulled me away. "They know, Travis, they know." I screamed.

By this time Noel had gotten to the one he knew as Gus and pulled him up off the ground in one swift move. He had him face-to-face, which was an incredible feat since Noel was at least 4" taller than Gus.

"You lying sack of shit. You played me. I hate liars, so tell me who hired you. And where is the woman your friend took?"

Gus's eyes were wide, but he only mouthed he didn't know.

"Yes, you do know, you son of a bitch. Either tell me, or I let my friend here continue to kick the shit out of your partner."

Gus looked down, as I walked back over to where the other man was moaning and complaining he was hurt. I kicked him again as hard as I could. I think I heard a rib crack. I moved up to his head and positioned myself for a kick to the face, when the guy on the ground yelled, "Tell them, damn it! Get her away from me."

Gus looked back to Noel. "Put me down, and I'll tell you what I know. I didn't take no girl. I was with you, remember?"

"Don't play with me."

"Man, I'm not. I was hired by this guy I know who has me doing odd jobs for him. I don't know his real name. He calls me, tells me the job, money gets delivered to me, and I do the job. This time, I was told to go where you all met me. I was told to move stuff to a truck that was already waiting for me. Honest, I didn't know about the stuff in the basement. I was told if the cops showed up to tell you the story of moving, but we weren't really moving anything. There was also a car there, the Caddy.

Larry was to leave the car near the park, then come pick me up after you left. Nothing else."

"Larry, huh." I was back in the man's face. "So where's the girl?"

"What girl? All I did was park the car."

"You mean to tell me you parked the car for hours and did nothing?"

He flinched when I took a step toward him.

"Yeah, I mean, nah."

"Which is it?"

"Yeah, I parked the car, then got a call to go pick up Gus. I was in a bar near there. It was raining like crazy, so I waited a bit until I thought it would let up. Then I ran to the car. I drove over to where Gus was, parked, and waited for him. We were heading back to Jersey, and Gus got a call to not take the tunnel but to go by ferry into Manhattan. I hate tunnels, so I thought what the hell."

I looked over to Travis, who shrugged his shoulders and shook his head. "I don't think these guys are smart enough to pull off an abduction. But they're definitely dumb enough to be set up."

Reluctantly, I agreed and walked back to the car trunk. I saw no signs of anyone being in there, plus the taillight wasn't broken. *Wait a minute, the car that picked up Gus allegedly had a broken taillight.* I ran back to Gus. "Who picked you up at the brownstone?"

Gus's face flushed and his eyes darted back and forth.

"Who?" I screamed.

"Larry did, honest."

"Then where is the broken taillight?"

"I don't know. I didn't understand what the officer meant by that. I said okay, just to get out of there. I ran down to the corner and met up with Larry and took off."

"The corner? Didn't Larry pick you up behind the brownstone?"

"No, the street was full, so I met him on the corner."

"Travis, Noel, there was another car! We need to get back to the cameras. I think we made a huge mistake. The asshole was right there with her, taunting us."

We arrived back at Xanadu. Noel had called ahead to get the DOT cameras back online. We each took a different view of all the streets near Elly's place.

Travis yelled, "I got it! There were two cars. In the dark they look almost identical."

I ran to his computer and saw the car make its way to the tunnel leading into Manhattan. The strange thing was it never came out.

Noel came over. "I have an idea." Noel looked up all the EZ Pass cars, then all the pay-by-plate cars. Nothing. "Here, let me see that camera." Noel flipped around a bit. "See, they never made it to the tunnel. They parked under the expressway. They might have had another vehicle parked there."

Noel radioed another officer, sending them to that area. A few moments later an officer reported finding an abandoned Cadillac with a broken taillight at that spot. No one was in the trunk.

Noel told them to secure the car until we arrived. I was torn. Should I go to the car that had once held Katerina or stay and look for the vehicle that may still have her? Noel must have seen my face. "C'mon, Fed, let's go to the car. If Katerina left any clues, you would know. I have a team here looking at all the cameras. They'll find the other vehicle."

We made our way back to Brooklyn. Travis stayed behind to keep up on the camera team. This car was definitely a look-a-like to Larry's car. Who knew you could have two 1975 Cadillacs of the same color in one area? Newer cars, sure, but a vintage Caddy? There must have been something significant about this type of car. I jumped out of the car and ran to the trunk. It was messy and large. I had my flashlight and hurriedly put gloves on. I moved some trash and saw blood. I felt lightheaded, but I knew I had to keep looking. Whatever had knocked Katerina out must have worn off. Her earrings were laying there with the backs on them, some red hair by them and a little bit of vomit. She had to have done this. In such a messy trunk, these things were too neat. The passenger side taillight was broken out. I looked at the inside of the trunk lid. Written in blood were the letters *JA* and a smear. I took pictures of everything and let CSU take over. I almost jumped out of my skin when my phone rang.

"Quinn."

"Jara, it's Tess. Any news?"

"Too much to tell you, but we haven't found her yet. Where are you?"

"I'm still at the brownstone. Jacob just got here. He looks a mess. He said he drove 90 all the way until New York traffic."

"Tess, where is Jacob right now? By you?"

"No, he went down to the basement. Why?"

"I have two strange things to ask, but please don't say anything."

"Okay."

I had been thinking back to the calls Tess and I made in the car. "Did you give Jacob the address to the brownstone earlier?"

"Well, I must have, he's here." Silence..."Jara, now that I think of it, I didn't tell him. I only told him we were going to New York. He has a police radio with him though. He could have heard it there. Is there a problem?"

"I don't know, Tess. I hope not. Did he drive a CSP car to Quantico or his own?"

"Yes, one of the unmarked. He checked it out this morning."

"Can you go and write down the odometer reading for me? I know it's a lot, but I really do need it."

"Sure, I guess. Just a second, let me call you back."

After Tess and I hung up, I called Amelia at the Quantico laboratory. "Hey, Amelia, glad I caught you. Did our evidence ever make it to you?"

"Hi, Jara. Yes, this afternoon."

"Can you tell me who delivered it?"

Amelia started laughing. "You losing track of your minions, Jara?"

I didn't laugh. "Just check for me, please."

"Okay, okay, I was just joking. Let me look. Bad day?"

"You could say that. Katerina has been abducted. We have no idea where she is."

"Oh my god, I am so sorry. Looking it up now... Interesting, all the evidence has a Detective Jacob Donovan's name on it and a copy of his ID, but that's not who made the delivery. It was an Officer Michael Thompson for CSP who was here."

"Thanks, Amelia, I owe you."

"I hope you find her soon, Jara."

"Thanks."

My phone rang again. It was Tess. "Hey, Jara, Jacob is being a dick and won't let me have the keys to the car. Also, the dumbass went downstairs without gloves. I think I'm going to kill him."

"Tess, don't kill him, but don't let him leave. Shoot him if you have to, but don't let him leave."

I was back at the brownstone in no time. I walked in and saw Jacob lying on the floor, face down in a pool of his own blood. Tess had a knee on his back and looked up at me. "He tried to leave." she said simply. Then she filled me in on what happened.

Tess pulled Jara's Rover in front of Jacob's car. She then had an officer block him in from the back. She found Jacob and had him escorted to the first floor.

"Damn it. What is the meaning of this? I need to see the crime scene too." Jacob growled. "Tess, what do you think you're doing?"

"Playing a hunch, Jacob. After your long trip, have a seat and rest."

Jacob pulled away from the officers. "I have had about enough of you and this. I'm leaving. Forget you."

Tess stepped in front of him. "Sorry, Jacob, but I can't let you leave yet."

"Bet me," he snapped and tried to push past her.

Tess grabbed his arm and turned him around, facing her again. Jacob began to lunge. In an instant, Tess met his nose with the heel of her palm, never letting go of his arm. She twisted it around his back and took him to the ground.

Chapter Thirty

Travis and Noel escorted Jacob to the back of Noel's car. I tried to explain to Tess what all was going on and what I suspected. I knew Jacob didn't do all the murders, but I was fairly sure he was involved in Elly's attack and the abduction of Katerina. We decided not to take Jacob to Xanadu, since it was such a well-kept secret. We arrived at a Brooklyn precinct and went to an interrogation room. Jacob argued loudly the whole way.

"What in the hell are you guys doing? I am an officer. I did nothing wrong. Are you arresting me? This is bullshit."

After Jacob was sat at the table by the officers, I calmly walked in. I knew aggression or threats wouldn't work with Jacob. He had too big of an ego for that. I sat down across from him, still being very quiet and as calm as I could be. I took a deep breath. "Jacob, I need your help, and only you can help me."

That got his attention.

"Something happened today that I think was a mistake. I think someone tried to abduct Elly again but instead got someone else who was wearing Elly's coat. I know whoever did this wanted Elly, but now they have a hostage they don't need."

Jacob looked at me for a minute, then dropped his head. "Jacob, I know you didn't go to Quantico today, but that's okay. The evidence got there anyway. I also know you are familiar with the brownstone we were just at."

Jacob looked at me defiantly.

"You know, Jacob, right now I don't care about all of that. I want to discuss this abduction." I stayed outwardly calm, although I wanted to leap across the table and choke the answers out of him.

"Am I under arrest?"

"At this moment, no. Should you be?"

"So I goofed off today. Last time I checked that's not a crime."

"You're right, Jacob, not a crime, but what did you do today...Goofing off as you put it?"

"Although it is none of your business, I was with my girlfriend."

"Your girlfriend, the stewardess? What is her name?"

"None of your business!"

"Well, Jacob, with that I disagree. Some really bad stuff went down today, and I believe you and your girlfriend know what I am talking about."

Jacob's face changed a bit, and a sinister smile crossed his face.

"Since we are talking about girlfriends, Agent Quinn, how is yours?"

It took everything I had not to smack the smile off his face. "Funny you brought her up, Jacob. I'm wondering if you know how she is and where she may be? I know whoever has her is probably pretty pissed off right now, getting the wrong girl and all."

His eyes blazed. I'd hit a nerve.

"I'm sure, Jacob, whoever is in charge won't let this mistake go unpunished. I know about the basement. It would be a shame if you ended up somewhere like that."

"Me? Why would I be held in a basement like that? I'm sitting here with you."

"Yeah, for now. But like you said, you aren't under arrest. I have a press conference to attend..." I collected my folders and started to stand. "And may I say what an amazing help you have been in this case. So, I guess, you're free to go."

I was playing another hunch. I knew the basement was bad, although I hadn't seen it, but Jacob had. He knew how ruthless killer was. The defiance that had oozed out of his body was now replaced by fear. He started to fidget in his chair. He looked at me with an almost pleading look.

"Can you at least uncuff me?" he asked.

I exhaled loudly, leaned over the table and spoke too low for the mic to pick up. "Jacob, I would. But honestly, you in cuffs is the only thing keeping me from beating you to death. I don't harm defenseless people."

His eyes widened. He knew I was serious.

"I know you aren't the brains behind all of this. You were probably only following orders, and right now, I don't care from whom. What I do care about is the location of Katerina. Can you help me with that? I don't have a lot of time. You know the press is waiting."

I knew Jacob couldn't be in charge. For the little time I'd known him, he'd shown a complete lack of motivation and confidence. The earlier bravado was his desperate attempt to be a badass. He wasn't a sociopath, but he wanted to be. Either way, he knew where Katerina was taken.

Suddenly Jacob blurted out, "I want a deal!"

"A deal? Jacob, you're not charged with anything. There is no deal. Either help me or take your chances with your friend. Your choice."

I heard a small knock on the interview room door and stood. "I guess it's time to meet the press, as they say."

Panic flew off his body. "I'll tell you."

"Tell me what?"

"Where Katerina is..."

I started to sit back down, when someone knocked again, harder. Even though I needed to learn what Jacob knew, I got up and opened the door. It was Tess. I stepped out of the room, frustrated as hell.

"What?! This better be good."

"Jara, I think we found her. We looked at the cameras where the Cadillac was abandoned. There is a motel about five blocks from that overpass that hid the Caddy. Jacob's car was there right before he drove to the brownstone. We're sending a team there now."

I wanted to be with that team, but I needed to finish with Jacob.

"Tess, bring her back to me."

I went back into the room. Jacob was still fidgeting. I looked at him and smiled. "Well, Jacob, I may not need you after all. Have you ever heard of a place called the Brooklyn Inn? Of course, you have. You were there today. Maybe with this girlfriend of yours."

Jacob avoided eye contact, and his lips twisted as if he was chewing on the inside of his mouth.

"We have a team, Jacob, going there now. Tess is going with them. She is going to make sure whoever is there knows how helpful you have been."

"I didn't tell you about that place, You know that."

"Yes, I know that, but they don't. This will make for a great press conference."

"Damn it, Jara, she will kill me!"

"She?"

"My girlfriend. I told you I was with her, but I wasn't. I was there with someone else."

Oh shit, I thought, *was Jacob not involved? Was his only crime cheating on his girlfriend in the fleabag motel?*

"We're going to find out soon enough, Jacob. The team is almost there. Anything you want to say to help yourself?"

I thought about telling him Katerina could ID him but thought better of it. If he got out of here, then she would surely be killed. Jacob fidgeted in his seat and looked like he was thinking.

"About what?" he asked.

I knew I was being recorded, so I had to be careful of what I said or did. I picked up my folders again and made a large motion of scooting back my chair. I slammed the chair back under the table and walked around to Jacob's side of the table. I got as close to him as I could and leaned on the table, bending over to meet his gaze.

"I swear, Jacob, if anything happens to Katerina, even a scratch or bruise, I will turn in my badge, hunt you down, and make you wish you were never born. You think the basement was bad? You just wait."

Jacob's eyes got as wide as saucers. He saw the crazy in my face. He knew I was serious. I walked out the door and didn't look back.

"Has anyone heard from Noel or Tess?" I asked the other officers.

Travis walked up. "They're just getting to the motel."

"Travis, I have to go there. If she's there..."

The radio crackled. "Travis, you there? This is Tess."

"Go ahead, we're both here."

I knew it was Travis's way of cluing Tess in on being careful with her words if it was bad.

"Katerina's not here," she said. "She was, but she's not now. We're checking the room for any clue on where they went."

I knew exactly who knew where they went. I headed back to Jacob. I slammed open the door, went around the table, and grabbed Jacob by the hair. I pulled back so hard it tipped his chair back, and he crashed on his back to the floor. I put a knee on his chest and my hands around his neck.

"Now, motherfucker, where is she? Either tell me or live disfigured."

I felt Travis's hands on my shoulders, pulling me off Jacob.

Travis yelled at Jacob, "Tell her, Jacob, or I'm letting her go."

Jacob tried to roll away from us but couldn't move past the table leg. Travis reached down and lifted Jacob up by the front of his shirt. Face-to-face, Travis growled, "Tell her!"

"I don't know, honest."

"You have an idea. You probably had plans to meet them there. Tell her!" Travis yelled, his face flushing red with anger.

I moved toward him...

"All right, all right, Connecticut, they're going to Connecticut."

"Where in Connecticut?"

Jacob put his head down.

"Where?" Travis demanded.

"The house," Jacob said gruffly. "Her house."

"Katerina's?" I asked.

"No, Toni's house," Jacob said hoarsely.

We all looked at each other, then back to Jacob. I shook my head.

"You mean Toni Branson? Her family home has been vacant for years. I thought it was up for auction."

"It is." Jacob sighed loudly. "There's a small cabin on the property. She used to play there as a child. No one knew it was Branson property. They have a lot of properties people don't know about."

Now it made sense. What better place to go than a place not known by police but very familiar to the killer?

"I need to know the exact location, Jacob, now!" I put a Google map in front of him. Jacob hesitated. My eyes flared, and I took a step toward him. "Now, Jacob!"

He pulled it up on the map and shoved the laptop to me. "Here. Right here in the woods, by the water."

I grabbed the laptop and ran out of the room. I knew we didn't have much time. I was sure the kill room was already set up, plus she had a head start. I grabbed my equipment and headed to my Rover.

"You're not going alone," a voice bellowed from behind me.

I turned around. Travis, Tess, and Noel were all standing there, equipment in hand. I gratefully whispered, "Thank you." Travis grabbed my keys again. He knew me too well. I would have probably had us killed in a wreck before we even got there. Jacob had pointed out a small, wooded area with a lake near the Connecticut, New York border. I called ahead for more FBI, and Tess called for CSP. She also got ahold of her chief and explained to him about Jacob. It was an ugly call. I then received a call from an unknown number.

"Jara Quinn."

"Jara, this is Anita."

A strange look came over my face. "Mrs. Burris, what can I do for you? We're kind of, well, in the middle of something."

"I know, dear, but Jack, I mean SSA Stewart, thought I could be of use."

"Oh, uh, okay, I'm not sure how. I thought you were maintenance. I don't understand."

"Well, dear, that's what Jack likes to call it." I could hear a laugh in her voice. "I am a fixer and a cleaner. I can help with this mess if needed, no questions asked."

I wasn't really sure what exactly she was talking about fixing, but any help was appreciated.

"Okay, we left Jacob, the CSP Detective that has been involved with abducting Katerina and possibly the attack on another person, at the Brooklyn precinct. We don't know his full involvement yet on any of the murders."

"I'll be on my way to New York then, Jara. Is it okay if I transport him somewhere else, someplace secure?" Anita asked.

I was sort of taken aback by her request but agreed anyway. "Whatever SSA Stewart agrees to."

"I'll be back in touch. Jara, good luck."

I put my phone down and gathered my thoughts. What in the hell did I just agree to?

We made record time to the road leading to the Branson family compound, at least that's what I called it. I wondered if Toni had cameras up, monitoring comings and goings. I knew I would. A CSP Emergency Response Team had arrived along with six more FBI officers. I explained to them the situation and the area where we were going.

"Danny, can you come here, please?" Tess asked one of the officers. A tall, muscular man walked over to our car, decked out in full tactical gear. "Danny knows this area like the back of his hand," Tess said to me. "Danny, would you be able to coordinate the best way into this area?"

He took the laptop and studied the map for a second, then pulled out a map of his own.

"No offense, ma'am, but you're map doesn't do much good. Mine has all of my off-road additions."

"None taken. Please, Danny, find us a way," I exclaimed.

We called out to the Emergency Response Team and the FBI agents. Travis took over, his voice being heard by everyone.

"Danny here is going to lead this extraction. He knows the area. Please follow his directions to the letter. We must get this victim out alive."

On hearing the word victim, my knees started to buckle. Tess grabbed me and leaned me against the car. I nodded in appreciation and closed my eyes. Victim, Katerina was now a victim.

Tess began apologizing to me. "I should have seen this, caught him. What was I thinking?"

"Stop, Tess. No need for apologies. You did nothing wrong. Jacob had us all fooled. Just help me to get Katerina back."

Danny had mapped out the entry points and assigned groups to each location. Part of it was rough terrain, and for the element of surprise, we needed to cover it foot. I felt it best if I stayed behind. With my mindset, if Katerina was hurt, or God forbid dead, her abductors would also be dead. We needed this to go well, not be fueled by emotion. My phone rang again.

"Mrs. Burris?"

"Jara, quickly, Jacob has informed me the cabin is wired with explosives and a tunnel leads out of the basement. Please be careful." I immediately radioed Danny, telling him about the explosives and the tunnel.

"Thank you, ma'am. I would bet the tunnel leads to the water. This lake has a river which connects to a much larger lake to the south. If she gets there, we could lose her."

"Don't lose her," I said, "but Katerina is first priority."

I got back in my Rover. Noel stayed behind, probably to subdue me if the time came. We waited for seemed like hours. The radio finally crackled. Danny's voice came over the receiver. "The cabin is in sight. Sound off if you are in position." Quietly, all six teams checked in. They were ready. Danny ordered team three to approach the cabin for a visual. Team three reported a vehicle was in the drive and lights were on in the home, but no movement. Toni had to know we would be coming. She was too smart not to know that.

Danny ordered all but team six to approach the house and report any sight of persons or explosives. Team six went to the water. It got eerily quiet as the teams approached. I was sure the radios were not being used, only hand signals. The waiting was killing me. I saw paramedics and ambulances pull up to our location. We were preparing for the worst but hoping for the best.

Waiting with a vivid imagination was worse than actually being there, but at least I wouldn't get shot in the Rover. I hoped. I was getting impatient and had my hand on the car door when the radio crackled again. "Go! Go! Go!"

They had breached the cabin. I looked over at Noel with pleading eyes. "I have to go. I'm sorry."

He let out a large sigh. "I know there's no stopping you, but I'm coming along."

I jumped out of the Rover, adjusted my vest, and made sure my weapons were loaded. I ran faster than I ever thought I could, ripping my clothes on brambles and branches. The team was inside, with two guarding the door. I shoved past them and headed for the basement. There was blood everywhere, old and new. My brain was assaulted by everything I was seeing, the tables, shackles, knives, scalpels...I felt myself becoming faint but powered on.

The radio crackled again. "Get the paramedics and ambulance. Now!"

Oh god. I found the room where Danny and Travis were. Travis saw me and tried to block my way. I heard a bolt cutter snapping metal.

"Travis, please."

"Give them a second. You don't want to see this."

I shook my head, my vivid imagination taking over. "I have to, please."

Travis tapped Danny on the shoulder, and he turned to let me through. Katerina was lying there, white as a ghost, blood everywhere. I couldn't tell where it was coming from. They kept her on the table, but the shackles were off. I knew not to grab her, so I touched her hand gently and bent over her face.

"My love. I'm here. Hold on. Please. Hold on."

Katerina's eyes fluttered open and her head turned and looked to my right. "Tunnel," she whispered. "Get them."

Them? God, does Toni have another partner? I kissed Katerina on her head and told her I loved her. "I'll be back, my love. I promise."

I grabbed Danny and Travis and pointed to the door. The paramedics were there, ready to get to work. We all moved back. I asked Tess if she would stay with Katerina. She nodded and took her hand. I looked at Danny. "I need your help and your map."

He pulled out the map. I saw that the door where Katerina was looking opened to the east. I followed where the tunnel would exit on Danny's map. It came out right before the intersection of the river connecting this lake to the southern lake. A dock could be there. The other ERT team was at a different exit point. They wouldn't get there in time. Plus, if Toni had a partner, they might go that way. We had to keep all exit points covered. Danny radioed them to be on the lookout. I bolted up the stairs and ran back to my car. Travis had barely got in when I took off.

"Where in the hell are you going?" he asked breathlessly.

"To the water. I think I know where she, or they, are heading. She is not getting away."

I followed the route I'd seen on the map around the edge of the lake to the river, parked my car, and headed to the water. I was right. Two small docks were on the lake that provided access into the lake or down the river. At the docks were small motorboats and a rowboat. I was looking around, trying to find the tunnel exit.

"Here, over here," Travis yelled. He'd found an exit door.

The makeshift door was broken. *Had she already made it out?* There were cobwebs and dirt all around it, so no one had been through it recently. Travis radioed Danny that we had found an exit. Danny was taking the tunnel from the house.

He radioed back. "The tunnel forks. We're splitting up. Not sure how many more splits there are. Also, there are explosives everywhere." Danny and Noel split up, and Danny radioed the possible exit coordinates of the tunnel split.

"Travis, you stay here. If the tunnel splits there has to be another exit. I'm heading to find it."

Before he could say no, I took off. The other possible exit was about a half mile from where we were, on the other side of the dock. I was exhausted, but adrenaline took me the rest of the way.

CRACK...POP...POP

Gunfire blasted right over my head. What the hell? I shot back in the direction it came from and found cover. I knew I had to get between the shooter and the water. I used the oldest trick in the book and threw a rock about twenty feet from where I was headed.

POP...POP...POP

At least they fell for it. I took off for the dock. A tall figure came out from behind a tree and headed to a boat. We were on the far side of the dock, so I had no idea where Travis was. Without thinking, I lunged at the figure, tackling them with all my might. I tried to point my gun while getting up. "FBI, freeze!"

I felt a sharp kick to my right knee and it buckled. I rolled and tried to get up but something heavy and large hit my head. I fell again, seeing stars. I tried to shake off the fog and saw the person raise a large rock over their head, readying to hit me again. I rolled, and the rock barely missed me. Rage flew through me like a bolt of lightning. I jumped up and tackled the person again, pounding them in the head with my fists over and over. In my rage, I didn't realize I was still holding my gun in my right hand. I felt blood but kept hitting them over and over until the person lay still underneath me. I felt hands grab my arms and pull me up. I struggled to get free until I heard Noel's voice.

"Fed, stand down. Please stop."

I got my bearings and looked down. It was Toni Branson, at least it resembled her. Her face was cut and bloody. My hands were covered in blood also, and I was still gripping my gun. I pulled it up and pointed it at her. My finger on the trigger.

"Jara, no!" Noel pleaded.

"She attacked Katerina...and Elly. She hurt them. Who knows how many others..."

"And she will pay, I promise. Please don't."

I stepped back but kept my gun aimed.

"I'm gonna check her now, Fed, then cuff her. Okay?"

I was crying by then and nodded yes. He bent down and checked her vitals. I could hear footsteps coming our way and Travis's voice. As much as I wanted to, I knew I couldn't kill this evil that was on the ground before me. We needed to know more.

Noel yelled out, "She's still alive. Get the paramedics."

At this point, both Danny and Travis were with us. I lowered my gun, as Noel cuffed Toni. "Where's Katerina?" I started heading for my car.

Danny answered, "Last time I saw, they were getting her ready to exit the basement and head to the ambulance. You might want to hurry."

Travis ran with me to the car, and we headed back to the cabin. Travis looked at me in shock. "Damn, Jara, what in the hell did you do?"

"I caught her, Travis."

"I know that, but my god, you're a mess. You need to get yourself cleaned up before Katerina sees you."

I looked in the mirror. I was covered in blood. I grabbed a towel from behind the seat and tried to clean the blood off my face the best I could. The towel wasn't helping. It was like sweeping a dirt floor. I kept smearing the blood everywhere. We came to a stop near the ambulance by the cabin, where they were just wheeling her out. I told Travis to tell them I was coming with them, as I got out and opened the back of the Rover for my first-aid kit. It dawned on me that this wasn't all my blood. Some of it had to be Toni's. I got a large piece of sterile gauze out of my kit and wiped my hands and face with it, then put the gauze in an evidence bag. I sprayed another towel with peroxide and tried to wash the rest of the blood off me. The cut on my head kept bleeding, so I stuck a large bandage on it, hoping it would help. I shut the door and ran over to the ambulance. I handed Travis the evidence bag. "Toni's DNA. It wasn't all my blood."

Tess was next to Katerina in the back. She stepped out, as one of the paramedics looked at me in shock. "Ma'am, you okay?" I pushed past him and climbed into the ambulance.

Katerina was covered with a blanket. She had an IV, an oxygen mask, and wires connected to her, but she was conscious and looking up at me. Sitting down beside her and grabbing her hand, I looked at Katerina and answered the paramedic.

"Yes sir, I am perfectly fine. I caught her." Katerina smiled behind the mask and squeezed my hand, then closed her eyes.

Katerina was rushed into the trauma center in Hartford. I was told I needed to stay behind, while they worked on her in a room. The nurse looked at me and put me in a room also. Noel and Tess had made it to the hospital a few minutes behind the ambulance and found me in the ER. Travis remained behind to help Danny with securing the scene and collecting evidence.

"Damn, Fed, you look bad," Noel said, shaking his head.

"Thanks, Captain Obvious, for the newsflash. Has anyone informed the SSA or the CSP chief?"

"Not yet. We wanted to check on how you and Katerina were doing first," Tess answered.

"I'm okay. Katerina was taken down the hall to another room. They're still with her. I need to call Victoria." They stepped out to make their calls and try to get an update on Katerina.

The call to Victoria was one of the hardest I have ever had to make. She was working at the Foundation, so I called ahead to make sure someone was with her. As I feared, she was not pleased with me having kept her in the dark this long. After I told her what happened and what hospital Katerina was in, she hung up abruptly. I assumed she was on her way. My next call was to Mrs. Burris.

"Mrs. Burris?"

"Jara, Anita, please."

"Anita. I'm not really sure about the parameters of your job, but I may need your services again. By the way, thank you for the cabin information. It came in very handy."

"You're very welcome, Jara." Anita paused. "I hope Katerina is okay?"

"Yes, ma'am, she is, at least physically, I think. She is still with the doctors."

"Keep me posted on her condition. Does Victoria know?"

"Yes, I just hung up with her. She is happy Katerina is alive but not pleased about just learning of the situation."

"I see. What can I help you with?"

"I caught the person we think is responsible for some of the murders, an attempted murder, and the abduction of Katerina."

"Yes, go on."

"Well. I...uh...I had to subdue her. She had shot at me, but I caught up to her. She hit me in the head with a rock and was about to again. I tackled her and well, hurt her."

"Killed her?"

"Honestly, I don't know. I tackled her and began hitting her. There was a lot of blood. I think both hers and mine. Noel found us and pulled me off. She wasn't moving by then. I didn't mean to...kill her, I mean, if I did. I left the scene to find Katerina before I was told the suspect's condition." I was crying. "Anita, what if I killed her? In my mind, all I saw was Katerina in that awful room. Hell, maybe I did mean to kill her. Can you help me?"

"Jara, first thing, don't repeat what you just said to anyone. Second, you were doing your job. You subdued a suspect. Let me make some calls and learn more. I'll get back to you."

I called Travis and let him know what was going on at the hospital.

"Have you called Victoria yet?"

"Yes, she's not happy. I also called Anita. She is going to do me a favor. I guess that's what you would call it."

Travis laughed. "I've heard some stories about her. If even some of them are true, she is one powerful and scary woman."

"Do I even want to know what that means? Forget it. No, I don't. And you don't spread those stories either."

"Fine, fine. So how are you feeling?"

"Actually, I feel okay, but I think it's just the adrenaline."

"Where is Katerina?"

"Still in with the doctors. They said they'll be down to talk to me very soon. How goes it at the cabin?"

"Jara, it's much bigger than we thought. They must have been using this place for years. I think there are some murders we don't even know about."

"So it wasn't just Toni and Jacob using this place?"

"There is at least one more person involved. Katerina told the team there were two people in the cabin, but Jacob is in custody. They also found more tunnels and more explosives rigged to a remote, but the trigger hasn't been found. Toni didn't have it, and so far, it hasn't been found in the cabin."

"So where is Toni? Is she alive?"

"Last I knew, she was still alive." Travis huffed. "You gave her quite the beating though. I'll find out where they took her and her condition."

I was thanking Travis when I heard a large noise in the background over the phone.

"Travis?! Travis?!" Nothing but dead air. I heard yelling and commotion, but nothing from Travis. I waited on the phone, hoping someone would pick up the phone and tell me what the hell was going on. Nothing but sirens and yelling. I reluctantly hung up and yelled for Tess, who was in the hall.

"Tess, there has been an explosion at the cabin. Please, call Danny. I have to know everyone is all right. I was on the phone with Travis when it happened. He's not answering me...Please, Tess, call someone."

She immediately started calling people she knew at the scene. "I'll find out, Jara."

Chapter Thirty-One

I lay back on the bed, fighting tears. "God, you know I don't pray a lot. Maybe it's because of my ego, but please don't let any more people die at the hands of this family. Please!"

I was getting myself together to leave the hospital and go to the cabin when a tall female in a white coat entered the room. She looked very familiar.

"Dr. Saroyan?"

"Hi, Ms. Quinn, I see you are keeping busy, which means I am keeping busy."

I wasn't sure how to take that, so I gave a sheepish smile.

"Dr. Saroyan, can you tell me Katerina's condition?"

"I can tell you she is critical, but stable. She had significant blood loss and contusions. We stopped the bleeding, gave her fluids and three units of blood, and she is stable now. We are going to do more tests to see the extent of the injuries. She needs a lot of rest. I am more concerned about her mental needs, once the physical injuries heal, but we will deal with all that when the time comes."

"May I go see her?"

"Not yet. It's your turn. I need to check you out."

"I'm fine, Doc. I need to see Katerina." I stood up but immediately felt weak and dizzy. I leaned back on the bed.

"Ms. Quinn, I believe you may have a concussion, so please don't fight me and lay back on the bed so I can examine you," she said sternly.

"I'm all out of fight now, Doc, so fine." I knew I didn't have much choice in the matter. A nurse then stepped in with an IV bag and a tray of first-aid supplies.

Dr. Saroyan ordered a blood draw and asked the nurse to clean me up so she could see the rest of the damage. I changed into a gown and started feeling a strange soreness creep through my body. Dr. Saroyan finished her exam and shook her head. "Were you in another car accident?" She pulled over the tray with needles and stitching thread.

"No, ma'am. I can't really talk about the details, other than that I was hit in the head with a large rock."

She lifted one of my hands, looked it over, and lifted the other. "So you were in a fight with a large rock?" She smirked. "Ahh no, it couldn't be that simple, could it? Your partner is here with all sorts of trauma, and you are walking and talking when you should be unconscious."

"Doctor, I really don't know what to say. It's this fucked up case I'm on. Katerina got caught up in it. She should never have been hurt." I started choking up and couldn't keep talking. Anger surged through me, and I could feel my face getting hot.

"Ms. Quinn, I am sorry I upset you. You need to calm down though. Your blood pressure is going to soar. Let me get these hands stitched up and get you down to X-ray. I am fairly sure you have some broken bones in your hands, not sure how many, and a concussion. I need to get a CT scan done on your knee and your head."

"Doc, is all this necessary? I really need to see Katerina, then get back out there."

"Ms. Quinn, Jara, I have left Katerina in good hands. Now, you have some serious things going on. You likely have broken bones and a concussion, and your knee is swelling up like a watermelon. Even if I did let you leave this room, you wouldn't get far. Let me at least get you sewn up, and we can talk about you visiting Katerina while we wait for transport to take you for your scan."

I realized I was still bleeding in a few places. Then it hit me how badly I felt. I looked down at my knee. I couldn't outrun any of these nurses, even if I tried.

"Okay fine, go ahead and sew me up, but please let me know if there is any change in Katerina's condition."

Dr. Saroyan nodded and started to glove up, but a nurse came in and whispered to her. Dr. Saroyan got a worried look on her face and asked the nurse to sew me up.

"Ms. Quinn, I'm sorry I must go. There has been an explosion and some of the victims are coming here. If I had to guess, you knew something about this before I told you."

"Like I said, Doc, it's this case. I wasn't there for the explosion. I don't know much about it, but I need to know." I closed my eyes and figured what the hell. "I was on the phone with my partner, Travis O'Ryan, when I heard the explosion in the background. I haven't spoken to him since. Now you see my urgency for getting out of here."

Dr. Saroyan's face softened. "If I learn something, I will come tell you. I promise."

"Thank you, Doctor, thank you."

The doctor left the room, and the nurse began numbing my hands. I must have passed out, because when I woke, I had a cast on my left hand and wrist. My right hand and head were wrapped in bandages, and there was a brace on my knee. It seemed surreal, like I had fallen asleep at a slumber party and awakened "decorated" by the other guests. A splitting headache confirmed the sobering truth. I looked around and no one was in my room, so I hit the call button.

"Oh, you're awake," the nurse said when she came in. "I'll get the doctor." I never even got a word out. A short time later, Dr. Saroyan walked into the room, looking exhausted.

"Glad to see you're awake. We weren't able to complete your concussion assessment, but we've been monitoring you. It is safe to assume you have a concussion with the injury you sustained. So be alert for any dizziness or nausea that may come with that and tell us if you start to feel worse."

I looked down at my hands and knee. "Those," she said, "are finally patched up. You have broken knuckles and cuts on both of your hands, and a distal radius fracture in your left wrist. With that large gash on your head, I want to keep you overnight and do another CT scan or an MRI tomorrow."

"What news do you have on the explosion?"

"I did promise you, didn't I?" She sat by my bed and sighed. "I treated some burns, broken bones, concussions, ear injuries, and a couple with internal bleeding. All typical for an explosion of that magnitude. You will be glad to know there were no casualties. They were very lucky."

At that moment, Travis burst into the room, yelling. "That bastard had the place double-rigged. While we were making sure the tunnels and the cabin were safe, the bastard detonated some of the evidence we were removing from the cabin."

He was talking even louder than usual, even for his excitement. I looked over to the doctor and mouthed *ear injury?*

She smiled and nodded yes.

"Travis," I yelled, "I am glad you are okay. Maybe you need to rest and get off your feet for a bit."

He looked at me strangely until I pointed to a chair. "Doc, can I see Katerina now? I promise I won't stay long."

"Fine, but only for a little bit," she said reluctantly. "She needs her rest, too, you know. I'll wheel you down there."

Dr. Saroyan sent Travis back to his ER cubicle to be checked for other injuries, then wheeled me to Katerina's room. I was relieved to see two officers standing guard on either side of the door. Tess was on her phone, and Noel was by Katerina's bedside, quietly talking to her. Noel's face was serious and his eyes red, as if he had been crying. My wheelchair rattled, startling him. He wiped his eyes and quickly regained composure.

"Wow, Fed, you must be special! A free ride from the doc."

Dr. Saroyan did not appear amused. "She can only stay a few minutes. Both of them need their rest."

Noel nodded. "I'll take care of it."

He wheeled me into the room. It was filled with even more beeping monitors and lines than in mine. Katerina looked so small. She never looked small. She was always bigger than life. I had Noel push me up to the side of her bed. She appeared to be asleep, so I carefully brought her hand to my lips and kissed it gently. I saw the contusions on her wrist and a little dried blood.

"I am so sorry, Kat. I am so sorry. Please get better, I can't live without you."

Her hand squeezed mine, and her brilliant green eyes flashed open. She whispered, "You have nothing to be sorry for. Just solve this thing. I am going nowhere. You are stuck with me, my love. So quit wasting your time wallowing in self-pity here and go avenge me."

I nodded my head and kissed her hand again.

"Your wish is my command."

I felt a hand on my shoulder. Victoria looked so strong and beautiful in the middle of this crisis. I pushed my wheelchair to let her get closer to the bed. She bent over and hugged me then whispered in my ear.

"I got this. You go and do what you do best."

She then turned to Katerina. "Now, my dear, let's see how we can get better."

I looked around the room, seeing almost everyone I loved, and all were safe. I backed the wheelchair out of the room as quietly as I could and rolled to my room. I found my clothes and my bag. Yep, gun and ammo were still there. I closed the door and pulled out my IV. As quickly as I could with a bum hand and leg, I changed into my clothes. I called Tess and told her to get my car and meet me out front.

"Girl, you're not discharged. What in the hell are you doing?"

"I'll explain when you pick me up. We need to get out of here before they notice."

"Fine, fine. On my way. I'll meet you on the east side of the building. It's not as busy as the front. No one will notice you."

I made it to the elevator and followed the signs to the side entrance. I walked, or should I say hobbled, slowly and found a bench to sit on and wait. Tess pulled up in my Rover.

"Wanna drive?" she asked.

"Hell no, I can barely walk right now, let alone drive. I need to get to the house and clean up. Catch me up on the way."

Tess explained that Toni was in an undisclosed place with Anita and getting medical treatment. Jacob was picked up from the Brooklyn precinct and was also somewhere unknown. The tunnels had now collapsed. No one could get back in them. There was some damage done to the cabin, but the basement was intact. The crime-scene techs were going through it again with the help of the bomb squad. The evidence that was destroyed in the blast was also being looked through.

"We're sure there was someone else at the cabin, but we don't know where they were when the bombs were detonated. According to the bomb squad, the bomber had to be close, due to the mechanism used, but they weren't found."

"Gotcha, let me make some calls. Hopefully, we'll get some answers." I dialed Mrs. Burris.

"This is Anita."

"Mrs. Burris, I mean Anita, it's Jara. I am wondering if there is anything else I am needing to know."

"Jara, are you discharged from the hospital?"

"Uh, well, I'm in the car with Tess heading to the house. So, yes, I'm out of the hospital. Where's Jacob? And Toni for the matter."

"I can't tell you that right now. Both are secure and where they need to be for the time being. Further interrogation will be done at a later time. But believe me, Jara, they are secure."

"Thank you, Anita. I greatly appreciate it."

"How is Katerina?"

"She's hanging in there. Victoria is with her. They both told me to leave. Anita, now what do we do? Have they said who else is involved?"

"I can't say right now, but build the evidence case, Jara. Follow the evidence and trust in what you know. Make sure it is clear and irrefutable. Keep in mind, things aren't always as they seem." Anita hung up. Tess drove to the house. After I got cleaned up, I collected my second gun, more ammo, and some Tylenol.

Tess watched me gathering my things. "Where are we going now?"

"We need to go back to where it all started, at least in the US."

"And that is?"

I looked around our makeshift headquarters. "Tess, I think we go back and see Andrew."

I called the facility which housed Andrew. He was out of solitary. I informed them we were on our way. I gave instructions to keep him out of solitary, no matter what, and to get him ready for an interview. I called Andrew's lawyer and informed him of our visit.

"Sir, we are going to talk with Andrew with or without your presence, but honestly, I prefer you to be there in case I have some questions for you."

"For me?"

"Yes, sir, for you. This is an ongoing investigation. Some things are adding up, and I have a feeling you can help. You do want to help, right?"

"Agent Quinn, of course I want to help, but not at the demise of my client."

"And what client is that, sir?"

"Andrew of course."

"But aren't you the attorney for the entire Branson family?"

"Well, yes, on paper, I guess I am. But I am Andrew's defense attorney. Why do you ask?"

"Sir, I have a feeling you will need to make a choice soon. Hope to see you at the interview."

Tess looked at me strangely. "What was that all about?"

"I'll explain in the car." I grabbed a few more things and loaded up an evidence box. I asked Tess if she would take it to the car. I had one more call to make.

I dialed up André and told him everything that was going on.

"Ah, *mon chérie*, what can I do? I can be on the next flight."

"Thank you, but I need you there. I need you to search Toni's house and gather everything you can. We have at least one more person involved. You may find something that can help. A warrant is on the way, but these are exigent circumstances. Please do what you can."

"I will *chérie*. Please stay safe...and keep me up to date."

"Thank you, André. Let me know what you find."

I had let Tess drive again. I don't think she minded. We got a few miles down the road before she demanded answers. "Okay, now spill it. What's all this about the lawyer?"

"Since we have Toni in custody, the lawyer, although attorney for the family, will need to choose who to defend. He can't represent both Andrew and Toni, because we believe these murders were all related. We need to learn if Toni was an accomplice to the older murders, and how, if at all, Andrew was involved in the newer ones and the abductions."

We pulled into the parking lot of the psychiatric center. Sure enough, Mr. Payne had beaten us there. *Must be nice to have one client so important you can drop everything and go.*

"Oh, Agent Quinn, are you okay? It looks like you were in an accident."

"Accident? Oh no." I smiled. "No accident, it was all intentional."

Mr. Payne gave me a funny look, and Tess snickered. I wasn't going to tell him about Toni yet. I wondered if he was baiting me and already knew.

The hospital administrator met us in the lobby. "Are you sure you need to speak to Mr. Branson? It is after hours. We usually don't allow visits this late."

I took a deep breath, looked at Mr. Payne, and back at the administrator.

"Sir, not to be rude, but this isn't your normal visit, and I don't give a flying fuck what time it is or what the rules are. We need to see Mr. Branson immediately. I can almost bet he is expecting us. So please, sir, if you don't mind, bring him to the interview room. Tell him Detective Tess Goodwin is here to see him."

The administrator looked at Mr. Payne, who nodded his head, and we made our way to the interview room. I set the box and folders on the table. "Tess, if you would, greet him and tell him you are doing a follow up. I am going to step outside for a moment."

She gave me a strange look, said "okay," and sat down. Mr. Payne sat on the other side of the table. I stood around the corner of the hall and watched as Andrew was brought in wearing shackles and a shit-eating grin. I moved to the side of the door, where I could hear their conversation and see through the window without being seen.

"Oh, Tess, how nice it is to see you." He smirked. "You alone?"

Tess didn't answer him but leapt right in. "Mr. Branson, I have some follow up questions for you from our last meeting that we need to get settled."

"Oh my, Tess, has something happened?" He sneered. "Why are you here all alone? Where is the nice lady agent that was with you last time?"

Tess smiled back and opened a folder. "Sir, I want to clean up a few things. You told us during our last visit your father killed your mother, correct? In France, I believe."

"Yes." Andrew started to fidget.

"You also said you witnessed this, but your brother and sister were both in the car when it happened, correct?"

"Yes, that's correct."

The lawyer spoke up. "Where are we going with this? This doesn't seem like the emergency I was told about by..."

Tess cut him off. "Sir, if you could be patient, I'm sure everything will become clear."

Andrew fidgeted more and looked at his lawyer. "Emergency, what emergency? Tess, dear, please don't tell me something happened to your agent friend."

Tess smiled like a Cheshire cat. "Well Andrew, I'm surprised at your concern about Agent Quinn, but please just a few more questions."

Andrew sat back and smiled but looked uncomfortable. "This better not take much longer. I have things to do."

"Oh really? Must tell! I'm curious about what happens here on a day-to-day basis."

"Get a hospital schedule! It's none of your damn business what I actually do. I'm getting tired." He closed his eyes.

"Okay, so we'll skip the daily activity questions. Have you heard from either of your siblings lately?"

Andrew's eyes flew open wide. "Why do you ask that?"

"Routine question. Actually, I see no one has visited you in a while other than your lawyer, ever since you attacked your brother."

Perfect! Tess was taking him where I wanted him.

"We're not that close."

"Seriously? After experiencing a traumatic event together, like your mother's death, and all of you knowing it was your father, plus having to keep that secret...I would think you three would be closer than ever."

"No, like I said, we aren't close. I saw Toni a couple of times at court, and Alan stopped visiting after I became angry with him."

"May I ask why you were angry at your brother?"

"I just was, okay. It's hard being cooped up here."

Tess turned to the lawyer. "And you, sir, have you heard from either Alan or Toni?"

"Come to think of it, I haven't. Like Mr. Branson said, I saw Toni at court and Alan here during visitation, but not since."

Andrew leaned over on the table, getting as close to Tess as he could. "What are all these questions about my siblings? I'm sure they are out there living their best lives."

I walked into the room, bruises, cast, and all. Andrew's eyes went wide.

I smiled at him as I walked to the table. "How nice of you, Mr. Branson, to show concern and to ask about me. Were you worried something happened and I couldn't visit anymore?"

I kept standing, trying to make him feel as small as I could. I walked around the table near him. He couldn't keep his eyes off my cast and bandages. I shoved my cast down in front of him.

"You want a closer look, Mr. Branson?"

He backed as far away from me as he could.

"Funny, Mr. Branson, all these questions to Detective Goodwin about me and you aren't even going to ask if I'm okay? Gosh, I thought you cared." I put my right hand on his shoulder and felt him jump and tremble a bit. "Did you think something happened to me?" I removed my hand and walked around the table again. "Oh, how rude of me. Detective Goodwin's partner, Jacob Donovan, sends his regards. He's sorry he couldn't be with us today. I believe that is why Detective Goodwin was asking about your daily routine. Detective Donovan, oops sorry, I mean former detective, will need to know the ins and outs of prison life. But then again, this isn't a prison, is it Mr. Branson?"

Andrew tried to swallow nonchalantly. "What do I care about the detective's fall from grace?" Andrew looked at Tess. "I hope it's not because of anything you did, or should I say wouldn't do anymore?"

Aha, he knew of Tess and Jacob's relationship.

Tess laughed. "No, Andrew, not because of me. You see, he has a new girlfriend, French I believe."

Oh, so she knew about the new girlfriend and must have put it together at the cabin. Andrew tried to keep his face unamused. "Well good for him, I guess, but what does this have to do with me?"

I had made it back around to Andrew's corner of the table. I leaned as close to his face as I felt safe doing. "Because, Mr. Branson, he was fucking your sister, Toni. Or should I say Anthony? I guess it is all about location."

Rage flew over Andrew's face, and he reached out to grab me. I slipped out of his reach and noticed a scar on the lower right side of his abdomen. I knew this meant something, but my brain was still a bit foggy.

"Oh, Mr. Branson, you don't want to fight with me."

"I want to kill you! How dare you disrespect my family." His lawyer did his best to calm him down and keep him quiet.

I laughed. "Wow. Two Bransons in two days wanting to kill me. Lucky me."

Andrew stilled, and a look of panic crossed his face as it went white. Mr. Payne, still having his hand on Andrew's shoulder, looked at me. "What are you talking about? I thought you said you had an accident?"

Tess and I looked at each other and laughed. "No, sir," I said, still laughing, "you said I looked like I had been in an accident. I said it was no accident and was all quite intentional. See, I don't take kindly to my family being disrespected either. Nor do I like to be shot at or have people I care about being almost blown up."

Then it hit me, accident. I almost stumbled getting back around the table to the boxes of folders. I grabbed the folder about the family history and started looking through it. I almost forgot I was in an interview.

"Oh, I'm sorry, agent, did someone you love get hurt?" Andrew tried to bait me.

I turned and glared at him. "Yes, Mr. Branson, they did. But they are safe and secure now. Can't say as much for the person who harmed them. Well...I guess I can say they are secure, but that's about it."

I couldn't read his face. Maybe he didn't want to ask me what happened or who it was. He leaned over to his lawyer and whispered something.

Mr. Payne nodded his head. "All right, are there any more questions for Mr. Branson?"

"Is he in a hurry? I would think he'd want to know more about what happened to his sibling. But fine by us, we can end the visit."

Andrew was furious by now and glared at me. He knew damn good and well that if I was here, someone was probably caught.

"I do say, Mr. Branson, your sister isn't much of a shot, hell, not much of a fighter either. You know what they say. If you think I look bad, you should see the other guy, or girl in this case. Actually, I'm not sure about that either."

Andrew was fuming. I could see I didn't have much time. I flipped through the pages in the folder, and there it was. I got him.

"So, Mr. Branson, I have only a couple more questions. then I will let you get back to your busy schedule."

He huffed. "Fine, out with it."

"After you killed your father's second wife in 2000, you held off for a few years. I admire that self-restraint. I was wondering what triggered you to commit another murder?"

"Do I really have to answer this? I have already gone through it all, and here I am."

"No, sir, you really haven't gone through it all. You only admitted to the bloody disfigurement murder in 2000 on our last visit." I put a crime-scene photo in front of him. "And confessed to five others for the court, sort of."

He went white again. I showed him a photo of the basement in the New York brownstone, along with crime-scene photos of Noel's other murders. Mr. Branson moved them around with his finger, not once asking about them. I added photos of the five he'd confessed to and of the most recent ones.

"Mr. Branson, you cleaned all these others up so well, but they do say your first always means the most."

I searched for the page with the timeline of all the murders. "Sir, your DNA was found at only one crime scene, correct?" I went on before he could answer. "That is when you were caught and confessed to that one and four others. Now you have confessed to the murder of your stepmother."

"My father's second wife was no mother to us."

"Us, okay, were your brother and sister as angry as you were? You all saw your mother dragged from the car. Toni was found walking in the parking lot with your mother's handkerchief, right? And you had your mother's purse, and huh...what did your brother have? He must have had something. And where was he found?" I pretended to look through the pages.

"In the car. Toni was in the car too."

"That's right, in the car. Interesting, there must be some mistake. It says here your mother's purse was found in the car. I thought you said you had it when you ran into the alley and saw your mother's body."

"I don't remember. I'm tired, and I want to leave."

I raised my voice. "You don't remember? You don't remember your father butchering your mother in an alley, taking her away from you? Leaving her like trash by a dumpster? You don't remember?!" I was shouting by now.

An odd calm came over him. "No, ma'am, I don't remember. May I be excused?"

"We're not at the dinner table where you can be excused. I will ask you again one simple question, where was your mother's purse?"

"With me, I had it."

Without giving me a full answer, he had answered my question. "I have only one more question. Mr. Branson, I read your brother and sister were in an accident before you were arrested. May I ask what injuries they suffered?"

Mr. Branson squirmed in his seat and pulled his institution sweatshirt down but didn't give an answer. I looked at Mr. Payne. "Sir, can you tell me those injuries?"

Mr. Payne looked confused, but answered anyway. "Alan had a torn artery in his liver and other internal injuries. Toni had severe internal bleeding and a concussion. Why?"

"I assume Alan had surgery to repair his liver. A laparoscopic surgery?"

"No, they had to go in and repair the artery because of the severity of the bleeding and the other internal injuries. They weren't sure where all the bleeding was coming from. Toni was given a blood transfusion. No other surgery was needed."

"I assume, Mr. Branson, you offered blood to both of them? You are triplets. I would think you would be a perfect match."

"I don't know what you are getting at, agent. I love my brother and sister very much and would do anything in my power to help them."

I smiled. "Of course you would. You are their protector, aren't you?"

Both Tess and Mr. Payne looked at me, confused. Mr. Branson glared and stood up.

"Oh, and by the way, the last time I saw your sister, she was unconscious and needing medical care to save her life. Thank goodness the second ambulance arrived in time, at least I think it did. I look forward to seeing her again. Don't you feel the same way, Andrew, I mean...Alan."

Alan Branson leapt over the table and lunged at my throat. I moved to the side and swung my left arm as hard as I could, hitting him in the head with my cast. This knocked him away from me long enough for Tess and the guards to take him down. I didn't move. I wasn't sure what I would do if I did. Tess had her knee in Alan's back and looked up at me mouthing, *what the*...I leaned over and pulled up Alan's shirt, exposing his scar.

I stood up and looked at Mr. Payne. "I think it's time you figure out who your actual client is because, sir, I'm coming for all three."

Chapter Thirty-Two

Tess and I considered the interview a success. When we reached the car, I immediately called SSA Stewart and informed him that Alan was locked up, not Andrew. And I had a hunch about Toni and her DNA. At first, he started to scold me for slipping out of the hospital but calmed down when he learned of our break in the case.

Tess called her chief and updated him. Her next call was to the Attorney General's office to tell the prosecutor that Alan was the one in custody. I could hear yelling and cursing on the other end of the phone. The question he had was what we should do with Alan and how culpable was he in these murders. My question was where in the hell was Andrew.

Alan was demanding to be released, saying he was falsely imprisoned. Mr. Payne was busy calling his office to find other attorneys to represent the siblings. No one knew when Alan and Andrew switched places or, actually, how many times. The prosecutor was able to find a judge who gave an emergency order keeping Alan where he was.

I texted Travis and told him to get Noel and meet us back at the house. I also called Mrs. Burris to see if I could get an update and to fill her in on what I'd learned. Someone else, who refused to give their name, answered her phone and told me Mrs. Burris was busy at the moment, but she would be at the house in a couple of hours. I asked where Jacob and Toni were and got dead air. The person had hung up on me.

The adrenaline had worn off, and I was feeling very achy and lightheaded. Without hesitating, Tess drove back to the house. As soon as we made it home, I went straight to the fridge, grabbed a couple of beers and headed to my boat. I told Tess to give me an hour to decompress and process. At first, she argued with me on how stupid it was to drink and go to the water in my condition. I agreed but never claimed I was smart. She gave up the argument, grabbed herself a beer, and sat on the back porch. She had some decompressing to do also.

I looked at my sailboat like a long-lost friend. I carefully went aboard and sat on the bow, then cracked open a beer and watched the harbor. I tried to quiet my mind and relax. I was missing Katerina. My arm and knee throbbed, and my head ached. Thoughts raced through my mind like Indy drivers. I closed my eyes and repeated out loud, "Follow the evidence, Follow the evidence." I had to cut through all the misdirection and distractions and go back to the physical evidence. We had to link it all together.

I kept hearing Mrs. Burris's voice in my head. "Things aren't as they seem." She was right: they weren't. We'd just proved that. I opened my eyes and saw Travis standing over me.

"You gonna sleep or are we going to solve this damn thing?!" He was still talking loudly.

"Damn, don't I at least get one moment of downtime?"

"Hey, you were the one who checked themselves out of the hospital. You must be fine. So let's get to work."

"Aye, aye, Captain." I even saluted him.

As we walked back to the house, Mrs. Burris's voice was on repeat in my head. Things weren't as they seemed. Alan was locked up and not Andrew. Jacob, a sworn officer of the law, was now a possible accomplice to murder and the attack on Elly. Toni was in the US, not in France as we were told. And was Toni actually Anthony? My head was pounding even more. What else was I missing? My phone rang, and *Dr. Saroyan* appeared on the display. I reluctantly answered. I barely got a word out—

"Agent Quinn, do you ever follow instructions? You could be making your concussion worse, and if you pull those stitches..."

"Doctor, I'm sorry. I couldn't lay in the hospital and do nothing. I promise, I will try and take it easy." I wasn't going to tell her I had already used my cast as a weapon against a person who wanted to kill me. "How's Katerina?"

"She is actually doing what she is supposed to, resting and recovering. Her physical injuries are going to heal. I am worried about her other injuries...the mental ones. She went through quite the ordeal."

"Did she tell you what happened?" I wanted to know, but at the same time I wasn't sure if I could handle it.

"Yes and no. I was in the room when she was interviewed. I wanted to be present in case Katerina needed sedation or a medical incident occurred."

"Sedation? Is she that fragile right now? And what medical incident?" I was out of my mind with questions and worry.

"As you know, during Katerina's abduction she was drugged. We still don't know with what or what the lasting effects are going to be. Also, when she was restrained, the abductor tried to cut or puncture her femoral artery. It wasn't successful, but she suffered significant cuts on her thighs and stomach. There are also signs Katerina fought back. She has bruising and cuts on her wrists, ankles, and hands. You two make quite the pair. You both could have internal injuries we haven't found yet. Katerina is in a CAT scan now. She definitely is a survivor, like her mother. I was glad I got to speak with Victoria." I remembered how helpful Dr. Saroyan was when we found Victoria after she was abducted and put in a coma. This family had been through so much.

"Dr. Saroyan, thank you so much for your care. She couldn't be in better hands. I promise, I will come back in as soon as I can."

"Jara, I am serious. I hope you are taking it easy. I didn't have a chance to finish your tests. I need to see you sooner, rather than later. Plus, Katerina needs you."

"Yes, ma'am, I understand. I'll be in soon." I had no idea when I would be there. I still had work to do. I went into the theater, where Travis and Tess were going over the timeline and all the institution's visitor logs.

"Visits were at least one week before and one week after each of the last four murders. Plus, it appears Andrew was still out during Elly's and Katerina's attacks. This can't be coincidence," Tess pointed out.

I agreed. "It's been Andrew the whole time, with Alan covering for him at the asylum. Toni was helping him, if not doing the initial abductions. And Alan committed the murder of the father's second wife."

Mrs. Burris walked in, her face very serious. I held my breath, not knowing what she was going to say. I started to pace, trying to keep myself calm.

"Jara, dear, please let's go into the den and sit down. We need to talk about some things."

"Can they come?" I motioned toward Travis and Tess.

"By all means, yes. You all need to hear this."

I sat on one of the couches, with Travis sitting next to me and Tess behind me. Where was Noel?

"Jara, I know you want to know everything, but we need to discuss Katerina's interview."

"Did you do the interview?"

"Yes, and I had another agent present," Anita said. "I am wondering if I am doing the right thing telling you about the interview. You are too emotionally involved."

I breathed a sigh of relief. At least Katerina knew Anita. "Anita, it's okay, I spoke with Dr. Saroyan. I know she was present for the interview."

Anita tried to give a comforting smile. "Yes, but not for all of it. I take it you know about Katerina's injuries, right?"

"Yes, I know what the doctor saw during her examination. Is there more?"

"Jara, Andrew was in the cabin with Toni. He knows you spoke to Alan and had the purse."

"Spill it, Anita. What did Andrew tell her?"

"He told Katerina he was going to ruin your family like you are ruining his. He said he is coming for you and all who you love." Anita softened her voice, "My dear, he's not done."

"Why is he so focused on me? I'm only a part of this team."

"If I had to guess, he knows you were figuring it out. He has had more contact with Jacob than we originally knew, but that information pipeline has been shut down."

"Anita, where are Jacob and Toni? What have you learned from them?"

"It's best you all don't know, dear. Safer that way. Jacob met Toni after Andrew was arrested. Toni convinced Jacob that Andrew was framed by Tess, and she needed help proving it." Anita looked at Tess. "He was very angry that you broke off your relationship with him. We will need to look through all the evidence Jacob was a part of."

Tess was fuming. "I framed Andrew...he really believed that? What a dumbass! He was that mad at me?! Anita, he was part of everything, Does this mean it is all tainted?"

"I'm not sure, dear, but we need to check. Toni isn't talking, can't really with a shattered jaw." Anita turned and looked at me, as she continued. "I know Jacob took a ring from evidence, said Toni needed it. She told him Tess planted it after taking it from one of the searches of the Branson house. Does a ring sound familiar, Tess?"

Tess thought for a moment. "Yes, it does. We found a ring I believe at the fourth crime scene. We never matched it to its owner. We thought it had been stolen from evidence, but we looked later and found it in another box. Jara, I think the ring was one of the discrepancies you asked me about." Tess punched the couch. "I should have known he was behind this."

"Dear, no one knew. Other than helping Toni take Katerina, and that was a mistake, I don't think he thought what he was doing was that bad. He was giving them information about a closed case and some about the current investigations. He took a ring he thought no one would miss from a closed case, then later replaced it with another."

"Anita, do you know the significance of this ring?" I asked. "Why did they want it back so badly?"

"No, dear, not yet, but I will. You spooked him when you asked for the evidence lists. Jacob is being moved to solitary in a federal facility today. Toni is receiving medical treatment and isn't going anywhere. She is securely confined and guarded."

I had really done it this time. Toni couldn't answer questions because I shattered her jaw. I thought I would feel bad, but I didn't. My main concern was that Andrew was still out there.

I decided I needed to see Katerina. She needed my support and honestly, I needed hers. Anita volunteered to drive me to the hospital. I wondered if she was going to scold me for my actions, but I took her up on her offer. Tess and Travis were going to go over all the evidence again.

We rode to the hospital without one word of condemnation. Instead, a softer side of Anita came out.

"Jara, I think it is in your best interest if the persons closest to you are protected. I believe Andrew knows Katerina and Victoria are your only family, but I wouldn't put it past him to go after Katerina's family or your team."

"Anita, I get that, but I can't hide or disrupt everyone's life every time a nutbag wants to come after me. I'll inform

Katerina's brothers, but could you help me protect Victoria and Kat?"

We were walking into the hospital, and Anita put her arm around me. "Yes, dear, I will protect them as if they are my own."

We checked in at the nurse's station. I was told to wait because Dr. Saroyan needed to see me. Anita went on into the room and hugged Victoria. I waited only a few minutes before Dr. Saroyan showed up.

"Agent Quinn, I'm glad you're here. I am making arrangements for you to get into a CAT scan today. Visit Katerina and I'll come to get you when we are ready."

I knew it was no use arguing, I reluctantly agreed and asked how Katerina was doing.

"She has slept off and on since she got here but has needed sedation to help combat some nightmares. They seem to be coming more often. I gave Mrs. Lansing the names of a couple of therapists that specialize in PTSD and trauma. I really would like Katerina to see one of them, sooner rather than later."

"Doctor, when can she come home?"

"I believe tomorrow. Medically, there is not much more I can do. She will need to feel safe though. That is of the upmost importance."

"Thank you, Doctor. I'll be here when you're ready for me."

Anita was sitting on the bed next to Katerina. Victoria saw me and gave me a huge hug.

"How are you?"

"Have had better weeks. How's Katerina? And how are you? You look exhausted."

Victoria gave a weak smile. "Never come to the hospital for rest, unless of course you're in a coma. This place unsettles me anyway."

I told her what the doctor had said about Katerina possibly being discharged.

"It will be good for us all to be home again."

Even lying in a hospital bed, Katerina was the most beautiful woman I have ever seen, though she still seemed so small. She looked up, and I smiled when she motioned me over to her. Anita remained by her side.

"I hear there is still one left," Katerina said matter-of-factly.

"Yes, Andrew."

She pulled her hand away. "Then why are you here?"

I was caught a bit off guard. "I... uh...wanted, well needed, to see you. I want to make sure you're okay."

"Okay is relative, I suppose. So yes, I'm okay." Katerina said flatly.

I looked over to Anita and Victoria. "Could we have a moment alone please, that is if Katerina is okay with that?" Katerina nodded. Victoria told her they would be right outside the door if needed.

"Katerina, are you mad at me? What have I done or not done? Tell me, please." I begged.

"Yes, I'm mad! I'm mad at being taken. I'm mad at this case of yours, and I am mad at you! Hell, I'm even mad at myself. It seems we are all still in danger, and you haven't caught the bastard yet. I had to be in that cabin with them and there was nothing I could do...and you...and you weren't there!" She started sobbing. "You weren't there."

"Sweetheart, I found you. I found you because you took me to you. You were smart and brave." I took a chance and sat on the side of the bed. She let me take her hand, then looked at me as if she just learned I was there. "Katerina, I'm here. I promise you. I am here."

She grabbed me and pulled me to her on the bed. She sobbed so hard she could barely catch her breath. All I could do was hold her tight. I wanted to say I understood, but I couldn't. I didn't understand what she really went through. I had never experienced it. I wanted her to know she was safe, safe with me, so that was what I said over and over. Her crying slowed and she loosened her grip on me to lay back on the pillows. I moved her hair from her face and kissed her forehead. She looked up at me and whispered, "I was wrong. You were there."

"Yes, my love, I was. I found you, then went after them."

She shook her head. "No, no, no, I mean you were there. You were always there, in my head and in my heart, telling me to fight, to survive, to come back to you. You were always there."

Now it was my turn to cry. I kissed her cheeks and told her how much I loved her. "Are you ready to come home tomorrow?"

A glow came over her face. "Can we go now?"

"I wish, but Dr. Saroyan wants me to do a couple of tests and needs you to stay here one more night."

"Stay with me? Stay tonight?"

Dr. Saroyan walked in and heard Katerina's request. She looked at me and back to Katerina. "Yes, she can stay. But right now I need her for a test. She'll be back shortly."

Anita and Victoria returned to the room and stayed with Katerina while I was gone. It seemed like the longest CAT scan ever. I returned to Katerina's room and saw blankets and pillows had been brought in. Anita pulled me aside. "I'm taking Victoria home and setting up security for the house. She has talked to Katerina's brothers. They are all going to go to the Islands in a day or two for Foundation business. It will be safer for them there. That way I can focus on Katerina's safety."

"Thank you, Anita. I don't know how I'll ever be able to repay you."

"You can repay me by catching this bastard."

I hugged both Anita and Victoria goodbye and started to pull up a chair to Katerina's bed. "Oh no, you don't. You are getting in here and holding me, bum arm and all."

"Yes, ma'am."

Chapter Thirty-Three

The nurses were in and out most of the night, checking the beeping and the IV. The bed was small, but it was nice to be holding Katerina again. About four a.m., I immediately woke up to Katerina hitting me and yelling. A nurse rushed in due to the spike in Katerina's heart rate.

"Katerina, sweetheart, it's me, Jara. I'm here. I've got you. I'm here."

Her eyes flew open, wild with panic, but she was trying to focus on me. I kept talking softly to her as she got her bearings. Another nurse entered the room with a syringe full of a sedative to put into the IV.

"Don't, please don't. Please..." Katerina cried.

The nurse looked at Katerina and me.

"Please, she is refusing it. Unless Dr. Saroyan specifically said to give it to her, then she refuses it."

"This is a PRN sedative for whenever she is suffering extreme anxiety. I won't give it to her if she refuses, but she will need to calm down."

"I'm right here, damn it. Talk to me. And do I need to calm down for you or for me?" Katerina yelled. "I don't want it. I will do what I need to do. Now will you please turn that damn alarm off?"

"That's my girl, the fighter."

The nurses turned and left after silencing the alarm.

"I can't depend on that stuff. It doesn't get rid of it anyway. I only feel woozy and out of it more. Did Dr. Saroyan ever figure out what I was drugged with?"

"Not that I know of, but the lab is still working on it. You know I'm here if you ever want to talk about any of it. I will try to be calm and listen." I said quietly.

"I know you will, and I do want to tell you about it, but not now and not here. Maybe at home when I feel safer. Too many people here, in and out. I think I told Anita and Noel everything I could remember."

"Noel? He was here too? He didn't mention it."

"Yes, he wanted to hear my story, then go to Elly's. I spoke with her earlier. He has been camped at her place since the interview."

"So that's where he's been. Good to know." I remembered I hadn't given him the burner number. I bet he was pissed. *Note to self, call Noel first thing in the morning.*

We drifted back to sleep, Katerina's head on my shoulder, her body intwined with mine.

Chapter Thirty-Four

We woke the next morning to Dr. Saroyan typing on her laptop.

"Dr. Saroyan?"

"Good morning, Agent Quinn. I wanted to check in on my patients. Looks like you both got some sleep. I hear Katerina had another nightmare and refused her PRN."

I started to answer, but Katerina was awake. "Yes, Doctor, I don't want to rely on that stuff to sleep. Do you know what I was drugged with yet?"

A concerned look came over the doctor's face. "I understand you don't want to take any medications, but I don't want you to suffer either. I will prescribe a mild sedative for you to have at home. You can gauge how many times you take it and when, as long as you don't overdo it. As for what was in your system..." She paused for several moments before continuing. "Your blood tests showed both ketamine and an opiate, so I don't blame you for not wanting to take anything."

My head was spinning. They could have so easily overdosed her. It dawned on me that they wanted her sedated enough to control her but have her aware of the horrors they subjected her to.

"As for you, Ms. Quinn, you have a moderate concussion. Your scan showed less swelling than I expected for your injury, but this is still very serious. If you don't get some rest, or worse are reinjured, you could cause permanent damage. So yes, you both can go home today, but no strenuous activity, and limit anything that requires concentration for the next few days. Katerina, allow yourself to build back your strength gradually with good nutrition and rest."

We both agreed. "So, Doc, when can we go home?"

"Neither of you are going anywhere until I get the go-ahead from Mrs. Burris that she is ready."

"Damn that woman has pull," I said to Katerina. "Doc, when you talk to Mrs. Burris, could you have her come see me if she can? I need to speak with her as soon as possible."

"Of course. I'll let her know."

Katerina gave me a sly smile. "You're up to something, aren't you?"

"As usual, my love, you're right. You may not like it, but I feel it is our best bet to catch Andrew and end this once and for all."

"Okay then, you'd better fill me in."

I told Katerina my plan. As I predicted, she wasn't happy but understood. We lay in the bed and held each other, feeling safe for the moment.

Chapter Thirty-Five

We awoke hearing Dr. Saroyan speaking to Mrs. Burris. She was going over each of our conditions and how we needed our rest. Mrs. Burris saw I was awake.

"You heard the doctor, right Jara?"

"Yes, ma'am. I plan to rest as much as possible..."

"You'd better," Dr. Saroyan said, while walking out of the room.

Mrs. Burris pulled up a chair by the bed. "I hear you wanted to talk with me?"

"Yes, ma'am. Are Victoria and the boys safe?"

"Yes, the boys and their families are now at the house, They will fly out tomorrow. I'm sure that is not what you wanted to speak with me about."

Katerina stirred and turned over, still asleep. I was so happy she slept through the night. I slowly sat up in bed and swung my legs over the side. "Can we go somewhere to talk? I don't want to wake her."

I allowed Mrs. Burris to help me stand and take the first few steps. I had totally stiffened up overnight. We moved past the guards standing by our door, and a nurse insisted I use a wheelchair to the sunroom down the hall.

"So, Jara, what are you up to?"

"Anita, I have a plan, but I need you to make it work. I promise I'll be careful."

"I'm listening."

I explained my plan and waited anxiously for Anita's reaction. She sat quietly, her face unreadable. I kept talking.

"My dear, please. I understand your plan, but are you sure? Is Katerina aware of it?"

"Yes, ma'am. She's not happy, but she understands."

Anita sighed loudly. "Jara, if you are serious, I'll set it up. But you will need to do exactly as I say or I will immediately pull the plug. Is Dr. Saroyan finished with your tests?"

"I believe so. We can double-check. What are you thinking?"

"To be safe, Jara, she needs to be involved. I know her and trust her. I have used her before."

"What? Dr. Saroyan? When? How?"

"That doesn't matter right now. Go home today, and be with your family. I'll be in touch."

My mind was spinning again. What didn't I know? I rolled myself back to the hospital room, where Katerina was awake and sitting up in bed.

"Jara, can we go home now, please?"

"Yes, my love, let's go home."

Chapter Thirty-Six

We finished up our discharge paperwork, and I called Tess to pick us up. She was there in an instant. I was able to walk out, but Katerina was still very weak and was rolled out in a wheelchair. The guards followed but were dismissed once Tess arrived.

"Your chariot awaits, my ladies," Tess teased.

"Tess, I hope you're not getting too used to my Rover." I chuckled. "I'll be able to drive soon."

We all laughed as if this were a normal day, but I felt something was off. We were definitely being watched.

The scene at home was almost festive. Katerina's brothers, CJ and Chase, were present with their families. The house was loud and full of life. It was good to see them again. It had been over a year since we last got together. CJ and Julia's son, Calvin, was taller and preparing for preschool. Their baby girl, Anastasia Leigh, was fourteen months old already, and a lot more active than the infant we saw before we had left for France. As soon as we entered the house, Calvin was on us to go sailing. Anastasia was right behind him. I promised him that, after his trip to the Islands, we would all go on another family sail. He was off running, Anastasia following him like a shadow.

We settled into our room, and Tess knocked on the door. "I'll be going now. Let me know if you need anything."

"Thank you, Tess, for everything," Katerina answered, "but please, stay here at the house. We have plenty of room. I'd feel better if you were here."

Tess looked startled for a moment, then thanked Katerina. "Okay, I'll stay for a while. We still have work to do."

Travis agreed to stay, also, although he was technically off duty due to his hearing loss. Noel was staying at Elly's place. Seemed like the bases were covered.

Another knock on the door sounded. "Hey, Sis, you doing okay?" CJ asked.

"Doing better, CJ, thanks for asking. Have fun on your trip. Sorry I can't go with you. I appreciate you dropping everything and going with Mom. I feel better knowing you all will be together." Katerina smiled weakly.

"Hey, who could pass up a free trip to the Islands? Calvin is over-the-moon excited. He was upset when he learned he couldn't bring his horse but quickly got over it."

I laughed. "Now that would be a sight, a horse on a plane."

"Hey, Jara," CJ's tone changed a bit. "When you get settled, can you come and talk to me and Chase? We have a couple of questions."

I looked over at Katerina. "Go ahead," she said. "I'm fine here, and it's better you tell them everything than me."

"Sis, I didn't mean to leave you out. We have some questions I think only Jara can answer."

Katerina scoffed. "Yeah, right, that is if she answers them at all. You know these Fed types."

I smirked at Katerina. "Thank you for helping me clarify my job, my love." I kissed her forehead. "I'll be back soon."

"Actually, I'll meet you in the kitchen. I'm going to clean up a bit and come down. I don't want to be cooped up."

CJ and I headed downstairs, and I saw Tess going into her room. "Excuse me, CJ. I'll be right down."

CJ went on downstairs, as I walked over to the room Tess was staying in and knocked on the door. "Hey Tess, do you have a moment?"

"Sure, come on in. What's up?"

I took a deep breath. *Well, here goes nothing. No turning back now.*

"Tess, I have a large favor to ask of you, and most of it you're going to have to trust me on."

"Uh, okay, sure, anything. What do you need me to do?"

"Speak with Anita as soon as you can. She is waiting for your call. If you tell her no, I will understand."

"God, this sounds ominous, but okay. I owe you. I'll give her a call now."

"Thanks, Tess. I appreciate it, but you don't owe me. Just don't tell anyone."

"Gotcha."

I breathed a sigh of relief and went downstairs, where I joined Chase and CJ in the den. Of course, they peppered me with questions about Katerina and the reason for the trip. Katerina was right. I answered what I could to put their minds at ease but left out a lot. They seemed satisfied with my answers, and we joined the rest of the family in the kitchen. It seemed like a holiday, everything seeming so normal. Victoria and Julia were cooking, and Abby sat with Katerina as the kids played around them. If they could look past the underlying concern, all the cuts and bruises, my cast, and our overall slowness, all seemed perfect.

Tess came down to the kitchen. She had met everyone earlier when they arrived. She pulled me aside. "You sure about this?" She had spoken to Anita. I nodded my head. "Okay then," she said, "Anita needs to see us right away. She is still at the hospital."

I looked over at the family with an odd forlornness. I hoped this gathering could happen again. I walked over to Katerina and whispered in her ear that I was leaving to see Anita. She nodded and forced a smile.

"Hey all," I said loudly over the voices in the kitchen, "I'm sorry, but I have to run back to the hospital for a quick moment. Dr. Saroyan wants to do one more test on me."

Everyone groaned and voiced disappointment.

"No worries. Tess is going to drive me. We should be back by dinner."

Calvin wanted to ride with us. "Sorry, little man, but I need to do this as quick as I can. Promise I'll be right back. You take care of Auntie Kat for me, okay?"

He ran over to her and climbed on her lap. "I take care of you 'til Auntie J gets back."

"Well then," she said, as she smiled at me, "I'm in good hands."

Travis walked in and yelled, "So here is where the party people are!"

"Damn, Travis, did you have to yell?"

He gave me a strange look. Tess and I started laughing and said at the same time, "Ears!"

"What?" he asked, his voice booming.

"Nothing, Travis, Hold down the fort. We'll be right back." Tess told him. She motioned to me with her arm. "After you."

Chapter Thirty-Seven

We didn't go to the hospital but to an address Anita had given. Tess pulled the Rover into a garage, and we went into a small, barren room. Anita and Dr. Saroyan were waiting for us.

I looked around the room, then to Anita. "I guess we're doing this. Thank you, Anita, Dr. Saroyan."

"Regan, please Jara, call me Regan. If we are doing this, we might as well be on a first-name basis. I want to voice my concerns now, for the record," Regan said, staring a hole through me. "Your concussion is serious. If anything happens..."

I nodded. "I know, I know. But this has to happen as soon as possible. I don't think waiting is an option. But thank you, Regan, for your concern. Now what?"

A team, dressed in all black, miraculously appeared and was instructed by Anita to go to my car. Another group came in with pelican cases and medical equipment. To say the least, I was impressed, if not a wee bit scared.

Anita had them put trackers on my Rover, and they installed multiple programs on my computer system. She also put a tracker in my cast and on my leg brace. Meanwhile, Dr. Saroyan hooked up an IV and brought in a few monitors,

"Now for the fun part." Regan had me lie down on the table. She hooked up some wires to me and started the IV. "You're going to need to be hydrated for this. I'm not very happy that you think you need to do this now. If your injuries get worse..." Her voice trailed off.

Anita took Tess aside and went over all the tracking equipment with her. Tess caught on very quickly to all of it, the monitors, the fail-safes, all of it.

Anita walked over to me to deliver another warning. "Jara, don't get too cocky or careless. All the equipment in the world won't save you if Andrew really wants to kill you. Please understand that."

"I do, ma'am. Believe me, I do."

Regan gave me two shots and what felt like another injection in my back, then returned to the monitors.

"All looks okay." She handed me two more syringes. "Take both of these after the family leaves tomorrow. If you have any issues, call me. I am still very worried about that concussion of yours. You need your rest."

"Doc, I know, but I won't really rest until Andrew is caught. You know that."

She smiled grimly and nodded her head. "I know."

Dr. Saroyan unhooked the IV and removed the wires while Anita and Tess went over some last-minute details. Anita walked back over and handed me a small capsule in a metal container.

"I know this is old school, but here is a capsule to put in your mouth as a last resort. If things seem to go sideways and you can't take it, bite down, but only as a last resort."

I hesitantly took the container. "Here's to hoping I don't need this."

We all sat quietly for a moment, knowing we had done all we could do. I stood up, trying to feel confident but only feeling a little woozy. "Let's get this show on the road."

I invited them both to dinner. Both declined, but Regan said, "When this is over, I will take you up on the dinner invitation." Anita agreed.

"Then it's a date. Put your food requests in with Tess."

We all laughed, and Tess and I headed for the Rover.

As we neared the liquor store, I said, "I think we need to make a stop, Tess. I'm going to need it."

We bought a bunch of different types of beverages and made it home before dinner was off the stove. We entered with two boxes filled with tequila, vodka, whiskey, wine, and beer. CJ met us at the door.

"Hospital, my ass. You went on a liquor run. It's a party now!" CJ took the box I was carrying.

CJ and Chase began fixing drinks for all of us. When we each had a drink in hand, Victoria proposed a toast.

"To family, all our family." She looked around at everyone, including Tess and Travis. "To health, happiness, and safety. May we enjoy and love each other."

We all clinked glasses, and Chase raised his glass again.

"I guess this is as good a time as any, since we are speaking of family and all..." A hush came over the room. I had noticed Abby was flushed and drinking only tonic water and lime.

*Oh wow...*I looked at Katerina and grabbed her hand. Glass still raised, Chase said, "To the surprise of all of you and myself, I have finally grown up and am going to be a father!"

Victoria about dropped her glass. "Oh my god, I'm going to be a grandmother!"

Calvin tugged at her. "But Granny V, you already are a grandmother."

We all burst into laughter and congratulated Chase and Abby.

"We don't know the sex yet," Abby said shyly. "I think we want it to be a surprise."

Good news, finally good news, but at the most awful time. Andrew had to be caught.

Chapter Thirty-Eight

We all turned in early. The family had an early flight to the Islands, and Katerina was exhausted. She snuggled up to me. "It's nice to be back in our own bed again."

"Yes, it is." I wrapped my arms around her the best I could with my cast.

"How long do you have to keep that thing on?"

"According to Regan, I will need to change casts in a couple of weeks, when the swelling is down."

"Regan now, huh?"

Snuggling even closer to her, I asked, "You jealous? She asked me to call her Regan. I guess since she has treated almost everyone in this family, we should be on a first-name basis."

"Uh-huh, okay, but don't forget I still have André," she teased.

"André! I forgot to call him. Will you call him tomorrow? He'd love to hear from you."

Katerina giggled. "You don't mind?"

"Of course not. There's an ocean between us."

"Damn you! I can never make you jealous!"

"My love, anytime someone looks at you, flirts with you, anything...I become torn between pride and extreme jealousy. I just don't let you see it."

She got very quiet. "What do you think about Chase and Abby? So happy for them." A tear rolled down her cheek.

"It's okay. they will be safe on the island."

"I know, I know. It's not that. Do you ever think we're missing out by not having a child?"

Damn, that came out of nowhere. "Kat, are you saying you want a child?"

"I don't know. With everything that has happened, it might be nice to settle down for a change. Put our energies into something other than ourselves."

I knew not to tease her about this, but children were the last thing on my mind. “Well, my love, if a child is what you want, we can discuss it. But can we table it until after this case?”

“Of course. I’m not saying I want a child for sure. It’s just crossed my mind at times.”

I held her tightly. “I love you. We’ll get this all figured out.”

Katerina kissed me good night and quickly fell asleep. I on the other hand remained wide awake. My arm was still hurting, thoughts of Andrew and this case cluttered my mind, and the bombshell of Katerina asking about children... *How in the hell could I manage a kid?*

I had just fallen asleep when I heard the familiar pounding of little feet running down the hall. Calvin burst into the room, Anastasia right behind him. Instead of leaping on the bed as was his norm, he tiptoed to the edge of the bed and stared at Kat. Anastasia gently crawled on my side of the bed and looked at me. Katerina opened one eye. Calvin was almost nose to nose with her. She reached out and grabbed him, pulling him onto the bed. Calvin and Anastasia squealed with laughter. Katerina tickled and kissed him over and over.

“My alarm clock. What did I ever do without my Calvin alarm clock?” Katerina said between kisses.

Anastasia was yelling, “Me too, me too,” so Katerina grabbed her and started tickling and kissing her. I tried to keep out of the way so I wouldn’t hit anyone with my cast.

Kat yelled, “Auntie Jara needs hugs and kisses.” And with that, I was swamped with two kids and a girlfriend. CJ and Julia finally came to my rescue, each trying to grab a child.

“We told them to be quiet and gentle,” Julia said, apologetically.

“It wasn’t them,” I said. “Blame it on their aunt.”

Chase had come in to see what all the noise and fuss was about.

“So Chase,” I said, “you ready for this? The mornings will never be yours again.”

He laughed. “Maybe we’ll get a late sleeper.”

“No chance, brother, no chance,” CJ said, a teasing note in his voice.

Finally, everyone left our room. Kat and I were tangled up in all of our covers. I was having a hard time detangling with the cast. I looked over at Kat and laughed. "So now, this is what you think you might want?"

"Right now, I'd settle for just you." She grabbed my face and kissed me. It felt good to experience passion from her again. I rolled over, still tangled in a sheet, and saw she had her shirt off. I put my right arm around her and pulled her to me. She pulled her hair in front of her, covering a cut on her breast. I moved her hair away and kissed the cut. We kissed deeply and Katerina moved to roll on top of me. She started either laughing or crying. "Oh honey, I want this so badly right now, but..."

"What, Kat, what is it?" I was concerned there was an issue because of her abduction.

"Jara, my hair is caught in your cast!"

We burst into such loud, hardy laughter, it brought the household back into our room. We laughed even harder then. The Lucy and Ethel show seemed to have returned. The guys and Julia grabbed the kids and hurriedly left, while Tess and Abby helped us untangle. We both turned as red as Katerina's hair. Tess was helping me get my leg brace untangled, when she started laughing. "So this is how the great Agent Quinn displays passion. Never thought I'd see you so, well, helpless."

"Shut up, Tess, and unhook that sheet from my brace." I wondered whether I was successfully grinning and glaring at the same time.

Abby was laughing so hard she could barely help Katerina cover up and detach her hair from my rough cast. Even if it was at our expense, it was good to hear laughter in the house. Thank God Travis was having ear issues and slept through this ordeal. I would have never heard the end of it.

Chapter Thirty-Nine

Victoria and the family headed to the airport with guards posing as their car service. Victoria promised to call when they reached the island. Anita had told me that the family was booked on a flight for the Caymans and another for the Bahamas, but they were actually taking a private plane to Nevis. Victoria knew money was spread throughout the islands, but she had a contact in Nevis and decided to start there. She had set up many meetings with multiple institutions, so no one would know where the family was at any given time. Again, Anita had worked her magic.

Travis finally woke up, and we all had a late breakfast. We contacted Noel. He had taken Elly somewhere, away from her home and business. He wouldn't tell us where.

Katerina spent most of the time on the back porch, working on her laptop. She had set up a couple of therapy appointments and was filling out paperwork for them.

Travis, Tess, and I went back to the theater and started separating the evidence again, double and triple checking everything. I called SSA Stewart and asked for an armored car to come out and get the evidence we had finished with. He agreed to send one out the next morning. I also left a message for André, checking on his progress with gaining evidence against Toni. I snuck off to my room and injected the shots Dr. Saroyan told me to take. My heart raced for a moment before it calmed down. *I probably don't want to know what I just took.*

We finished up with all the evidence, finally, and I went to join Katerina on the back porch. She was crying.

"Kat, what's wrong?" I sat at the foot of her lounge chair.

"I'm not strong enough for this," she said, continuing to sob. "I can't get that cabin out of my head. Now I must go to therapy and remember it more."

I moved closer to her and reached my hand out to touch her thigh. She pushed me away. "Kat, what? Are you mad at me again?"

"No, but I don't think you'll ever want to really touch me again."

"What are you talking about? It's driving me crazy not to touch you now. I just don't want to push you. I don't want to hurt you any further."

"I can't be hurt any further, Jara. He tainted me," Katerina said, her eyes still full of tears.

I closed my eyes, trying not to explode. As calmly as I could, I asked, "Kat, tell me. What did he do?"

She sobbed and pulled back her shirt, showed me the cut I had kissed earlier. "Kat, cuts and bruises will heal. You know those things don't matter to me. You are my love, my soulmate."

"I have other cuts and marks," she said. "He wanted to ruin me for you."

"He could never ruin you for me." I inched closer. I wanted to hold her and make this all better.

"But he may have ruined me for me. He tried to cut me down there."

Wait, wait. I knew Dr. Saroyan and Anita told me about multiple cuts and bruises. I thought they were going for her femoral. Were they trying to cut her genitalia, also? "Sweetheart, can you tell me what they did? Do you want to tell me?"

Katerina stood and took my hand. She led me upstairs to our room, where shut and locked the door. She slowly undressed. I sat on the bed, nervous about what I'd see. Could I handle it? I guess I had closed my eyes.

"Look at me." Katerina said.

I opened my eyes slowly. I saw cuts and bruises on her breasts, stomach, and thighs. I could see distinct bruise marks on thighs in the shape of handprints and a gash to the right of her pubic bone. My body shook with anger, and tears filled my eyes.

"See." She grabbed a blanket. "You think I'm ugly. And there is more. Like I said, he tried to ruin me for you. You won't want to touch me again."

I slowly stood up and took her in my arms. "No, my darling, I think you are the most beautiful and sexiest woman in the world. I am so lucky to have you. I cry for the pain and doubt they put you through. I shake in the anticipation of one day holding them accountable for what they did to you. No one, no cut, nor scar will ever make me see you as any less beautiful."

She relaxed in my arms and began sobbing, "I love you. I will always love you."

We sat on the bed. I was holding her as tightly as I could. Katerina relaxed more, moved out of my arms and laid her head on the pillow. I tucked her in and started to get up. She grabbed my hand. "Please stay until I fall asleep?"

I smiled and kissed her. "Of course."

She fell into a deep sleep quickly. I had a feeling she had taken a sedative. I walked downstairs, too angry to settle. I grabbed a beer and a bottle of tequila and went to the back porch. Tess saw me. "What in the hell are you doing? You can't drink with a concussion."

"Watch me!" I downed a shot of tequila and drank half a beer. I wanted to punch something, anything.

Travis had made his way to the porch. "C'mon, Jara, chill out."

"Fuck you, Travis. I'm angry, and I feel helpless. Maybe getting shitfaced will help my attitude a bit."

I finished my beer and took another shot of tequila.

"Jara, please slow down," Tess begged loudly. "This isn't good."

"Yeah, yeah it is for me." I threw the beer bottle down and opened another.

Travis shook his head. "I'm not going to watch you get drunk."

"Then don't! You can leave." I downed another shot.

"There's no reasoning with you. C'mon, Tess, let her have her pity party by herself."

Tess and Travis went back into the house as I continued to drink. I looked out at the water and knew I needed to be on my boat. I made it to the bow and set down the tequila bottle. A sharp pain went through my head and down my body. I found myself lying on the deck of my boat as it was motoring away from the dock. I tried to throw the tequila bottle to shore, but it shattered on the dock, then I passed out.

I have no idea how long I had been out, but I woke up restrained to an oversized chair, almost like an old barber chair.

"Oh, look who's awake. I have been waiting patiently," said a voice from the shadows.

Andrew. I pulled on my restraints a bit. *No breaking out of these.* Andrew had cut off my cast, and it was on the floor in pieces. He saw me looking at it.

"Silly girl. Did you think I wouldn't check you for a tracking device? Yes, I found them all, the one on the boat, in your cast, and on your brace—all destroyed. And armed...Wow, are you that scared of me?" He held up my two guns and the knife I'd had in my cast. "Were you going to cut me or shoot me?"

I laughed. "Cutting is your territory, not mine. And I don't have to shoot you to down you. Just ask your sister. Oh, that's right, you can't. Plus she couldn't answer you anyway, shattered jaw and all."

He became red with anger and hit me across the face.

"Andrew, what has happened to you? After Mommy died, you couldn't be with a woman unless she was dead?"

Andrew yelled in my face. "Don't talk about my mother."

"Why not? Alan did. He told me how she cheated on your father with a lowly baker. Who else did she sleep with? Daddy not satisfy her?"

"She wasn't a whore," he screamed. His face was aflame with anger.

"Oh, Andrew, such strong words. I never called your mother a whore. Is that what your father called her? Heck, maybe she was a whore."

I knew I was getting to him, because he started pacing around me and talking to himself.

"So, Andrew, have you ever killed someone on your own, or did you always need help? Seems Toni, or is it Anthony, is the only one who ever really had the balls to do it. No pun intended."

"Shut up, just shut up! You ruined everything. I want to kill you, but I'm not yet. I'm going to kill your family, your precious Katerina, and let you live to see it." Andrew's eyes were crazed.

"Andrew, I have no family. You know that. And you already tried to kill Katerina and failed. So tell me, who are you going to kill?"

His eyes raged and his nostrils flared, as he hit my broken arm with a hammer. I yelled out, more from surprise than pain. I felt a little dizzy but gathered myself.

"C'mon Andrew, tell me what a killer you are."

And the rant began...

Chapter Forty

When Jara left the porch, Tess went to the room next to Granny's and pulled up the computer. The trackers were beeping, showing Jara on the boat. Then, one by one, they stopped.

"Damn it. He found them fast." She ran down the stairs and into Katerina, who was at the base of them.

"The boat's gone. Did she take the boat? Where is she?"

Tess nodded. "I know it's gone. I followed it up the coast, but I've lost her. The trackers have been disabled." She grabbed the Rover keys and headed to the driveway. "Katerina, stay here."

"Like hell I will."

Tess was busy calling Anita and pulling up the Rover computer when Katerina jumped into the car. "I'm going."

"Fine, fine. Anita, Tess. Yes, he has her. He definitely thought she was drunk. She got rid of the bottle though. Uh, huh. okay..." Tess typed a password into the computer, and a locator appeared on the screen. "Got her, Anita. I'm on my way."

Katerina looked at the dot on the map. "She's on the coast, north of here."

Tess threw the Rover in gear and took off. She kept Anita on speaker and followed the signal. "How is she doing?"

Anita was with Dr. Saroyan. During Jara's meeting with them, they loaded her with things you'd only think possible in the movies. The trackers Andrew found were decoys in a way. The real trackers were inside of her. One was embedded under the skin on her back, and the others were literally inside her. The internal trackers transmitted readings of her respirations, heart rate, blood pressure, and the like. They could tell if she was asleep, moving, in pain... The other devices were microbots. They would deliver painkillers to her system whenever Dr. Saroyan saw on the monitors that she was in distress. The microbots latched down on the intestines and, in regular use, would give an extended, but constant release of pain medicine. In this case, they were boosted to give out more drugs if needed.

"This is Regan. She has had a couple of elevations but is holding her own."

"Thank you, Doc," Katerina said, not meaning to say it out loud.

"Katerina, is that you?" Anita yelled. "Why are you there? Damn it!"

"Auntie Anita, I couldn't let her go through this alone. I'm fine. I have to be here."

"Stay in the car!" Anita ordered but likely knew her words fell on deaf ears.

Regan cut in. "Hurry, Tess. Her vitals are rising."

Tess found where the tracker was stationary. She didn't see the boat, but there was an old, abandoned lighthouse ahead.

"I think she is in the lighthouse. Here are the coordinates. I'm leaving the car and approaching the building." Tess turned on her watch, which of course was also a tracker.

"Sending backup to the area by land and water. Be careful," Anita said.

Tess left the car and looked back at Katerina. "Stay here." Tess snuck up to the building, made her way inside, and hid outside the room Jara was in. She heard almost all of Andrew's ranting.

"Andrew," I taunted, "you're boring me. I enjoyed talking to Alan and beating Toni a helluva lot more than listening to your bullshit."

This time he hit my bad knee with the hammer and continued his rant.

"I am the mastermind. I avenged Mother. Alan killed the freak in New York who said she was going to be our mother. But I killed all of my father's so-called girlfriends in France. And Alan, well he was so messy. Mother wouldn't have liked that. And hell, Toni is so fucked up, she never knows from one minute to the next whether she's a boy or a girl. They made her a girl when she was born, but she still never really knew. She hates everyone. She wanted everyone to know what it felt like to feel different. But I was the one, Agent Jara Quinn, I was the one who changed people. I made art. Mother would have loved my art."

"Why didn't you kill your last mother?"

"My last mother?" he thought for a moment. "Oh her, she wasn't my mother. She was our nanny. She took our last name a long time ago to make sure caring for us was as easy as it could be. She was always good to me."

"Did she know how fucked up you all are, Andrew?"

He hit me again. "You are too mouthy, Agent Quinn. Maybe I'll cut your tongue out, let you watch everyone die in silence." He was going toward a knife.

Think fast..."But Andrew, I can't tell you where Toni is if you cut my tongue out."

He stopped for a moment. "Where is she?"

"How about this, you show me how you plan on killing my so-called family, and I'll tell you where Toni is."

He hauled off and hit me again. "I'll make the deals around here. Sure, I'll show you..." He brought over a laptop. It showed the front of the Foundation. "Tomorrow, when Victoria and Katerina step into the building...Boom! They all die and the legacy dies with them. You all tried to trick me. I know Victoria didn't go to the Caymans. No one was on that flight."

Whew, he didn't know Victoria was in Nevis.

"So, Andrew, we get to chat then, until tomorrow?"

"Oh, I have other plans. Mother and daughter get to go first. Although, I'd love to have more time with Katerina. She was so lovely. Did she tell you what we did together? Such beautiful skin." Andrew continued to taunt me as he ran the tip of the knife down my shirt, cutting it like paper.

Okay, so he was getting to me now. "You fucking bastard, you'll pay for what you did!"

Andrew cackled. He set down the knife and stepped out of the room. Tess appeared and grabbed the knife, cutting through the restraints.

"Get out of here," I whispered. "He'll be coming back. Stop him. Get me later."

Tess turned to leave, and we heard a large commotion in the hall.

"Well, look who I found. I'm not going to wait after all. Oh and Detective Goodwin, how lovely it is to see you. You know, you made my list too." Andrew had found Katerina, who had snuck in after Tess. He dragged her into the room by her hair. He backhanded her with the hand holding the hammer, and she fell into the wall. He came toward Tess, and she stabbed him in the chest just below his shoulder. With the knife still sticking out of his chest, he hit her with the hammer, knocking her to the floor. He'd raised the hammer to hit her again, when we heard the cock of a gun. Katerina had not been knocked out as Andrew had thought. She was able to grab my.357 revolver that was on the table and had it pointed straight at him.

"Stop it!" she yelled.

He turned to her, and an evil smile crossed his lips. "Little girl, you don't have it in you."

"I said stop, Andrew. Let her go." Katerina's virid-colored eyes blazed as she focused on him.

Andrew backed up to me, hammer still in his hand, slowly raising it above my head. "Beautiful Katerina, unable to save herself or the one she loves." Andrew's muscles tensed to bring the hammer down on my head.

I heard a sound like lightning hitting a metal roof, then I felt hot liquid all over my face. I blinked to get it out of my eyes. Before me was the most beautiful woman in my world, still holding the smoking gun out straight. The man who haunted our nightmares now lay in a heap at her feet, blood pooling beneath him. Katerina's chest heaved with each breath, as the shot still echoed in the small room. She had pulled the trigger...for the first time.

I slumped in the chair, bruised and bound, but alive. Sirens wailed in the distance, faint, but getting closer. Tess reached out and touched Katerina's extended arm. She flinched and pulled back. Her eyes searched Tess, trying to regain recognition. Tess continued to slowly talk to her, her voice anchoring us both. Katerina dropped the gun. It clattered to the floor, louder than it should have sounded.

Tess grabbed the gun from the floor and put it in the back of her waistband, as she continued to gently talk to Katerina.

"Tess," Katerina whispered, as her shoulders relaxed and recognition took hold. She turned to me and staggered forward, dropping to her knees beside me. Her fingers fumbled, hands shaking violently, as she worked to untie my restraints. Tess checked Andrew's pulse, making sure he was dead.

My voice was only a whisper, ragged but steady. "Kat...look at me." I tried to reach out to her but was still bound. "Katerina, please look at me," I pleaded.

"I warned him," Katerina mumbled, her eyes still focused on my restraints. "I warned him to stay away from you. I warned him."

I knew she was talking about what she had said to him in the cabin. I was sure she'd warned him about a lot of things. Too bad for him, he didn't heed her words. Grateful and in awe, I looked at her, studying her and trying to find a trace of what she was feeling.

She looked up, her eyes wide and flooded with tears, and found my gaze. Those emerald pools were now full of pride, not fear.

"You found me," I said, my voice cracking. "You saved me."

Katerina shook her head. "I didn't think I could do it. I've never..."

I saw her eyes change to something I didn't recognize as the last restraint fell to the floor.

I reached up, cupping Katerina's cheek with a bloodied hand. "You did what you had to."

Katerina's eyes flared again as she clenched her fists. "I hated him so much for all the pain he caused."

I took Katerina's trembling fist and pressed it to my heart. "Love pulled the trigger, Kat, not hate." I said. "You found your strength in our love, and you aimed it at the darkness and into the nightmare."

I glanced over at the body, then back at Katerina. My voice dropped to a whisper, full of finality, full of love. "And this time, the monster won't walk away."

Our nightmare ended with a bullet. But our story? It would continue with love.

Epilogue

Katerina and I were driven to a secure, top-secret building. Tess followed in my car. Anita and Dr. Saroyan were waiting for us. Tess had audio of all Andrew's ramblings and the shooting. She was downloading the recording for Anita and SSA Stewart. When told of the outcome, his only words were, "Well, at least it saved the taxpayers some money." Dr. Saroyan took X-rays of my arm and informed me surgery was in my future. She put another cast on it and pumped up the remaining robots in my body.

"This will help with the pain for the next few days. I want to see you later in the week for surgery. That will give the bots time to leave your body naturally."

I started to open my mouth.

"And before you ask, no, you won't be able to see them."

I was bummed, but at the same time relieved.

We contacted Noel and told him all was safe. He decided to bring Elly to the house. It was good for Kat and Elly to be together after all of this. I called Victoria and told her the outcome. If Kat wanted her to know the whole story, she could tell her. We also sent the bomb squad to the Foundation. One device was found, and the building was cleared. Victoria said they had good luck with finding some of the Foundation's stolen money. She and the family would stay on the islands for another two weeks before returning home.

I was removed from duty again until I was cleared physically and mentally. Per SSA Stewart, he wasn't expecting me back any time soon. I was totally okay with that. After my surgery, Kat and I took it easy and attended therapy together. It was very good for us.

Travis's ears got better, and he returned to active duty. Tess left the CSP to work with Mrs. Burris and Dr. Saroyan.

Since I have more time off and therapy helped, Kat and I made the decision to go back to France for a while. Figured I could thank André in person for all of his help. Surprisingly enough, Victoria and Anita decided they were going to come with us.

Kat and I discussed it, and since I couldn't drive for a bit and we were going to France anyway, I sold my Rover to Tess for a dollar. Hell, she deserved that and more. I figured I'd get another one once we got back.

My career was now uncertain. Two cases, and both myself and the people I loved were hurt. I wasn't sure I could put them through another case. But for now, I was still FBI and with the love of my life. I looked forward to recovering while surrounded by my family. I could worry about whatever would come next later. Much later.

Author Notes

Thank you for joining me again in this series. I want to take a moment to speak directly to you about the journey that shaped this second book.

First and foremost, this story is total fiction. Every character, event, and plot twist exists only within the pages of this book. That said, I poured significant effort into grounding certain elements in real-world research to make the world feel lived-in and authentic.

Much of the inspiration for the scientific and investigative aspects came from studying DNA research, law enforcement methodologies, and forensic science. I explored how DNA analysis works and how it's used in contemporary investigations to help frame key moments in the story. I also spent more time learning about police and FBI procedures, aiming to portray investigative work in a way that is respectful of real protocols while still serving the narrative's dramatic needs. On a very different note, I even dove into the world of perfume composition and fragrance crafting because it plays a symbolic and sensory role in this book that was too intriguing to overlook.

With this second installment, I intentionally made the tone darker and more serious than the first. I wanted to push deeper into the complexities of human nature—to explore not just what my characters are capable of achieving, but also what they struggle with internally. This book reveals both the strengths and weaknesses of Jara and Katerina, testing them in new ways and forcing them to confront shadows from their pasts as well as their own vulnerabilities.

If the first book was about the beginning of a journey, then this one is about confronting the costs of walking further down that path. It asks: What does it take to stand firm when everything you believe is tested?

Thank you for reading and for believing in these characters and this world. I can't wait to continue the journey with you.

About the Author

I still live in Indiana with my partner, Mary, and our doodles, Truffle and Roux. Since the release of my first novel, *Hornet's Nest*, my life has become a whirlwind I never imagined. I've had the opportunity to travel from Indianapolis to Omaha, New York City, and California, meeting readers from all walks of life and hearing their thoughtful, passionate responses to my work. Along the way, I've also had the honor of appearing on podcasts with Andrew Eborn from London and *Quinn Lemley's Secrets of the Stage* in NYC.

Writing has opened doors, sparked conversations, and deepened my love for storytelling. I'm thrilled to share book two of *The Jara Quinn Series*, *Forbidden*, and I hope you enjoyed reading it as much as I loved creating it.

Note to Readers

Thank you for reading a book from Launch Point Press. We have made every effort to edit this book. However, typos do slip in. If you find an error in the text, please email publisher@launchpointpress.com so the issue can be corrected.

We appreciate you as a reader and want to ensure you enjoy the reading process. We would like you to consider posting a review on your preferred media sites and/or your blog or website.

For more information on upcoming releases, author interviews, contests, giveaways and more, please sign up for our newsletter and visit us as at Launch Point Press: www.launchpointpress.com and "Like" us on Facebook: Launch Point Press.

Bright Blessings

www.ingramcontent.com/pod-product-compliance
Lightning Source LLC
LaVergne TN
LVHW010459070526
838231LV00035B/596

* 9 7 8 1 6 3 3 0 4 0 8 4 7 *